You Have No Idea

Scott Carlin

First published in 2025 by Blossom Spring Publishing
You Have No Idea
Copyright © 2025 Scott Carlin
ISBN 978-1-917938-14-3
E: admin@blossomspringpublishing.com
W: www.blossomspringpublishing.com

'You have no idea.' Four little words. Words that could be questioning, or maybe responsive. But in the context of their discovery, undeniably cryptic.

Chapter 1

Heavy snow had been falling for just over two hours, falling fast, like the sky couldn't wait to get rid of it. Covering everything it fell upon in a blanket of velvety white.

In a sleepy forgotten town on the outskirts of Munich, it had been as normal a day as the locals had become accustomed to. The shops and businesses had closed, the locals returning to the warmth and comfort of their homes and settling in for the night. Well, most of them.

Philip Langer was standing on the front porch of his house, and his springer spaniel, Poppy, was sitting at his feet like a ball of energy, filled with anticipation for her final walk of the day. As usual, their walk took them to the edge of town, over three miles there and back, normally a one-hour walk, maybe longer with the heavy snow that had fallen.

As Philip reached the street at the bottom of his garden path, he turned left and made for the centre of town. He headed past the old church and down Main Street, past the main square, and continued to the end of the town, which was quiet, still and white. They crossed the small Victorian bridge at the end of the road, leaving both foot and paw prints on it, and entered the wooded footpath locally known as 'Bluebell Woods'. Philip had walked the same walk every night for the past three weeks as autumn had turned to winter and the days had grown shorter.

As normal, Poppy would run in circles, eager for her master to throw her favourite ball ahead for her to chase. Due to the darker nights and the dense woods, Philip's wife had purchased a rubber ball from a local market designed with a light inside that lit up a bright neon red when thrown or was moved abruptly, making it easier for the dog to find. As Philip threw the ball, the excited dog took off in pursuit. The ball bounced high and straight on the recently covered snowy path, lighting up red as it hit the ground, and illuminating the trees way above the reach of Poppy. As the ball landed a second time, it took a different bounce, possibly from hitting a rock or tree branch beneath the snow. It bounced high, but this time to the right, deep into the trees, and the excited dog followed, knowing no better.

As Philip reached where the ball had entered the wooded area, he stopped and called out the dog's name. The red light had gone out. He waited. Ten seconds went by, no sign of Poppy. A sliver of light from the moon lit up the dense area. Small streams of light cut in narrow rays between the massive trees, like strobe lights but nowhere near as bright. He called the dog's name again, louder, and waited: silence. There was no sound of paws crunching on the untouched snow, no barks or yelps. He crept onward, large precise steps, like a cartoon version of someone creeping into a house and trying to be silent. Again, he called out, and again, silence. He stood still; it was as good as pitch black the further into the woods he crept.

Then, like a firework in the night sky, from twenty feet to his right-hand side came a beam of blood-red light. The dog's ball was close by, more like thirty feet when he focused his eyes. He headed towards it, quicker steps, but not by much. Still, there was no sound from Poppy, no heavy panting from running through the snow.

As he finally reached the red glow, the light went out

again, and the forest was again doused in darkness. Philip fumbled his glove off and fished in his pocket for his mobile phone. He opened it and clicked on the torch feature. He pointed it outwards in the general direction of where the ball had lit up. The torch on the phone was not great and lit a small area, five feet in front of him maybe, not ideal, and he still couldn't see anything. He shone it across the whole area, side to side. Still nothing. He carried on cautiously.

Then he heard something, quiet, close by on his right-hand side, a small movement brushing on the snow, maybe a hesitant footstep. His heart began to pound. He pointed the light from his phone in its direction, at head height, but still nothing. Then he lowered the phone, and there she was. His excited dog, Poppy. She was sitting in the snow, alert and panting and covered in white speckles, her tail gently brushing the top of the snow beneath it. He reached down to pet her. She had the ball in her mouth. As he leaned down, the dog moved slightly. As she did, the light inside the ball was triggered and once again pierced the darkness with a blood-red beam. Philip froze. The red light was better than his torch by a long way. As he went to straighten back up and get his bearings, he noticed something in the snow, a darker patch of the red colour that the ball was giving off, over to his left-hand side, a few feet wide. He leaned forward and was reaching out to touch it when something further to his left caught his eye again. He turned, a quick movement, more worried than curious. The second he turned, however, the light went out. He pointed the phone that was still in his hand towards it, but with the cold and sudden apprehension, he dropped it. The fresh snow swallowed it up, and again, he was in complete darkness.

He steadied himself and took another step closer to the dark patch he had seen. No noise, only the whistle from the softest of winds meandering between the trees. He paused. Behind him, he heard a crunch. Something or someone was close: the dog following him, he thought. He carried on, and again, another crunch. Then suddenly, like a spotlight, everything in front of him became visible.

With fear in his eyes, he stumbled backwards, falling onto his hands, scrambling backwards in panic, kicking his legs like a swimmer learning the backstroke for the first time. He focused his eyes and stared, at the same time knowing he didn't want to see the horror in front of him, not really. But it was too late. At the foot of one of the massive trees was an area of snow that had been cleared, only a few metres long and a metre wide. A misshapen circle of dirt from the forest floor remained, dark, like a hole in the ground. But it wasn't a hole. Maybe at some point it had been, but not now; now it was a grave. And not the kind you would see in a graveyard, no cross or headstone at the top telling you a name, not like that at all. The reason that Philip was certain it was a grave was that protruding from the dirt was a partially decaying body, but not a whole body; it was the top half of a body lying at an angle. What he could make out was a head that was both partly decayed and partly frozen. Below the head was the chest cavity, with a thin arm hanging from it, withered and partially eaten. The rest was not visible. From what he could see, the body had been half-buried.

Philip lay for a second, in shock, taking in the terrifying sight before him. He finally got to his knees and looked back at the dog, who was staring at the corpse. He crawled forward, not knowing what to do. His first thought was to run, but instead, he crept closer to it, unsure why. Just as he was a few feet from it, he reached out his hand. To do what exactly, he didn't know; maybe touching it would clarify it wasn't a nightmare. But just as he did, the light from the ball went out, throwing the woods into darkness.

Then he heard the crunch of the snow behind him again, and again, he thought it was the dog. He got to his knees and sat upright, now shaking from the cold and the fear. He got ready to stand, but before he managed to, he felt the weight of a hand grabbing at his shoulder.

They say if you scream in the woods, will anyone hear it? It was safe to say the scream that came out of Philip Langer when he felt that hand touch him was heard by the entirety of the sleepy town, and maybe the neighbouring one too.

Chapter 2

Detective Thomas Lahm was waiting at the foot of the small Victorian bridge at the far side of Schwaberwegen as the river below bounced and creaked. Ice had begun forming at the banks, but the current was too strong for it to freeze over completely.

Lahm was looking back up towards the small town, a former mining village on the edge of the Ebersberger Forest, one of Germany's largest woodlands. The town was now occupied mostly by couples who had moved there to retire. It was far enough outside of Munich to be quaint and smaller than neighbouring towns enough to stand out.

The call had come through for a detective to attend a crime scene just over an hour ago. A police inspector had received a call at 7 p.m. from a local man who said he had discovered the remains of a dead body out in the forest. Lahm, who was on patrol nearby, was first on the scene. He spoke briefly to the man who had called it in, but he was still in shock. A second man had also been present when the body was found but had quickly fled the scene.

After speaking to the inspector in charge to get some information, Lahm made his way towards the scene, but just as he approached the bridge, he received a call on his mobile phone. It was from his partner, Detective Anna Muller. She had been on duty working a murder case from a few weeks back that they were close to getting a result on. When the call went out for all officers to attend, she had left immediately. Lahm had told her the location and said he would wait until she arrived before checking it out.

Detective Muller drove her cherished Seat Leon through the back roads towards the location Detective Lahm had given her. She knew that for a call to go out for all officers to attend meant it had to be serious.

After passing through several small villages, she finally saw the street sign for the town of Schwaberwegen. The sign was washed out and faded.

The Ebersberger Forest was on her right as she entered the town and made her way towards Main Street. As the shadow that was cast from the trees next to her cleared, she was met with a sea of flashing lights. There must have been twenty patrol cars gathered in a car parking area in the centre of the town. There were forensic team vehicles, patrol cars, unmarked police cars, and an army of officers patrolling the entrance to the footpath that led to the crime scene. She was directed into a space and parked her car. She showed her ID after getting out and was shown where to go. Further down the street, she could see Lahm standing on the bridge; he was leaning against it with both hands, staring down into the river below. The forest as a backdrop behind him made it look like a picture from a Christmas card, she thought as she approached.

'Hey, thanks for waiting,' she said, interrupting his train of thought.

'No problem. How are you?' he replied.

'Unsure of what we are about to witness.'

'Seems to be a big deal,' Lahm said.

'You have any details?' Muller asked.

'Only that it was a half-buried body.'

They crossed the bridge and entered the forest. The

area where the body had been discovered, they found out, was known to the locals as Bluebell Woods, due to the flowers that bloomed there in the summer months.

The snow on the footpath was now churned up and melting with the foot traffic it had seen. Many officers had been walking back and forth, setting up parameters and lighting rigs, taping off access points and making sure that no one could pass through. Lahm led, watching his steps carefully. The path was still slippery, even more so now. The overhanging trees that were just above their heads were dropping fresh snow as the wind whistled and agitated the branches.

They turned right at the end of the path where the tape told them to stop, then across a small ditch and over thirty feet of deep snow. They could see footsteps in the snow, not as many as they had on the first path; only a few people would have been to where the body was found.

Lahm walked on, Muller close behind and struggling to stay on her feet. As they approached, they could see markings in the snow off to their right-hand side, as if someone had fallen or been knocked over. Up ahead they could see a massive oak tree, six feet wide and almost a hundred tall. The police floodlight only showed the first twenty feet, then was swallowed by the darkness.

Muller pulled alongside Lahm as they reached the body. They could immediately see it was worse than from the brief description they had already.

It was indeed a partially decomposed body of what could be a middle-aged man, half-buried in a makeshift grave. His head and the top half of his body were sticking out from the ground as though whoever had put him there had buried as much as they could manage and then just left, possibly fleeing after being disturbed.

Lahm stepped closer. He took off one of his thermal gloves and swapped it for blue plastic ones. He knelt and felt the dirt in front of the body, which was loose but beginning to freeze. He looked up at the tree: no markings on it, or at least nothing they could see from the light that the police floodlight was giving off.

Muller crouched down next to him. She also put on a blue glove as she stared at the horrifying sight of the body.

'Any ideas?' she asked.

'None whatsoever.'

She leaned closer to the body, a shiver running down her spine. This was like nothing she had ever worked on before; she was shaken but didn't want to show it in front of her partner.

'We're going to have to let forensics in here soon. I'm not sure what we can discover with a body in this state,' Lahm said.

Muller wasn't listening; she thought she had noticed something. She took out a pen from her coat pocket and knelt as close as she could to the body without stepping on the grave itself. She placed her gloved hand on the forehead of the skull.

'What are you doing?' Lahm asked.

'Can you see that?' she replied.

'See what?'

She took the pen in her right hand, slid it into the closed mouth of the body, and pried it open, just a little. At the corner of the mouth, there was something visible, something white.

'I wouldn't start pulling at that. Leave it for forensics.'

Muller again didn't listen. She gently tried to grab whatever it was with her thumb and index finger. It was a piece of paper. It was damp, so she had to be careful. After a few seconds of trying not to rip it, she was able to remove it. She dropped the pen and turned to face the light, Lahm side-stepping to be next to her. She opened it up gently. On it was some writing, slightly washed out and faded, the same as the Schwaberwegen town sign she had passed earlier.

Muller carefully set the piece of paper down on a sheet on the ground. Scribbled on it in black writing were four words that read, *You have no idea.*

Lahm and Muller were now standing at the back of one of the forensic team's vans. The piece of paper Muller had found and removed from the dead body had been passed to the head of the forensics team. They had processed it and bagged it to be sent to the lab for examination. Meanwhile, they had sent in the forensic team to thoroughly sweep the scene and gather any evidence they could find.

Lahm and Muller were writing up their statement when their boss arrived. He was an ex-army officer named Andreas Schmidt.

'Good evening. How are you?'

'Fine,' said Lahm.

'That was a good find, Muller. Great work.'

'Thanks, boss,' she replied. 'This isn't like anything we've seen before; it's pretty bad.'

'I've been down to the scene, and I agree; this is going to be a big case, with lots of exposure and a large media presence. I've told all officers to keep the journalists out until we get a handle on this.'

'Good,' said Muller.

They all stood awkwardly for a second.

'What do we do now, then?' asked Detective Lahm, sounding a little shaken.

'Now we call Stam,' Schmidt replied.

Chapter 3

Oliver Stam was sitting in a strip club in the centre of Munich on what was the second day of a week-long holiday that was three years overdue, and this was his idea of how a holiday should be: drinking and smoking in dimly lit bars where no one would recognise him. He didn't go for lounging about at overcrowded pools in overpriced resorts with overstimulated people.

Not that his holiday would continue in this way, as his daughter planned to visit him and was flying into Munich airport the day after tomorrow. He couldn't wait, seriously couldn't wait. She had been travelling across Asia for the last four years, and this would be her first time back in Germany since she had left.

The strip club he was in was like all the rest he had frequented: murky lighting, murky smell and murky people, all of which he didn't mind. He wasn't there for the girls; he was nearly sixty years old and past all that. A few months back, he had told one of the girls who had made advances towards him for sex that if he had to choose, he would rather have a bowl of soup than sex at this point. The girl had briefly looked repulsed before moving on to the next punter along the bar.

The reason for drinking in strip clubs and not bars was mostly down to his past. He had pissed off a good few people in his time as a detective, and thanks to a big case a few months back, his face had shown up in more than a few tabloid newspapers, which was the last thing he had wanted. He knew that no one paid that much attention to who you were in a strip club.

There was always the option to drink in the bars that

the local police drank in, but if he was honest, off-duty police officers pissed him off just as much as the journalists and photographers did. He enjoyed his own company, and this was where he preferred to spend his time.

On the bar in front of him was a double whisky with a mouthful out of it, a half-drunk bottle of Beck's lager, and a twenty-pack of cigarettes with three left inside. There was also his work mobile phone. He said it was his work mobile, but the truth was he didn't have a mobile of his own, so it was his only mobile, and for the last twenty minutes, it had buzzed with incoming messages, over and over. It was vibrating from one side of the bar to the other.

'You going to answer that?' asked the bartender after the latest buzzing started. He was a short, stocky man aged anywhere between thirty-five and forty-five, with a round face, a bowl cut and an eyebrow piercing that didn't suit him.

'I'm on holiday,' replied Stam, not looking up.

'From what?'

Stam looked up.

'Sounds like someone is trying to get hold of you pretty bad.'

'I'm on holiday. If anyone wants me bad enough, they'll find me.'

'Fine. You want another drink?'

Stam glared at him.

The bartender wandered off to the other side of the bar and reappeared with a bottle of beer after a few seconds. Stam had drunk the remainder of his whisky in the time he had taken to do so.

'Can I have another whisky too?'

The bartender looked annoyed.

'What? You're not on holiday; you're working, right? Can I have twenty cigarettes as well, please, sir?' Stam said sarcastically.

'You're not supposed to smoke in here. You've been told already,'

'There's a lot of things you're not supposed to do in here. You want me to start naming them?'

The bartender paused for a second before fetching the whisky and cigarettes, and when he returned, said, 'Whisky's on the house.'

Stam smiled at him, again, sarcastically.

The bartender set the cigarettes on the bar in front of Stam before scurrying away to the other side of the bar to deal with one of the strippers who had punched one of the patrons for grabbing her inappropriately.

Stam knew he was going to check the messages; it was in his nature to be curious at the best of times, and when it came to his job, even more so.

He took a long draw from the cigarette he had just lit and followed it with a mouthful of whisky, both burning his throat in different ways. He cherished the sensation for a minute before reluctantly getting up from his bar stool. His phone buzzed again as he looked at the screen. It was a number he didn't recognise that had left the six missed calls and six subsequent messages. He picked it up and headed towards the door, the bitter cold hitting him like a punch as he exited the club. The snow had stopped, but with the clouds lifting, it had made the temperature drop even more.

The mobile buzzed again in his hand, the same number as the previous seven calls, now eight. Reluctantly, he answered and provisionally ended the holiday that he had only just started.

'Is this Detective Stam?'

He thought he recognised the voice straight away.

'You're the one who called me.'

'Oliver, it's Inspector Schmidt from the Munich police office. I believe we have a case that would best suit your expertise.'

'I'm on holiday,' Stam replied.

'I think this is the kind of case that would make most detectives cut their holiday short, especially if that person is you.'

'What are you trying to say?' replied Stam.

'I'm trying to say that you are definitely going to want to take this case, is all.'

'I'm four whiskies deep and have another waiting on me.'

'You're going to want to see this,' Schmidt repeated.

Stam looked up at the clear night sky. It was black and littered with bright stars and small drifting clouds. He thought about his holiday, about his daughter who was visiting. She would understand; she had before, and more times than he would have liked to remember. He then thought about his cigarette and his double whisky, the burning sensation in his throat trickling down into his chest.

'Okay, send a car,' he said, before heading in to grab his jacket and pay his tab.

Chief detective Oliver Stam had worked for the German police for thirty-eight years, except for a two-year absence from duty for 'personal reasons' in his mid-thirties. To all accounts, he had enjoyed it, not that everyone he had worked with along the way would agree.

Detective Stam had a reputation and a demeanour that wasn't quite angry, but which moody didn't quite cover. Some said it sat somewhere between pissed off and agitated, and he was fine with that. Many also thought that he wasn't particularly happy to be doing what he was doing, but since his wife had died of cancer ten years ago, this couldn't have been further from the truth. Work was the one thing that made him content, for want of a better word. The problem that other officers who had worked with him in the past had trouble with was that they didn't always like his approach. Some people aren't used to being told how things are, especially in the blunt manner Stam was known for.

He did appreciate hard work, dedication, and an overall sense of doing the right thing, no matter the cost. This was why he was now regarded as one of the best criminal detectives in Germany, and when all was said and done, every one of his superiors was more than happy to have him at their disposal, despite his methods.

Detective Muller had heard of Oliver Stam, the infamous German detective; everyone in the force had, and not just from the media. He was known as much for his unwavering dedication to a case as he was for his excellent investigative skills. She had heard plenty of stories of his previous cases but hadn't worked with him yet.

Muller pulled up to the kerb of the strip club, one she had attended many times in the past to arrest drunk patrons who had started to get a little handsy.

She had driven there in her Seat Leon after telling the inspector the police patrol cars were pieces of shit. He chose not to argue and let her go.

After beeping her horn four times, each beep getting longer, she was about to get out when a man she presumed was Detective Stam came striding out the door of the club, smoke and bright lights escaping from behind him, and he was not what she had expected. He seemed a little younger than she had first pictured. He looked to be in his late fifties and had thick grey hair which crept down to a thick grey beard, not trimmed but not messy. He looked a little under six foot tall, maybe more, she thought, as he was hunched up against the cold. His long jacket pulled closed meant she couldn't guess his weight.

He opened the door and lowered himself inside. He stank of whisky and cheap cigarettes.

'So, you're Detective Stam?'

'And you must be Detective Muller?'

'That's correct. It's a privilege to work with you.'

'Who said you're working with me?'

He said it in a tone that Muller wasn't sure how to take. She smirked it off and pulled away from the kerb.

They drove along the back roads towards Schwaberwegen. A snow plough had been out already and cleared the roads, but the dip in temperature meant it was already beginning to ice over. Muller drove cautiously, her winter tyres gripping the worsening road as they passed through the outskirts of Munich. The road skirted in and out of the edges of the forest which was now the most direct route to Schwaberwegen.

As the tree line got tighter, the dark skies above narrowed, then were blocked out by the denseness of the foreboding forest as it began to encroach on the small car. Visibility was poor, which meant Muller was driving with her lights on full beam, the glow darting with every twist and turn of the road.

'So, what's your opinion on the crime scene, then? I assume you've seen it yourself?' Stam finally said after twenty minutes of driving in silence.

Muller had checked three times during the journey to make sure he wasn't sleeping.

'I have witnessed the scene, and from my initial thoughts, I have a few queries regarding the circumstances.'

'Like what?'

'Firstly, the positioning of where the body was buried, thirty feet from a path that's used regularly by locals from the town, and when you have thousands of acres of forest around you, it doesn't seem right to me.'

'And secondly?'

'Why half bury a body and leave a note with it? It doesn't add up. If you go to the bother to dig a hole, then dig a hole. Don't half dig it and then try to bury a body and at the same time leave a cryptic note that would never be found if you buried it correctly in the first place.'

'You think it was staged, then?' Stam asked.

'I'm not sure about staged, but it's odd.'

'Who found the note?'

'I did. It was concealed inside the mouth.'

'Good for you, Muller,' Stam replied.

Muller didn't know if it was sarcasm, but she assumed not.

'My name is Anna, by the way.'

'Also good for you, Muller,' Stam replied.

Which she knew for sure was sarcasm.

As the trees released their grip and the road ahead opened, they approached the town of Schwaberwegen, this time from the opposite end from where Muller had first arrived earlier today. Up ahead in the distance, they could see the glow from the lights of the town centre lighting up the sky.

The sign that welcomed them was almost as faded as the one on the other side but still legible.

Muller edged her small car through the even larger collection of police vehicles that had now gathered in the centre, some parked on the main road, which had been partially blocked off.

Muller got out and was met by Inspector Schmidt.

'Everything okay?' he asked her quietly as Stam was getting out of the car on the other side.

'I think so.'

'What do you mean?' Schmidt asked.

'I think he might be drunk,' she replied.

'How come?'

'He didn't really speak much, and when he did, it was mostly sarcastic comments.'

'That sounds about right, drunk or sober.'

Stam approached them from the front of the car and stopped the conversation. The men shook hands before the inspector spoke.

'Detective Stam, thank you for coming despite the short notice and interruption of your holiday. As I said on the phone, though, I believe this will be a case that you will want to see for yourself.'

'Okay. Firstly, I would like to know who has been to the crime scene?' Stam asked abruptly.

'Detective Muller and Detective Lahm are the only ones to have examined the body. Anyone else that's been there was there to set up lighting and take photos.'

'Okay, and the person who discovered the body?'

'They're waiting to be interviewed. We're just looking

to set up a temporary office in the town church; I believe it won't be much longer.'

'I want a copy of his statement as soon as possible, please.'

Stam took notes in a small black notebook he had taken from his jacket pocket.

'I'm going to check the scene; I want Detectives Muller and Lahm with me.'

Inspector Schmidt nodded and signalled to Lahm to come over. Stam shook his hand before asking Muller to lead the way.

The three detectives made their way from the main square, down the street towards the Victorian bridge at the bottom. They crossed the bridge and entered the forest. Stam walked slowly between the two detectives, taking in the scene as they followed the tight path that was now starting to ice at the edges. As they reached the police tape at the end of the path, they turned right into the wooded area and carefully made their way towards the makeshift grave, which was brightly lit by two light stands on either side.

Apart from the path made by the police, Stam could see several imprints in the snow as they approached, further back and off to the right a few metres away.

All three of the detectives followed the trail and stopped as they reached the grave.

Stam walked around it, first looking from the opposite side, then around the massive tree and back to where Muller and Lahm stood. He took out his notebook and wrote a few words inside. He then kneeled close to the corpse, tilting his head a few times as if mimicking the position of the body. He took his pen and leaned in further, and with the pen, he opened the mouth of the corpse, as Muller had earlier.

'Was the note fully concealed?'

'Not completely. I noticed the smallest piece at the bottom right-hand corner of his mouth,' Muller replied.

Again, Stam wrote in his notebook, after taking the pen from the mouth of the decaying body.

He stood again, looking around at the imprints in the snow and then back at the grave.

'What do you think?' Lahm asked.

Stam didn't reply. He was now concentrating on the protruding arm of the corpse, the one with the biggest part of it still buried in the ground.

'Do you know what I mean now with it being odd?' Muller then asked. 'Why would you half bury a body, then leave it?'

After a minute, Stam stood.

'I don't believe they did half bury it; I think it was fully buried.'

Muller and Lahm looked at each other, confused.

'I believe that someone has tried to dig it back up and failed.'

Chapter 4

The Gothic church was over two hundred years old and spectacularly haunting. Large stained-glass windows on both sides, creating a fusion of dark colours, combined with the vaulted ceiling to add to its grandeur. Two small heaters on the outer walls at the entrance were all there was to heat it, which only emphasised the cold, empty atmosphere within. The room that the officer had set up, which appeared to be some kind of storeroom, was at the rear of the church, next to a grand organ.

Inside the makeshift control room were Inspector Schmidt, Detective Lahm, Detective Muller, and Lead Inspector David Klose, who oversaw the whole police operation but left the investigative operations to Inspector Schmidt. And of course, Detective Stam.

They were all anxious and eager to begin, and all looking at Stam, knowing he was the one who knew *where* to begin.

'I've spoken with the head of forensics, who was making her way to examine the crime scene. As you will all appreciate, with the nature of the crime, this will not be done in a hurry. I've told forensics to take as long as they need. We need them to be thorough,' said Stam.

He looked at his watch.

'It's now 7:44 p.m.. The earliest we can hope for them to be finished is by midnight. Anything before that will be rushed, and I've told them as much.'

'What do you suggest we do in the meantime?' asked Detective Lahm.

'In the meantime, we do our jobs,' replied Stam.

'We need to make sure that the media does not obtain

information from the crime scene, and absolutely no pictures; this is important. Tomorrow we will release a statement reassuring the public that although there has been the discovery of a body, we don't believe there to be an immediate danger to them and that more details will follow in due course,' said Schmidt.

Stam now remembered where he had worked with Inspector Schmidt previously. It was on a missing persons case ten years ago in a small town in the north of Frankfurt. For three weeks, they had worked on the case, and in the end, they got a positive result. A teenage girl was found safe and well in an abandoned warehouse and her abductor caught. Schmidt had been recently promoted at the time, and Stam could understand why. He was an exceptional inspector who led with authority and gave the case his all.

Lead Inspector Klose agreed with Schmidt's plan of action and excused himself to organise his team.

'While we wait on forensics, I suggest we start by interviewing the man who discovered the body. I believe all we have is the initial statement the first officer at the scene took from him. We can use this office as an interview room,' said Stam.

'Who will be interviewing along with you?' Schmidt asked Stam, expecting that Stam would be the one doing the interview.

'I want Detective Muller only.'

'Sure thing,' he replied.

Detective Lahm looked across at them, slightly annoyed that Muller had been chosen but now also in need of instruction.

'Lahm, can you make sure that the forensic examiner has contacted the coroner? Also, ask them to make sure they have a forensic pathologist ready to examine the body.'

'Yes, boss,' Lahm replied, a little less annoyed.

'Inspector Schmidt, can you get me a detailed overhead map of the forest? I need to see all access and entry points to the area.'

Schmidt and Lahm both stood and headed for the church door.

Stam stood and began to rearrange the chairs. Muller helped with the table, placing it between the two sets of chairs, making it look like a police interview room.

'It's a privilege to be working with you,' Muller said as they set the huge table down. She said it with a smirk on her face.

Stam stared back at her. They were going to get on just fine, he thought.

***

Philip Langer was a tall stick of a man in his early sixties with an ashen face and square shoulders from which the rest of his body seemed to hang loosely. From his initial statement, they knew he was retired and lived north of the main square with his wife and his dog.

As he took his seat, it was clear that he was still visibly shaken. He had arranged for his wife to collect the dog while he was being checked over by the paramedic and was then held in a police van, waiting to be interviewed.

'Mr Langer, my name is Oliver Stam, and this is my colleague, Anna Muller. I appreciate that this is a challenging time, but I must get a statement from you while it's fresh in your mind.'

'No problem at all, I understand. I'm just a little on edge.'

'Understandable. We won't be long,' replied Stam. 'Can you take us through the events that led up to you discovering the body in the woods?'

'Certainly. As I've done every night for the last three weeks or so, I took my dog on our nightly walk. Down to the end of the town and over the bridge into Bluebell Woods.'

'The same walk every night?' Muller asked.

'Exactly. We carry on up the path until we reach the start of the pond, then we circle it and return on the same path home.'

'Okay, and tonight, did you see anything different?'

'I can't say that I did, no.'

'And had you noticed anyone else out on any of these walks in the past three weeks?'

'I don't think so, no.'

'What about the site where the body was discovered? Have you ever seen any footprints leading into that part of the forest?'

'Again, I'm not sure I have, sorry.'

Muller was writing everything that Mr Langer said down in the incident report.

'I understand that the dog chased after the ball into the forest. What happened as you arrived at the grave?'

'After I followed my dog, I noticed a darker patch on the ground. It was highlighted because everywhere else was thick with snow.'

'And then what happened?'

'The light from my dog's ball lit up, revealing that I was almost standing on top of the grave. I stumbled backwards, falling as I did. Then, after composing

25

myself, I got closer to it, to see what it was exactly.'

'And?' asked Muller.

'And then I felt a hand on my shoulder.'

'There was someone else with you?' Stam looked at Muller to check back on the statement.

She looked at him and shook her head.

'You haven't mentioned this to us.'

'I'm sorry. From the second it happened, I must have been in a state of shock. He wasn't with me, though.'

'He. So, you're sure it was a man?'

'Yes.'

'And this man, did you see him while you were out on your walk tonight before he touched your shoulder?'

'I can't say I did.'

'Could you describe him to us?'

'I can do better than that. His name is Hans Fischer. He lives in the old hunting lodge on the outskirts of town.'

Chapter 5

After Mr Langer had left, Stam called in the same five people that had been part of the first meeting and revealed that a second person had been at the crime scene. As everyone took their seats, he told them of the newly discovered details.

'We need to check the name Hans Fischer with the local police records. Mr Langer has also given us his address, which we need to confirm. I would also suggest sending a patrol car to watch it until we can check it for ourselves,' Stam said.

Lead Inspector Klose was frantically writing down what Stam was saying.

'Lahm, how did you get on with the forensic examiner and what I asked?'

'Good, boss. The examiner said they should be done in an hour, and they've been thorough; she wanted me to tell you that. She also said that the Ebersberg coroner's office is in the next town over and will be ready for us to use. She then mentioned that one of the most distinguished forensics pathologists in Germany is on her way. She'll be here in a few hours.'

'Dr Angela Park?' Stam asked.

'I believe it is, boss.'

Stam had worked with Dr Park on a few occasions. The last time had been on the death of an Interpol agent found behind a bar in Dusseldorf, where she had found a vital lead in the case. He also knew she was highly regarded in her field by other detectives who had worked with her.

'Okay, good. Schmidt, how are we doing with the

map?' asked Stam.

'We have the forestry commission en route with one. It should be here shortly.'

Schmidt then instructed that Lahm be the one to drive out to the old hunting lodge with a local officer to keep an eye on the house. Klose and Stam agreed.

'For now, we wait for more information to work with, and we meet back here in an hour. If anything comes up beforehand, come and find me.'

Lahm exited the church along with Schmidt and asked Inspector Klose for an officer to accompany him to the old hunting lodge. Klose told him he would assign an officer as quickly as he could.

Schmidt then conferred with Inspector Klose regarding the statement they would release to the now-gathering media.

After they had left, Muller organised the chairs in a semi-circle. She had found an old whiteboard in a back storeroom and pulled it into the room they were using. She set it up in front of the chairs and began writing up all the information that they currently had.

Stam was standing at the side entrance to the church, smoking the second-last cigarette from his packet. He blew the smoke up and out into the frosty night sky, watching as it swirled up and away before being caught in a light wind and being pulled back down and dancing in front of him.

He gazed through the smoke, thinking about the case. The possibilities of a dead body being dug up and why someone would go to such lengths, such risks. He took another drag of his cigarette and switched his thoughts briefly to the burning sensation of the whisky. He was glad he had answered his phone. He would rather be here than anywhere else right now.

His thoughts were interrupted, however, by the sound of Muller's voice behind him.

'Boss, the forensic examiner has finished. She wants to see you.'

Stam glanced at his watch. 11:05 p.m.: early, but not by much.

'Tell her I'm on my way,' he replied.

Stam walked back through the church and out onto the street. The police cordon had been pushed back even further up the street, at both ends. Stam crossed the road and headed for the hub of police vehicles. The forensic examiner, a middle-aged woman called Helen, got his attention and waved him towards a large white van that had *Forensic Examiner* written on the side. He climbed up and into what was a shiny white office fitted in the rear of it, all high gloss and lined with monitor screens. There was a table in the middle, surrounded by stools, and a large screen mounted on the wall that lit up as Stam and Muller took a seat. Helen clicked the screen on and took a seat.

'What have you got for us?' Stam asked.

'Something we haven't seen before, and rather interesting, for want of a better word,' Helen replied. 'We now believe you were correct in your initial assessment: the body appears to have been dug up after being buried, maybe even as long as four months after.'

***

Deep within the Ebersberger Forest, hidden under the seclusion of dense trees, a grave that had been dug and then filled in was once again being dug up. Protruding from it was the decaying corpse of a 42-year-old man. The hooded figure who was currently in the process of digging it up knew time might be against him.

Being careful not to break any of the now rotten and fleshless bones, he gently pulled at the underarms, delicate movements, slowly but surely uncovering the rest of the skeletal body. The smell was horrific, as always, but he was starting to get used to it.

Far off in the distance, the sound of sirens was bellowing over the treetops, and now and then, the spray of a blue police light would dart through the woods. Time was limited, but this part couldn't be rushed.

As the body was unearthed in its entirety and then laid out on the snowy ground, it could then be checked. A small torch was required for this.

First was the skull, which looked intact: no bullet holes or lacerations and no deep compressions in the bone. Then down to the chest area: no visible puncture wounds or bullet holes. From the state of decay on the neck, it wasn't clear if any strangulation marks would be evident; more than likely they wouldn't be. After a final check of the lower part of the torso, all seemed okay, with no sign of any obvious injuries, and so began the painstaking task of burying the body for a second time. Although the grave was still partially dug, this didn't make it any easier, especially in the current conditions.

After twenty minutes of digging, the body was finally back in the ground, lying out flat. All that was left was to refill the grave, and after what had happened with the last body he had tried to bury a few days ago, there could be no mistakes. Even with the police less than five miles away, he had to be sure. It took a further twenty minutes before the body was completely buried. The grave now stood out in the whiteness of its surroundings. He had to cover it with snow. Finally satisfied with the result, the figure packed his things into the small rucksack and headed further into the forest, away from the sirens and lights.

The concerning thing now was the noise that had been distant two minutes ago but was growing increasingly louder, and it was the distinct sound of a helicopter circling. He turned off the torch, throwing the path into darkness again, which wasn't an issue, as the figure knew these woods like the back of his hand. He headed west, further into the heart of the forest, before heading south, but not to his destination; it was too risky. Instead, he stopped at a small shelter that was dug into the earth, concealed from above. After crawling under a camouflage sheet, he waited, the buzz of adrenaline flowing through his veins. He would give it an hour for the police presence to clear. Not that he could return home just yet: he still had one more job to take care of.

Chapter 6

Inside the back of the forensic examiner's van were Helen, Muller, Stam, and Schmidt. Stam had called Schmidt over to hear the examiner's findings, and although the van was spacious, it was now feeling cramped.

When they were all settled, Helen began.

'So, from our initial examination of the scene, I'm afraid we don't have that much to go on as far as physical evidence goes. There are a few smudged footprints beneath the recently fallen snow, but nothing we can get a size or imprint from. As you all witnessed, the body is heavily decayed, but we will leave that for the pathologist to examine in detail.'

'And what about the timeline of the body being buried?' asked Schmidt.

'As I said, we believe that the body was buried close to four months ago, then dug up as recently as a few days ago. The reasons for these findings are that when we began excavating the body, we could see small traces of blue, both underneath the body and attached to some of the clothing that remained. We believe this to be bluebells, the flower that this area is named after.'

'Is that even possible, for them to still be intact?' Muller asked this time.

'It is. If buried deep enough, where the soil stores enough heat, then it is possible. We also checked when it's in bloom, which seems to be from early April to early September, which means the latest it could have been buried, in theory, would be fourteen to sixteen weeks ago.'

Stam wrote the timeline down. He knew that it was of importance and was glad the examiner had been thorough.

'What about the note that was found? Do you have any evidence that can be taken from it?' Stam asked.

'The paper is of common stock. The type mostly used in food packaging or greetings cards would be my guess. It absorbs more ink than the more standard paper that you would find in notebooks or invoice paper.'

'Is there anything within it specifically that could narrow it down?'

'Not that we can see. Maybe a specialist in such a thing could help. The colour is off-white, but that's about all we can tell.'

'And the handwriting?' Stam asked.

'The handwriting could be significant. From my initial checks, I would lean towards the person who wrote it being left-handed, but again, a specialist could tell you for sure. The pen itself could be a fountain pen, not common but not rare either. I'm still in some confusion as to why whoever wrote it would take such risks to leave it in the first place.'

'Would we be able to match the handwriting?'

'It could be something you could compare with suspects, but you'd need to find their handwriting in something written before today. If they think it's something we're looking at, they'll try and change it. Experts can usually tell, however.'

'Okay.'

'I've taken a copy and sent the original to our offices, where we'll have one of our specialists look at it more closely and send you the findings.'

'Thanks,' said Schmidt.

'In the meantime, we'll close the scene but keep it cordoned off and wait for the coroner's office to lift the body. We'll be in touch.'

Everyone knew this was their cue to leave.

As they crossed the main road, they walked in silence, all thinking, most likely, of a half-dug-up body, the note, and the second man at the site.

'Muller, can you contact Lahm and make sure he's on his way to the hunting lodge, and to be in touch when they've got eyes on him?' Stam asked.

'Can do, boss.'

Stam hated the 'boss' thing, and his patience was running thin with it.

Muller carried on down the street, taking out her phone to call Lahm.

Schmidt was called on by Inspector Klose, hopefully with the overhead map they had requested.

Stam stood on the steps of the church. The sky above was threatening again; it looked like snow or possibly a thick fog that was beginning to descend on the small town. He took out another cigarette and lit it, breathing in the hot smoke. Just as he exhaled, his mobile pinged with a notification. It was a message. He took out his dated phone and looked at the screen. It was a message from his daughter, and he clicked it open. It read, *Hey dad, my flight is tmrw morning, I should be landing in Munich just after 2 pm, will see you then, maybe lolz, love Monica xx.*

He closed his phone. He had almost forgotten that his daughter was visiting.

Detective Lahm was in his beat-up Volkswagen Golf. He had been promised a new car from his department weeks ago but was still waiting. It was a work vehicle at the end of the day, so he couldn't complain too much.

He and Officer Hunter, a recent trainee who had only qualified a few months ago, had made the short twenty-minute drive to the outskirts of town. The roads were treacherous due to another snowfall that the local radio station had warned them to expect, along with another snowfall due in the early hours.

As they approached the old hunting lodge from the south, they slowed and drove by the front. It was situated twenty feet back from the only road out of town. As they passed, Hunter had a good look.

'What do you see?'

'Not much. There's a double garage on the ground floor, which is closed, with what must be the living area on the first floor, I'm guessing.'

'Any lights on or signs of life?'

'No lights on. There's a car in the driveway to the right of the house, some kind of four-by-four with snow on the roof, so I doubt it's moved recently.'

'Okay.'

Detective Lahm drove his Golf another mile up the road before he found a turning point in the road. He straightened the car up and slowly made the journey back to the house, approaching now from the north.

'What's the plan?' asked Hunter.

'We watch. Our instructions are not to make contact, which we will follow.'

The old Golf slowed as it reached the lodge, creeping at ten miles an hour, as they looked for a safe place to wait and watch.

From the opposite side, they could see the front of the lodge a little better. The painted white walls were now starting to fade, and the garage doors were a shiny white but also fading. A light mounted above the garage door was on.

'We'll pass by and park up on the verge across from it.'

Hunter nodded.

They were now coming parallel with the driveway, still moving slowly, still watching. They passed by: still no lights on inside, no sign of life. The only difference to the previous drive-by was that the four-by-four was gone.

'Shit, where did it go?' Lahm asked himself more than Hunter.

'I don't know.'

Lahm stopped the car and reversed slightly so he was parallel with the driveway again. He got out and headed up towards the house. The fog was beginning to form, lowering itself menacingly to ground level. Lahm saw a side door to the house. He tried the handle: locked. He traced the path to where the car had been sitting. He stopped and stared. There were no footprints or track marks to or from the house or to where the car had been sitting. He quickly shone his torch around the back, where a small fence surrounded a large garden. He couldn't see anything. He headed back down the driveway, confused, and climbed back into the car, blowing into his hands to take the chill from them.

'You see anything?' Hunter asked, looking a little wary.

'No, nothing. The door's locked, and there are no lights on at the rear. There are also no footprints from the house to where the car was sitting.'

'What does that mean?'

'It means that when we passed by the first time, someone was sitting in the car.'

'Waiting for us?'

'Maybe, I'm not sure.'

'What do we do now, then?'

'Nothing changes: we wait.'

Just as he said it, his mobile rang. It was Muller.

The owner of the old hunting lodge was sitting in a small cabin he had built himself many years ago. It was just over one hundred yards from the lodge, hidden amongst the trees and now by the snow.

He had watched from inside his car as the two officers passed by in a beat-up old Volkswagen. When they had passed, he started the engine and moved the car to the lockup he owned, which was halfway between the lodge and his cabin. He watched as one of the men got out and tried the handle of his door and then checked the back of the house before returning to the Volkswagen. He saw it all clearly through the scope of his sniper rifle, which was pointed straight at the man. In hindsight, he shouldn't have run last night when he approached the man in the woods; he had known instantly it was a mistake. But he knew he shouldn't have been there in the first place, and now it looked like he may have been recognised, if that was in fact the police that had shown up at the house, which was definitely not helpful.

Chapter 7

It was now approaching midnight, and yet the locals had not moved. They were still gathered in groups outside on the frozen streets behind the police cordon, watching the events unfolding in their small town.

Lead Inspector Klose had decided to release a statement to the media first thing the following morning. This meant that even though people would still be curious, it would keep the media presence at the scene relatively low for now. When the news got out, however, they would have every news reporter in the country with their eyes on them. This was also why they had decided to release only the information that there had been the discovery of a body. Revealing that the body had been half-buried, or half dug up, would create a media frenzy, which was the last thing they wanted.

Stam, Muller, and Schmidt were all sitting in the makeshift police office inside the church. They were now joined by Mike, one of the employees from the forestry commission, who had brought the overhead maps of Ebersberger Forest and a map of the Bluebell Woods. The three detectives were all staring at the whiteboard that Muller had dragged in earlier, drinking coffee from paper cups that Muller had managed to find. Mike sat motionless, not sure of his role. After dropping the maps off, he had been asked to wait, as one of the detectives wanted to speak to him. He was now sitting looking at a half-empty whiteboard and the two maps he had brought, not knowing which detective it was who wanted to see him.

Stam sipped some of his coffee before beginning.

'Mike, my name is Oliver Stam, and I'm one of the detectives currently investigating the discovery of a body, which you may or may not be aware of, in the wooded area of the Bluebell Woods.'

Mike turned his gaze from Stam to the map of the Bluebell Woods, not speaking.

'I'm going to be honest with you and tell you upfront that no one knows the location of the body yet, and we want it to stay that way. You understand?'

'Yes.'

'Okay. What I need from you is your experience of the area I mentioned. Besides the main route across the bridge, can you tell me how many more entrances there are that you would consider a common route, shall we say?'

'Sure,' Mike said, a little nervous. 'If you access the woods from the entrance after you cross the bridge, it will take you towards an opening that leads onto a small pond. From there, you have three options that lead from it.'

'Which are?'

'You can head west, which is a rural path that brings you out five miles along in the town of Anzing.'

All three detectives looked at the map of the Bluebell Woods, trying to follow the route Mike was describing.

'Or you can head east, which is a path that's just under two miles and which brings you out onto the ST2080 road that splits the forest and brings you out in Ebersberg itself.'

'And the third option?'

'The third option is to head south, which is not recommended; it follows a trail that takes you into the forest's heart. Many hikers use it in summer, but it can be very disorientating.'

'And what if you crossed over the ST2080'? Is there a path that follows on east to any other towns?' Stam asked, knowing that the hunting lodge was set in the town to the east of Schwaberwegen but not wanting to let Mike know.

'There is. It picks up on the other side of the road and eventually brings you out to the village of Forstinning.'

Bingo, Stam thought.

'And how long would it take someone to walk from the bridge in Schwaberwegen on this path before they reached Forstinning?'

'Normally, one hour. In these conditions, ninety minutes, give or take.'

'Thank you, Mike, you have been extremely helpful. Remember what I said earlier, though.'

'I will.'

Mike stood up and left. He was escorted out of the office and then through a side exit of the church, in the hope that if any media were present, they wouldn't see him.

Schmidt finished his coffee and set the cup down on the floor.

'You thinking this is the route our possible suspect has taken, then?'

'Would be my guess,' Stam replied.

'We should check it out in the morning.'

'I agree,' replied Stam. 'For now, I need an update on where we are, though.'

Muller took the cue and spoke first.

'I've spoken with Lahm. He and a young officer, Hunter, drove out to the hunting lodge, which they passed by slowly and saw no sign of life, no lights, and a four-by-four parked in the driveway. They drove a little further up the road to turn and then headed back down. When they returned to the lodge, the four-by-four was gone.'

'Interesting. Did he get out?'

'Yes. He walked up the drive to the side door and checked the back garden too.'

'His initial thoughts?' Stam asked.

'Felt eerie, he said, like they were being watched.'

'Anything else?'

'Yes. He said that it had begun to snow on the way there. But when he got to the top of the driveway where the car had been sitting, there were no footprints anywhere close to where the car had been parked.'

'That means whoever drove it away must have been inside when they passed,' Stam said.

'That's what they thought.'

Stam wrote down what he needed to and closed his notebook.

'Tomorrow morning, we will visit Mr Fischer. In the meantime, try and get a registration number for the four-by-four and pass it to all patrol vehicles. Until then, tell Lahm to call it a night and head home and to be here tomorrow at nine a.m. If Mr Fischer was clever enough to leave without being seen, then he will be clever enough to stay away until it's clear.'

'Okay,' replied Muller.

'Are you sure we shouldn't be out hunting for him?' said Schmidt.

'I'm always sure,' Stam replied. 'Where are we with the coroners?'

'I've just spoken with one of them. They're in the process of collecting the body now. They say they'll have it back at their lab tonight, and Dr Park will start to process it immediately.'

'Good. Does she have both our numbers?'

'She does,' replied Schmidt.

Muller nodded.

'I recommend for now that we keep a high police presence on the scene and in the town until we speak with the media tomorrow morning. Make sure the crime scene remains sealed off until we decide it's clear. For now, we need to try to get some rest. Tomorrow will be a busy day.'

'What are you going to do?' asked Muller.

'I'll find a bed and breakfast somewhere in town for the night and sort something more permanent tomorrow.'

'You're more than welcome to stay with me,' said Schmidt.

'I'll be fine, thanks. It's still early for me anyway. Just make sure you're all here tomorrow at nine a.m.'

Both Schmidt and Muller got up and headed out to the front entrance. Stam looked at his watch: 00:12. He knew he wouldn't be able to sleep, not this early.

He grabbed his coat and made his way down through the pool of police vehicles and onto the bridge. He crossed over it and entered the forest. A ninety-minute walk to the lodge in these conditions, Mike reckoned, give or take. He could manage that, he thought, give or take. He hunched the collar of his coat up, pulled his woollen hat down over his ears, and made for the hunting lodge.

Chapter 8

Detective Schmidt met with the coroner as she was leaving the forest. She was walking behind two men carrying a stretcher with the remains of the body, now concealed inside a black body bag.

They had managed to get their van as close to the old Victorian bridge as possible, to stop prying eyes from getting a closer look.

'How did you get on?' Schmidt asked.

'Okay. It was a slow process with the condition of the body, but we managed to get it out intact.'

'How long will it take to process, if you don't mind me asking? I understand these things can't always be rushed.'

'Our initial examination will take an hour. As for Dr Park's examination, that could take as long as three hours.'

'Thank you.'

'We'll be in touch,' she replied before helping with the body bag.

Schmidt talked with Lead Inspector Klose about what the coroner had said and what he and Stam had discussed about the crime scene. Klose told him he would organise the team to work through the night and they would meet again first thing in the morning.

Schmidt thanked him and headed for his car. He got in and turned the heaters to full. As the windscreen thawed, he put it into drive and headed for home. Stam was correct: tomorrow would be a busy day.

Muller left the church and made her way to the square

in the centre of town, which was still a sea of police vehicles and officers. They had now set up several tents, mostly for privacy but also for shelter. The clouds were low, and the temperature had dropped to minus one.

After meeting with her boss, Lead Inspector Klose, and telling him she had been told to finish for tonight, she asked who oversaw IT for the case. She was told that a specialist from Munich would be dealing with all IT communications and was given their number. Muller dialled it and gave them the name Hans Fischer and the address of the hunting lodge. She asked for a full report on him, convictions and cautions, and any vehicles registered to that name.

She then met with Detective Lahm, who had returned from the hunting lodge but had been told to head home. Muller told him she would do the relative paperwork and see him in the morning.

After he left, she headed back into the church, passing two uniformed officers who were standing at the front door. She spent half an hour updating the incident file with what Lahm had explained had taken place at the lodge.

When she was done, she left the church, knowing she had to be back again early tomorrow morning, and decided to call it a night. She grabbed another plastic cup of hot coffee and made for her car. She climbed in, turned her heaters on and waited, cradling the hot coffee cup for instant heat. She glanced at the clock: it was 01:48. She was shattered. She had been on shift for fifteen hours and she needed to sleep. Then something began to niggle at her; it was what Stam had said before she and Schmidt had left him earlier, how it was 'still early for him'.

She kept the car running but got out and walked back

up the hill to the church. She passed the same two officers at the door. Inside was a third officer, who looked like he was on the phone. Stam hadn't been inside when she had been filling in the incident file, and he still wasn't. She then went looking for Klose, whom she found after ten minutes of asking.

'Have you seen Detective Stam, sir?'

'Last I saw him was when he entered the church with you and Inspector Schmidt. Maybe he's gone to find somewhere to stay tonight?'

'I get the feeling that that's the last thing on his mind right now.'

'If I see him, I'll tell him you're looking for him.'

'Okay, thanks.'

Muller knew Stam wouldn't be looking for somewhere to stay. She wandered back up to the tents that had been set up and asked a few officers if they had seen him, but they had not. She then turned towards her car but passed it by and headed for the bridge. She walked over and stopped at the entrance to the forest. Up ahead she could see several officers securing the path that led to the crime scene. She walked along until she reached the police tape. A young officer was standing on patrol. He looked frozen and tired.

'I don't suppose you've seen anyone passing through here? Not in uniform: a detective named Stam.'

The young officer looked for a second as though he had actually frozen over.

'He's in his late fifties, grey hair and a beard, looks annoyed most of the time,' she added.

'My colleague did tell me when we changed shift that a detective had passed through. He said he needed access to the path surrounding the crime scene. My colleague said that he looked particularly angry.'

'That's him. When was this?'

'Well over an hour ago, I'd say.'

'Thanks,' Muller replied and headed back to the car. She put the car in gear and headed out of Schwaberwegen. She knew where he was heading. And it would take ninety minutes or so, give or take.

***

Stam was cold, annoyed and stubborn, all at the same time. He had completely underestimated what a ninety-minute walk would take out of him, especially in these conditions. He was certainly not in the prime of his life, and his fondness for whisky and smoking didn't help. But he had still felt he could make the trek with no problem. He was wrong.

With every step in the deepening snow, he could feel his energy being sapped and his legs burning with pain. It also didn't help that most of the walk had been on a slight uphill gradient.

After passing through the cordon and past the incompetent officer who was on duty, he had carried on up the path and through the wooded tree line towards the pond. Just as he was ready to stop and catch his breath, he saw a sliver of light up ahead and what looked like an opening. Begrudgingly, he traipsed onwards, moving with heavy, purposeful steps. The trees began to clear, and he could see the faintest of light from the heavy clouds reflecting off a partially frozen pond. It was maybe thirty metres in diameter and a deep, icy-blue colour, the sky reflecting from it like a mirror.

Stam leaned against one of the trees closer to the pond

and caught his breath. He tried to stretch his legs to release some of the pain, but it didn't help. He was conscious of stopping and wanted to carry on. Then, way ahead of him in the clearing, he could see three clear openings in the trees, three paths, he imagined. Not that you could see any paths on the forest floor because of the snow, but that's what it appeared to be. After working out which route would be south, he headed off in that direction.

After another long mile, the path began to narrow, the trees creeping in on him along with the darkness that they brought. The sliver of light from the pond was now far behind. He suddenly became aware of the silence of the forest, and a light wind gently whistling through the trees gave it a haunting, lonely feel. He was not easily scared, but right at that moment, he could understand the temptation to feel such a way.

Just when doubt had started to creep in that he may have taken the wrong path, he noticed a sliver of light, faint and hovering above the trees. He took another step and stopped. He heard something, far into the woods: a deer, he thought, possibly. Surely no one else was stubborn enough to be out here in these conditions, at this hour. He listened hard for a whole minute: no more sounds. He carried on again, checking for any tracks in the snow, but he couldn't see any, human or animal.

The light he had seen began to grow brighter the closer he got to it, and at first, he wasn't sure exactly what it was until he heard the guttural sound of a diesel engine working hard in the cold, far off in the distance. It turned out it was the ST2080 road that divided the forest into two sections. When he finally reached the road, he stood at the curb and looked both ways. Miles of grey tarmac slalomed through the forest like a river, A snow plough had already been through and cleared a path, pushing the snow onto the verge. He stepped onto the road, walked to the middle, and stopped. Every fifty yards, there were lampposts, alternating from one side of the road to the other. With the darkness circling above, it reminded him of a tunnel.

He checked his phone again: 01:35, and the battery said it had eight percent remaining. Again, he could hear the sound of an engine, a whirring noise, a long way off. He hurried to the other side of the road and found an entrance in the trees. The snow was just as deep on this side. From the map, he knew the path that Mr Fischer might have taken would lead him straight to the town of Forstinning, which was only another ten minutes from his current location. He hid behind the snowy embankment and waited as a small car flew by. It was travelling so fast that he couldn't make out the registration or the make of the vehicle.

He looked above as the snow began to fall, light flakes floating in the air. Stam stood and shook off the snow from his trousers and headed into the forest again, towards Forstinning and the hunting lodge.

***

The hooded figure stood watching from the trees as Detective Stam reached the road. He watched him look both ways before crossing and hiding behind the embankment as a car sped by. He then stepped behind one of the thick trees at the same time, out of sight. When the car had passed, he re-emerged to see Stam turn and head into the trees. The figure copied the same movements but on the opposite side of the road, heading deep into the forest from where he had just come.

Chapter 9

Stam had trudged through the last of the forest, and thankfully, after what seemed like an eternity, he could see the flicker of lights, which he presumed was from the village of Forstinning. As he reached the edge of the tree line, the small village became visible. Sporadic lodges were situated at random and tucked away behind rolling hills and groups of large trees. There weren't a lot of lodges in the village, no more than ten, and a small shop and pub, which was typical for small rural villages. He could see where the main road that wound through the lodges was situated by a dark line in the crisp white snow, heading east. He thought better of making it easier on himself and walking along the smooth tarmac. This seemed like the size of a village where even before his boot hit the tarmac, everyone would know he was coming. Instead, he stuck to the edge of the forest and headed east himself. Hidden from the far-off lodges, with the forest as a backdrop, that should help to keep him out of sight.

Walking was slightly easier now, as the snow wasn't as deep close to the tree line. Stam could also make out that there must have been a path that ran alongside the forest line before the snow had covered it up.

It took him ten minutes until the lights of the lodges began to fade and the road began to narrow up ahead. He saw a clearing in the snow that a tractor must have made between two fields at some point earlier in the day and began to climb the hill toward the main road. Again, not wanting to be visible, he crossed over the road and walked alongside it. Now, to his left, was the hillside stretching high up to the sky above. He walked slowly, as he knew the hunting lodge was close, and he was wary of any cars that might approach, specifically any four-by-fours. The good thing was that he would see them well in advance, as the headlights would stand out from a mile away.

After a long curving bend and then a sharp left turn, Stam could see the hunting lodge. From Lahm's report to Muller earlier, he knew roughly where it was located, and he had a brief description of what it looked like. As he approached, he fell back further into the trees that led to the back gate of the property, stepped over a small fence, and walked on with a lot more caution now that he was so close to the house.

From afar, over the fence, he could see a large garden that had two long rectangular sheds, with a garage on the far side, big enough for two cars. The house was in darkness, and considering the time of night, this was not a surprise, but he did think he could hear a low buzzing noise, maybe a generator. He crept on slowly, his hands shaking with the long exposure to the cold. As he reached the outer fence, he crouched and peered over. He could now see clearly over the opposite fence that led to the driveway, but still no four-by-four.

He stepped over awkwardly, due to the height of the fence and the age of his old bones, and stood still on the other side where his feet hit the ground. Still no movement from inside, no alarm sounding to warn off intruders, so again, he crept forward. The two long sheds on his left looked sturdy, almost industrial. The garage was made of the same wood as the house, solid oak, Stam thought, all built at the same time many years ago, by the looks of the exterior wood. To the left and right of the porch were steps that led up to it, meeting in the middle. Under the porch was a worn-looking seating area, old cheap wooden chairs with a wooden dining table in the middle. On the wall to the right was a brick barbecuing area, built by hand. In the centre, on the rear wall of the house, was a large window, two metres wide and a metre high, which looked into a kitchen area. Stam took the first step up to the porch. No creaking from the old wood or alarm sounding, he took another, still the same, and then the last step that took him onto the porch. Still no creaks: decent quality wood, and well built, many years ago.

He took another step and knew the next step would take him into view of the kitchen window and anyone who may be inside looking out, but he took it anyway and looked in from an angle. The reflection from the white snow on the hills made it difficult to see inside. He took another step and stopped. The house was in darkness, still and silent. He turned back and headed down the stairs to the gate that led to the driveway. He swung it open and turned right on the path next to the drive. The side door to the lodge was also made of wood but with no windows, and he stopped next to it. Knowing full well that he was in no place to do so, he reached out and tried the door, his shaking hand stretching for the handle. That's when the silence of the cold night was disturbed by the definite sound of a rifle firing, long-range, far off behind him and to the right. A cloud of white snow sprayed at his feet as the bullet hit just in front of his left foot. Stam recoiled at the sound and fell backwards. He had only hit the ground for a split second before he was back on his feet and scrambling down the driveway. From the sound of the gun, he knew the direction would put the shooter far up on the hillside, so he knew heading down the driveway was the safest direction to head. The trouble with that plan was it was leaving him more exposed, as the road had no covering. As he reached the gate, he paused, grabbing at the lock, and again, he heard the pop of the rifle, again far off in the distance. The bullet was much closer this time; he could feel the air that it generated pass by his left leg, and it smashed into the fence in front of him, no more than a few inches from hitting him. He was opening the gate, unsure of his next move, when heard the screech of an engine racing up the road from his right. As it reached the last turn before the hunting lodge, he could hear it braking hard. The car came to a halt less than a foot from him. It was a Seat Leon; it was Muller's Seat Leon. He clambered in and had barely shut the door before Muller hit the accelerator and sped off.

'What the hell was that?' Muller said, not looking at Stam.

'It was a warning, I presume,' he replied.

'Or someone who's a bad shot.'

'I'm sticking with the warning. How did you know I was here?'

'I'm a good partner. I think about stuff like that.'

'Like what?'

'Like the best investigative detective in Germany saying he's going to find somewhere to stay, when it was quite clear that that was the last thing on his mind.'

Stam looked at her. She looked like a rally driver the way she was sitting, crouched forward, negotiating the tight corners. He had thought to himself earlier that day that they would get on just fine, and now he was actually beginning to like her.

'So, where are we headed? The town is in the other direction,' Stam said through relieved breaths.

'My house. You can sleep on the couch,' Muller said as the next corner approached, her eyes glued to the road in front.

Stam didn't reply. They carried on into the night, the forest passing them by on both sides.

Eventually, they approached the village of Herdweg. Muller slowed shortly after entering and turned right. The road sloped down and weaved through the side of a hill, scatterings of trees on both sides with a small outhouse on the left. As she entered the wooded area, the road peaked and then turned sharply before opening out onto the view of a large lake that was situated at the bottom of the village. Lodges were spaced out sporadically across the side of the hill, looking out onto the lake.

Muller pulled into the short drive at the front of the house, and they got out of the car and went inside. Without any talking, other than Muller showing Stam where to sleep, they both climbed into their beds and fell asleep instantly.

**

Hans Fischer had panicked when he saw a second man, whom he presumed was another police officer, approach the rear of his house on the same night. He was also aware that the man was trespassing on his property and that he had the right to protect it. He never intended to fire, but when the man had reached out to try the handle, he couldn't stop himself. There was no way he was letting anyone into that lodge, not until he had cleared a few things out first.

Soon after the man had fled in the car that had arrived, he thought better of hanging around the lodge in case anyone turned up to ask questions. His four-by-four was moved and parked in his lockup half a mile from the lodge. He could sleep in the small cabin he was currently occupying, but if they showed up and started searching the area, they would come across it eventually.

So, he packed his rifle and locked up the cabin, fastened his jacket, pulled his hat low and headed for the safety of the forest.

Chapter 10

The exact coordinates of the metal hut were as close to being in the centre of the Ebersberger Forest as possible. This had been chosen by design, not by chance. The positioning was to not only create somewhere that was hard to stumble across, but it was also the exact same distance to reach in every direction. Or to escape from, should it be required.

The hut itself was constructed with sheet iron that had started off grey, but through the years, faded to a mouldy green colour that hid itself effortlessly within the foliage of the forest. It had a large steel door with a padlock and a slide bolt across the length of it. The interior, though, was nothing like it would appear from its exterior. The inside was neat, organised, and clean, or as clean as such a place could be.

On the walls was reinforced aluminium sheeting with no windows cut out of it and designed to take the weight of long, heavy shelves that ran the length of it. The shelves were filled with all kinds of tools, both power and manual, all of which were neatly positioned in their specific places. There was a workbench running along the back wall with a vice and a lathe attached, well-worn but spotlessly clean.

The hut was eight feet by twelve feet and more than big enough for its purpose. In the centre stood a wooden table, decent quality wood, well built decades ago and still doing its job. It had fixed legs that were bolted to the concrete floor beneath, solid and strong, the same as the table. It had five leather straps secured to it that were positioned on both sides, two at the top and two at the bottom, with one at the very top, in the centre. These were important in keeping whoever was tied to them secure, not only for the procedures that they might be put through but because most of the people who found themselves in this location could find themselves there for at least a couple of days.

This was the case for the person who currently found themselves there: three days, to be exact. His name was Robert Ewing. He was a big man, over six foot and strong, but not strong enough, as it had turned out. He had feathery grey hair and large grey mutton chops which were quintessentially German looking.

The hooded figure who was responsible for bringing him there had spent almost six months trying to do so, which had made it even sweeter for him when he finally had.

The sedative that had been injected into Robert Ewing's neck the night before was now wearing off, the same as it had the previous two nights, and he was now coherent but drowsy, exactly as was the intention.

Robert could make out the outline of the figure standing over him, but he couldn't make out any features; it was merely a black silhouette lurking. As the sedative began to fade, Robert could feel some strength coming back into his muscles. He could feel the blood rushing through his veins and the fog beginning to lift. And with the realisation and now sudden fear of the situation that he found himself in, he tried with the little strength he had recovered to free himself, but it was no use. The straps were just as strong as the wooden table, and his efforts were futile.

Robert watched as the figure circled the table and then stood in front of one of the shelves. The figure knew it was now the perfect time to execute what he had brought Robert Ewing here for, to execute the second step of their revenge.

He reached up and took down a set of angled pliers from one of the shelves, along with a hacksaw. The thought crossed his mind to sedate Robert again before the removal of the teeth and the tips of the fingers, but on reflection, he didn't think that he deserved such a luxury, especially after his own actions.

As he returned to the table, Robert was now a shivering wreck and looked half the size he actually was, with his body trying to recoil. The figure placed one hand on his forehead, the other holding the pliers. After a struggle, he grabbed the first tooth with the pliers, gripped hard and pulled. The instant explosion of blood was immediately serenaded by a scream that came a split second after it. It took two further pulls and a twist at the end for the tooth to come free, and another fifteen minutes to remove the remaining seventeen teeth. The other reason for the location of the hut in the centre of the forest was that any screams from within wouldn't be heard by anyone.

With all the teeth removed, the figure lifted the hacksaw and began to remove the fingertips, one at a time, slowly and intently. At this point, however, Robert was drifting in and out of consciousness, which meant the screaming had subsided but the blood not so much. If anything, it had got heavier as the blade of the hacksaw sliced and then crunched its way through tendon and bone.

When all ten fingertips were removed and placed in a plastic bag to be disposed of later, the hooded figure took the power drill from the shelf and came round to the top of the table, positioned directly behind Robert's head. Robert looked up at him, now conscious again, fear screaming from his eyes. The drill started up, but the figure took his time to find the exact spot behind the ear; he had to be precise. When he found the spot, he touched the skin with the sharp metal and very slowly began to drill.

When the main artery that runs over the top of the skull is punctured, it doesn't cause a person to die straight away. The blood starts to starve the brain of oxygen as it begins filling it, shutting the brain down slowly. Nerve endings begin to die and stop sending signals to other parts of the body. After an hour, the blood floods the cavity of the brain, eventually causing the brain to shut down completely.

Just over an hour later, this was the case. Robert Ewing's body was hanging lifeless over the shoulder of the hooded figure. The body was heavy, which was obvious from its size, and for this reason, the location of the grave that had been dug was not too far from the hut: still far enough away to be safe, but close enough that he would be able to carry it there relatively quickly. The figure trudged on slowly, the terrain hazardous but not impassable.

The hole that had been dug the previous night, after the sedative had been injected into Robert's neck, was more than big enough to fit his body, but somehow, in the middle of the gaping forest, it felt small. That was until Robert's body was dropped into it, and now it seemed strangely large again, but still, the body had to be manoeuvred back and forth to fit it all in.

Now finished, the hooded figure stood above the grave

and looked down into it, happy that he was one step closer to what he had set out to do many years ago. Three down, one to go, he thought to himself.

Before beginning to cover the body, he reached into his pockets and brought out a small note which had four words written on it. The words read, *You have no idea*. He crouched down close and placed the note inside the bloody mouth of the body before standing back up and reaching for the shovel. The hooded figure then spent the next twenty minutes filling in the hole, with a feeling of pleasure and satisfaction washing over him.

*****

Dr Angela Park received the body from the coroner at 02:55. She marked the time down in her file. The examination made by the local coroner's office was attached to her file, not that she would read it before she had conducted her own examination. She never did; she knew it could influence her own conclusions.

Dr Park had worked as a forensic pathologist for over twenty years, and she knew it was what she was meant to do with her life. Not because she had been infatuated with all things dead and broken when she was a kid, which was merely just a goth phase. It had more to do with the fascination she had with being able to discover things that no one else was able to: to be told that something was a certainty and being able to prove that, in fact, it was not.

After graduating from university, she had begun working in her local hospital in Hamburg. After five years, she retrained to become a forensic officer at her local mortuary. Fifteen years later, she was one of the leading forensic pathologists in Germany.

The half-decayed body was now lying on the table in front of her, and she could honestly say she hadn't come across many bodies in such a state in her time. Some of the flesh was partly frozen even now, and some was still intact but half-chewed at by the animals. However, the majority had gone, revealing the skeleton underneath.

She took her own measurements and the weight of the body and marked it in her file. She established that it was of a man in his mid-forties, still with his teeth intact, which they could hopefully match in their records and determine the identity. She then checked that all the digits were attached and checked the body for any tattoos or distinguishing features, which she noted down in the file. Then came the part of the examination that she had been called here for in the first place. From her initial checks and the local coroner's autopsy, a cause of death had not been discovered, which was common for coroners but not necessarily for her.

She leaned over and clicked her speaker on. She then pulled up her mask, lowered her visor, and got to work.

***

Detective Lahm was on his way home. He had intended to call it a night straight after dropping Officer Hunter off, but he still had a few things left to tidy up before he could finish.

He had been reluctant to go home; the house still didn't feel the same, even after all this time, but in the end, he was pretty much ordered to finish for the night by Inspector Klose and to return at 9 a.m. the following morning to meet with Detective Stam.

It was now the middle of the night, and he was exhausted, so he drove slowly and steadily, deep in thought. His thoughts were mostly on the case. He couldn't get his head around why someone would dig up a body that had been murdered and buried in the first place. His mind wandered, and he began thinking of the hunting lodge, the moving of the car from the driveway and where it could have been moved to, and so quickly. He was eager to be heavily involved in the case and had wanted to stay at the scene, but he had been awake now for nearly twenty hours, and he was functioning purely on caffeine and adrenaline.

Lahm pulled into his village, drove across the gravel road to his lodge and parked the car. His house was in darkness and almost hidden against the backdrop of the surrounding forest. He got out and stood on the porch, slipped off his shoes, and turned to look out at the lake. The moon was full and reflecting off the water. He looked around at all the other lodges. They were all in darkness. He looked at his watch; it was late, and he needed to get some sleep.

He opened the door, took off his jacket and hung it on the coat hook, then stood for a second and listened: all quiet, same as always when he came home now. He skipped showering and headed for the bedroom. He climbed into his side of the bed and pulled the covers up. Just before he fell asleep, he turned and reached his arm out to the other side of the bed, out of habit, or hope, but the bed was empty, as always. He rolled back over again, closed his eyes, and fell asleep.

Chapter 11

Dr Angela Park was now three hours into her examination of the body, and she still had a while to go. So far, the circumstances of the corpse had certainly been out of the ordinary but the examination not so much.

She had travelled nearly two hours from her home on the west side of Munich. After she had finished her supper, and before she headed out for drinks with a friend, her mobile had rung. She had had to call her friend and apologise before leaving her apartment and heading to her office to collect her equipment.

The lab she was using not only accommodated the Schwaberwegen forensic examiner but also those of another five villages in the local area, and it was not the worst she had worked in, not by a long way. Being used by five different villages meant that it was well equipped but also well used. It was spotlessly clean, however, and smelled of bleach.

From what she had found so far, the body had an old fracture to the left ankle, more than likely happening years ago in the victim's late teens. The appendix had been removed, and from the scar tissue, Dr Park surmised that this had also happened in their late teens or early twenties. She hadn't discovered any other old breaks or fractures, but she did notice a small crack in the right-hand side clavicle. By the looks of the break, it had happened after death and not more than a few days ago. She noted it down in the file and circled it. She had not yet discovered what the cause of death was, which she wasn't worried about; she still had the neck and skull to check before she was finished.

Firstly, she checked the neck and the top of the spine. The small bones at the top of the neck were all intact, and what remained of the windpipe had no damage, which ruled out strangulation. Then she moved onto the skull. No impact fractures or cracks. She checked the back of the skull with the same result. Next were the sides of the skull, which she checked closely, taking her time as she always did, and eventually, something caught her eye: a small mark behind the left ear, hidden by some hair. She noted it down on the diagram in the file and brought in the magnifying glass. She looked through it and zoomed in as close as she could. It was a small hole, only a millimetre in size, very easy to miss. She measured the tiny hole before taking a picture of it and jotting it down before returning to the magnifying glass. The hole was minute and not a bullet hole: far too small. She thought back to a case she had worked on over ten years ago, with an equivalent size and placement of hole to this one. She concentrated on it for a minute longer before filling in the rest of the details in the file and signing it off. She was certain she knew what it was that had caused it.

After cleaning up and uploading the file to the computer database, she looked through the police file. The detective in charge of the case, she saw, was Detective Oliver Stam. She had known Stam for many years and was happy when she saw his name. She wrote down his number and checked the clock on the wall: 6:40 a.m. She knew it was early, but she still dialled his number. It rang twice before he answered.

'Hello?'
'Detective Stam.'
'Dr Park.'

'I thought you might be awake; you haven't changed, I see.'

'Why change what works? How did you get on?'

'Good. When can you get here?'

'That good?'

'Something like that. I need to see you.'

'I can be there later this morning.'

'That will have to do. See you then,' Dr Park said and hung up the phone.

She collected her briefcase and told the receptionist she was finished for now but would be back in a few hours.

The sun was beginning to rise as she left the coroner's office. She walked to the first café in the nearby town and sat at the window. She ordered a waffle with bacon and eggs and a pot of coffee. When it was served, she poured a mug of the hot coffee and drank half of it before she began eating. As she ate, the town slowly came to life. People came in and bought drinks and muffins and reluctantly left again for their offices or trains. She always felt grateful for her job and was happy she had put the effort in at the beginning of her career. Now it had paid off, and she was doing what she loved.

She finished up, drank the last mouthful of coffee, and took out her mobile. She held it in her hand, contemplating. From the second she had found the hole in the skull, she had been trying to decide if she should phone her old boss. He was now the security minister for the German government, after all, and was also well aware of the case she had worked on ten years ago, with the same cause of death as this one. In the end, she knew that she had to call him. The one thing that was stopping her was that he was her ex-husband, and she hadn't spoken to him in nearly eight years.

Chapter 12

Detective Anna Muller was thirty-two years old and had been a detective for almost eight years and a police officer for twelve. She loved what she did for a living, maybe not as much as Stam, but she had always known that she wanted to join the police force. Her father had been a detective, and her mother had worked in the Munich police force as a translator for over thirty years.

She had worked her way through the ranks quickly before becoming a detective, and more recently, had been considered for inspector, which at such a young age was rare.

She had been born in Munich but lived most of her life in Schwaberwegen, and a few years ago, had moved to a smaller town with her then partner, Patty. After they separated, she had kept the house and had done what she could to be able to afford to live there, and she was glad she had worked hard enough to do so. She was now happy and content with how things had turned out and focused most of her time on her work.

The morning fog had struggled to rise, almost as much as Stam when the call came in from Dr Park. He wasn't too happy about staying on Muller's couch, but last night, he hadn't had much of a choice. The sofa bed he had slept on wasn't particularly comfortable, or big, which meant that at any given point, at least one part of his body had been hanging off the side.

He had woken just before his mobile rang and thought it may have woken up Muller, but he was wrong. Just as he ended the call with Dr Park, he smelled the aroma of strong coffee which was meandering its way through from the small kitchenette to the living area.

The house itself was practical and cosy without being overly sleek. The living area was sectioned off by a partition wall that had been put there to divide the open plan. The furniture was small, tidy, and fashionable, which to Stam meant uncomfortable and expensive.

A hall beyond the kitchen led to a bedroom on the left and a bathroom opposite it on the right. The perfectly positioned window in the living room framed a picturesque view of large oak trees and cascading hills topped with snow. Stam thought he would be content living in a place like this.

As he entered the kitchen, he saw Muller attending to the coffee. She was standing at the counter, waiting on pastries heating up.

'Hey, you're awake. Who was on the phone, if you don't mind me asking?' she said, a little too cheery for the time of day.

Stam smirked at her lack of courtesy. She reminded him of his daughter. All the confidence in the world at such a young age.

'Morning to you too,' he replied.

Muller turned and smiled at him as she handed him a mug of coffee. She then turned and set a plate on the countertop between them with two croissants crammed full of butter and jam.

'It was the forensic pathologist. She wants to see us.'

'Us?' Muller replied.

'Well, me, but I feel I'm going to have a hard time leaving you behind.'

'Got that right, boss.'

'Enough with the boss, please. I don't like it.'

'Sure, boss.' She smiled as she took a bite of croissant.

Stam lifted the plate with the other croissant and headed for a small table opposite the kitchen area that had three chairs around it. He sat and Muller followed.

'Did she tell you anything on the phone?'

'Yes, she wants to see me.'

'You know what I mean.'

'She wouldn't. The fact that she wants to see me means something is out of the ordinary. Normally, you get sent a report of the findings and that's that.'

'Sounds ominous,' Muller said as she sipped her coffee.

'Helpful is what I'm hoping for.'

They both sat and watched as the sun began to creep over the top of the trees. The haze coming from the snow on the treetops was mixing with the fog.

'So, what's the plan today?'

'First, we have another coffee, and then we make our way to Schwaberwegen and check in with Inspector Schmidt. I want everyone on the same page.'

'What about last night and the incident at the lodge?'

'After we meet with the inspector, that's the first place we're going.'

'What about Dr Park?'

'She's been working all night, so another hour won't do any harm.'

'Sounds good to me. I'm using the shower first, though.'

She got up and headed through the kitchen and down to the bathroom. Stam took his mug and headed out onto the porch. He could now see the view in all its glory. Further down the side of the hill, he could see a lake and hills reflecting off the icy water. He went back inside and rinsed his mug in the sink. The rear of the house backed onto some more lodges and the forest beyond. By the looks of it, all the lodges were pretty much the same, with maybe a few additions to make them individual. He looked out and could see some smoke coming from the chimney of the lodge directly behind Muller's. He put the mug on the draining board as he heard a car starting up close by. He stepped into the hall and past the bathroom door, the shower now running inside. He reached the end of the hall, which had a long window. The car in the next lodge over was idling, but he couldn't see it. It was behind the lodge, the occupant starting the heaters and then heading back inside until it had defrosted. Sitting at the front of the neighbouring drive visible to Stam was a faded yellow VW Beetle that looked like it hadn't been started in years, an old model, more than twenty years old. There were trees and fallen branches covering the roof, and all of its tyres looked flat.

Muller called to Stam that the bathroom was free as she walked across to her bedroom. Stam went in and got into the shower that was still running. He closed his eyes as the warm water ran over his face.

***

Detective Lahm hadn't slept very well, as had been the case recently. It was just after seven, and he was stirring under his covers, restless and overthinking the previous night. He knew he had an early start and needed to be at the church for the briefing, but he was shattered and had hardly slept. He looked at the alarm clock again: 7:10 a.m. He reluctantly sat up and slid to the edge of the bed and stretched before heading to the bathroom. He brushed his teeth and stared at his reflection in the mirror. He felt old and faded and worn out, which he was. Recently, the lack of sleep and long hours were beginning to show. After a quick shower, he changed and headed for the kitchen to pour himself some coffee. He stood and drank it slowly as he looked out at the lake, still and silent and cold. He then headed out to start his old Golf. It took a few more turns than normal due to the frost, but the old engine finally kicked in and began defrosting. After a second mug of coffee, he walked up the hall and considered entering the second bedroom but decided against it and walked back to the kitchen. He felt that the house was slightly different this morning, more so than usual; it felt still and silent and cold, much like the lake outside.

He closed the front door and locked it before making his way to the car. The frost had gone, but the cold remained, and after a few minutes of idling, he pulled out of the driveway and turned onto the icy road. As the old Golf trundled along, Lahm looked through the rear window and saw his neighbour turning out of their drive too.

***

Inspector Schmidt was standing at the side of the grave in the Bluebell Woods. He had made sure he was first on the scene so he could check it in the daylight to see if there was anything else that may have been missed or not picked up within the reach of the police floodlights that had been set up late last night. But from his first walk around, there hadn't been. He knew that forensics were still on site and would be making a more thorough search of the surrounding areas themselves.

After twenty minutes he made his way back to the centre of town. The soft, flaky snow of the previous night had now turned to hard, compacted snow which was far worse to navigate. He crossed the bridge and walked up the small rise to the main square. The street was still swarming with police activity. As he reached the relative shelter of one of the tents, he could see Detectives Muller and Stam getting out of the Seat Leon on the other side of the square. Detective Lahm had already arrived and was standing under one of the tents, looking tired and anxious.

As they convened, they all stood awkwardly for a few seconds before Schmidt suggested they heard for the church.

The old church was still as unwelcoming as it had been the previous day, and with it being much earlier in the day, even colder. There was also a mist forming high up in the ceiling, lurking over them as they entered one by one and made for the makeshift office. They all sat in the chairs that were positioned in a small arc facing the information boards, and Schmidt began.

'Morning, everyone. Thanks for being here so early. This is going to be a busy day. I will begin by saying that we have two hours before the media are told of the incident. Until then we need radio silence. Any updates or statements will come through our correspondent representative. That clear?'

No one spoke, but they all nodded.

'Good. Stam, do you want to begin?'

Stam didn't want to, but he did.

'Okay, before the statement is released, I want myself, Detective Muller, and Detective Lahm to pay a visit to the hunting lodge that belongs to Hans Fischer. After we concluded here last night, I walked the trail from the grave site here in Schwaberwegen to the town of Forstinning and the lodge itself. I did not receive the best of welcomes.'

No one asked him to elaborate.

'So far, Hans Fischer is our only person of interest until we uncover evidence stating otherwise. I want him to explain his reasons for being in the Bluebell Woods last night and then fleeing the scene. After last night I believe him to be dangerous, so everyone must approach him with caution.'

Everyone again nodded but didn't speak.

'Dr Park has asked me to attend the coroner's office in Erding today, which I shall do after we have spoken with Mr Fischer. I'm confident we will know more about the identity of the corpse and the circumstances that led to their murder when I have. Apart from that, I have nothing else to add.'

Head Inspector Klose was writing everything down, and Muller was too. Lahm was listening intently, just glad he was being included in the inquiries today.

Schmidt spoke. 'Okay, we can meet again in the afternoon. Stam, I need to see the forensic report. Can you make sure it's passed to me when you receive it?'

'Okay.'

'Anything to add?' Schmidt asked.

Head Inspector Klose looked up from his pad.

'Is there any possibility that these could be the actions of a serial killer? The note placed in the mouth of the body is bothering me immensely.'

'I've also been deliberating that,' Stam said. 'One step at a time, though. Let's not begin to manifest theories; we work with the facts to find the answers for now,' Stam said.

Klose was happy enough with the reply and thanked everyone for attending before he exited.

'Okay. We will convene again in the afternoon, hopefully with more information to go on. As soon as the media are involved, we'll be under pressure to get answers; you're well aware of that, though. Be smart and stay in touch, please,' Schmidt concluded.

Everyone got up and left the office. Muller and Lahm headed out of the front door of the church. Stam hung back and gestured for Schmidt to wait. He paused until everyone else had gone.

'How much do you know about Head Inspector Klose?' Stam asked.

'He seems straight up, worked most of his days in the local police, seems fair and dedicated, and has the respect of his officers.'

'What about you?'

'I respect him as a boss.'

'Personally?' Stam asked.

'To be honest, I haven't met him outside of work and don't know too much about his personal life other than what the report tells us. What are you thinking?'

'I'm just thinking, same as I do with everyone,' Stam replied.

'Me included.'

'Yes, but I did that the last time we worked together and have no need to again,' Stam said as he began walking to the door.

Schmidt followed, knowing it must have been the comment regarding the serial killer that had prompted Stam's questions.

Chapter 13

The icy road that led through the trees to the town of Forstinning was already proving difficult enough for Muller to navigate, but now the thick freezing fog at ground level was making things even worse. With every turn, she slowed, driving cautiously, nursing the small car onward.

Inside the car were Muller, Detective Stam, who was in the passenger seat, and Detective Lahm, who was in the back behind Stam. Thus far, no one had spoken on the journey.

They approached the hunting lodge from the main road that ran east and then passed by it. All three had a good look before Muller turned the car on the road further up, in the same place that Lahm had yesterday, and crept back down. On the way back she slowed and stopped in the same spot as Lahm had yesterday. The four-by-four was back in the driveway.

The lodge looked quiet and unoccupied except for the large double garage door, which was open but at the same time looked uninviting. They all got out of the car and crossed over the road. The fog was still floating low in the sky and was now crowding the lodge and the open garage; they stopped short of entering and peered inside.

On the floor to the left were all kinds of machinery, from lawnmowers and power tools to diesel generators and compressors. On the right-hand wall was a long cabinet of mahogany-brown wood filled with various rifles locked behind glass doors, maybe ten in total, all polished wood and gleaming metal on display. The rest of the garage, however, was filled with something a little more sinister. Neatly stacked on the floor were rows and rows of deer antlers, with some suspended from the low ceiling, in varied sizes and shapes. It gave the garage an eerie feeling, Muller thought.

'I know it's a hunting lodge, but I didn't think it was still used as one. Why would he have so many antlers lying around?' Muller said.

'I assume it would be to sell. Even with it being illegal in Germany, I believe there to be a market for this kind of thing,' replied Lahm.

'There's an illegal market for everything nowadays. I wouldn't think deer antlers would be high on the list, however,' Stam answered.

'You'd be surprised,' said Lahm.

Stam stepped forward and was about to enter the garage when the sound of footsteps in the snow stopped him. He turned to see who he assumed was Hans Fischer appear from the side of the house.

'I take it you have good reason for being on my property?' Hans Fischer said in a low, husky voice that didn't match his appearance.

He was a small thin man in his late fifties, with long dirty brown hair that hung below a woollen work hat. He was dressed in dark green colours and wore heavy boots; he looked serious but efficient in his manner. Stam immediately disliked him.

'I would assume that you are clever enough to realise that you were identified two nights ago in the forest outside of Schwaberwegen. Maybe not clever enough to realise that fleeing the scene would make you a prime suspect, however.'

'A suspect in what, exactly?' Hans replied.

Stam could already feel the contempt in the man's

voice from the few words he had spoken.

'Even if it weren't you in the forest that night, we both know that you would have heard about it by now.'

'People around here like to keep to themselves,' Hans replied.

'I tend to find that small towns that use that statement as an excuse seem to know everybody's business nonetheless,' Stam replied.

'Well, you got it wrong here; I don't have any idea what you're talking about.'

'I find that hard to believe.'

'And how might that be?'

'Because someone spotted you. You know fine well that there was someone else in the woods and that they would have identified you.'

Hans Fischer seemed defiant in his manner, but now a hint of doubt was etched onto his face.

'This sounds like one man's word against another, and one man is mistaken.'

'You got that right,' replied Stam.

Hans walked over to the garage doors and stood inside, the backdrop of the deer antlers making him seem even more menacing.

'So why are you here?' he asked.

'We're here to ask for permission to search your premises.'

'Do you have a warrant?'

'We don't.'

'The answer is no, then.'

Muller looked round at Stam, who was staring at Hans.

'And if you had any evidence more than mistaken identity, then you would arrest me.'

Stam smiled at him.

'So, I'm going to ask you to leave now.'

Now both Lahm and Muller looked at Stam, who was still staring at Hans.

'If you have any travel plans in the near future, inform the police. Otherwise it won't just be a conversation we'll be having.'

Hans now looked rather pleased with himself as the three detectives turned to walk away. As they reached the road, Stam turned back towards the house.

'I don't suppose you know who would have tried to shoot at me last night, in the early hours, from way up on that hill?'

'Someone with a bad shot, I would imagine; you're still standing,' Hans said as he grabbed the rope that was attached to the handle of the garage from the inside and pulled it, slamming the garage door shut.

'Shit!' Hans said as soon as the door had closed, out of earshot of the detectives.

Outside, the Seat Leon started up. Muller pulled onto the road and headed for Schwaberwegen.

'Can I ask why you didn't bring him in for questioning?' Lahm said from the back seat.

'Can I ask why you didn't smack him in the mouth?' Muller said in a high-pitched voice.

'You saw the anger in his voice and the contempt he has for us. Bringing him in will only escalate that, and we won't get anything from him,' replied Stam.

'So how do we get anything from him now?' asked Muller.

'We wait and we watch. I want eyes on him until we get enough evidence for an arrest or at least a warrant to search that lodge.'

'And until then?' asked Muller.

'Until then I want Philip Langer and his family moved out of their house and into a safe house. I also want 24-hour surveillance on Hans Fischer.'

'Okay,' replied Lahm.

They drove on and had reached the outskirts of Schwaberwegen before Stam spoke again.

'Lahm, I want you to speak to Klose and arrange the safe house for Mr Langer and his family and to be the one to escort them there safely and discreetly. Muller, I want you to come with me to meet Dr Park.'

They dropped Lahm off at the top of Main Street. Muller didn't want to have to negotiate the endless rows of police cars, so she circled and headed north for the town of Erding.

'You know where the coroner's office is in Erding?' Stam asked.

Muller didn't reply; instead, she turned and gave him a look. Stam understood.

'What do you think of Hans Fischer?' Stam asked her.

'I know I don't like him. Seems to be one of these men who assume that everyone else is beneath him, like he doesn't have to answer to anyone.'

'What do you think of him for the murder of the body found in the woods?'

'Being there when it was discovered seems too coincidental, but we aren't going to get any answers unless we get some evidence from the pathologist or forensics.'

Muller drove on.

'If anyone finds something that no one else has, it will be Dr Park,' Stam replied.

Dr Angela Park had reluctantly made the call to her ex-husband, the security minister, Karl Ballack. She had made it as soon as she left the café, and they had spoken for twenty minutes, the length of time it had taken her to walk back to the coroner's office. She explained the situation she found herself in. She also explained that the case was not yet public knowledge and that he would have to discuss the details of it with the detective in charge. Karl had said, after the initial awkwardness, that he was happy to hear her voice again and he would do what he could to help. She had agreed to forward the number of the detective to him and also a copy of her findings if authorised to do so, as she was meeting him in the next hour or so. She told Karl they would speak soon and ended the call.

As she entered the coroner's office, the receptionist informed her that there was a message for her.

'Dr Park, the results from the coroner's DNA test will be here within the hour. The lab called when you were away to say they had concluded their examination and would arrange for them to be sent as soon as they were filed on the system.'

'Excellent, thanks. I have someone on their way for a meeting. When they arrive, can you let them through, please?'

'Of course.'

'If the results arrive, can you send them to me also?'

The receptionist smiled and returned to her computer.

Dr Park walked through to the meeting room at the rear of the office and arranged the chairs. She sat at the back of the room next to the projection screen. She took out slides of the images she had taken of the small hole and the break in the clavicle and laid them out on the table. Suddenly, she felt uneasy and a little overwhelmed at the prospect of seeing Karl again. The way it had ended was by no means bitter, but it was the end of something that she had cherished for such a long time.

She refocused and took out the local coroner's report, which she was happy to read now that she had conducted her own examination.

The report was thorough and detailed. It showed the old break in the left ankle and the scar from the appendix being removed. The break in the right clavicle was picked up but wasn't highlighted as being a fresh fracture, which she knew it had to be – the break was too clean. The most important thing that was missing was the cause of death: the pin-sized hole behind the left ear. Without being arrogant, she wasn't surprised.

The silence was broken by the phone in the corner of the room ringing, which Dr Park answered. The receptionist told her that the coroner had arrived with the results of the DNA and wanted to discuss the findings with her.

The coroner entered the meeting room and sat opposite Dr Park. Her name was Linda Strum, and she had been the local coroner for the past twelve years. She was a short frumpy woman with small features and a loud voice, and she looked out of breath but eager to talk. As she sat, she smiled warmly before shaking hands with Dr Park.

'I trust that with your decision to come in person, what you have discovered may be rather important?'

'You trusted correctly.' Her voice filled the room. 'Before I begin, did you find a cause of death?'

'I did, but I am expecting a detective shortly. If you wish to be included, then I can discuss my findings.'

Linda went to say something but stopped and focused again on the results.

'We ran a DNA test on a sample of blood and hair from the deceased, along with dental records, and we got a match.'

'That was quick.'

'It turned out that we didn't have to look very far.'

'Go on.'

'We checked the dental records first and got a match almost immediately. We then waited for the blood and hair samples to come back to confirm, and we got a name: Frank Mayer.'

Dr Park printed the name in the file.

'He's forty-five years old and from Dortmund. A missing person's file was opened on him eight months ago, but as far as any other information regarding him or his whereabouts, it all appears to be restricted.'

'How did you manage to find out as much information in such a short time?'

'Because Frank Mayer was a police officer with the Stuttgart police force when he went missing.'

Detective Lahm was standing under one of the tents in the centre of Schwaberwegen, sipping a warm drink from a cold foam cup.

After being dropped off earlier, he had explained to Inspector Schmidt what had taken place at the hunting lodge in Forstinning and that Detective Stam had instructed him to get the Langer family to safety. Inspector Schmidt agreed with the decision and spoke with Head Inspector Klose, who made the necessary arrangements. It was explained that the details and the location had to be kept between the smallest number of people possible. For obvious reasons, Inspector Schmidt said he would be the one to escort the family to the location.

Schmidt was the one that made the call to Philip Langer, and after a lengthy discussion, it was agreed that with them having no immediate family in Germany, they would be moved to a nearby safe house for their own protection. It was also arranged that Inspector Schmidt would find suitable lodgings outside of Schwaberwegen, and in the next two hours, would collect Philip and his wife and escort them to it. He told them to pack clothes for at least a few nights and to be ready to leave.

Philip Langer had protested until it became clear that the inspector was not going to take no for an answer and after he had relayed their concerns regarding Hans Fischer and the Langers' proximity to the hunting lodge in Forstinning.

After the call, Detective Schmidt spoke to Head Inspector Klose out of earshot of Detective Lahm, who had gone to find coffee. They agreed to keep Detective

Lahm out of the finer details, which he was more than happy with, to let him concentrate on the case.

'I'll have one of the communications team find lodgings, and I will escort the family in the next few hours. Until then, do we have anything back from the piece of paper that was removed from the mouth of the body?' Schmidt asked.

'I know that Helen sent it away late last night to her office to test for DNA. I also believe that it was being passed to a specialist when it was done, regarding the handwriting,' Lahm replied as he returned with a foam cup.

'I need that to be your top priority for now, Lahm. Make contact and get an idea of when we can expect to see the results.'

'Okay, boss. Will we let Stam know what's happening?'

'He's occupied; we can fill him in when he returns later. He'll have enough to deal with for now,' replied Klose.

***

The receptionist at the coroner's office asked Detective Stam and Muller to wait a moment as she dialled through to the meeting room. Dr Park told her to send them through.

She greeted them both at the door and asked them to take a seat, which they did, both directly across from Dr Park and a second woman whom they were introduced to as Linda Strum, the local coroner whose practice they were using.

Dr Park was still in her early fifties and looked good for her age, according to Stam at least. She was tall without looking gangly, and she was thin without looking skinny. She had long chestnut brown hair that was brushed to the side, with a streak of pink dye down the middle. He also noticed that she had three piercings in her left ear and one in her nose that had been removed, maybe for work reasons. Her right ear was covered by her hair, but presumably, it had the same piercings as well.

She spoke first and did so with an air of confidence that had been cultivated over many years in order not to come across as arrogant.

'Thank you all for joining me. I understand that you are all busy, but I think what I have to discuss will be better heard in person.'

Stam liked the sound of her voice; it was soft but serious at the same time.

'Linda and I have carried out our examination of the body, and apart from a few small differences, have come to the same conclusions.'

Stam had introduced Detective Muller when they came in. He addressed her as a detective who was working alongside him, which she liked hearing but didn't show it.

'Linda, if you would like to begin?'

Linda passed out photocopies of her examination report. Outlined at the top was written:

Name: Mayer, Frank. No middle name.
D.O.B.: 16/7/1977
Sex: Male
Height: 6ft 2in
Weight: 190 pounds.
Cause of death: Unknown

After the other three had read the brief description of the injuries that had been discovered, Linda began to speak.

'Upon concluding the examination, I sent samples of DNA to the lab for testing, and as you can see, we got a hit fairly quickly.'

'Very quick,' Muller said, more as a question than a statement.

'The reason for this was that the first database we checked came back with a hit. Frank Mayer was a police officer for twenty-three years and worked out of the Stuttgart office for all of them. He was reported missing a little over eight months ago, and since then there has been no further information regarding him.'

Muller stared at the photocopied sheet of paper. Stam fought the urge to swear and struggled with the thought of an active police officer being buried in the forest, which instantly turned the case into something much bigger.

After what felt like an hour but was only a few minutes, Stam said, 'We'll have to investigate Frank Mayer. If he was a former police officer, then there must be a file somewhere regarding his disappearance.'

'We tried and came up with nothing.'

'What do you mean, nothing?'

'As I said, the first database gave us his name and date of birth, but apart from that, it's like he doesn't exist.'

Stam wrote something down in his notepad before continuing.

'What was the cause of death?' he asked, fully knowing that Linda hadn't found one but with the knowledge that Dr Park had called him here because she had.

'The cause of death was from a hole drilled into the skull, piercing the main artery to the brain from behind the left ear. This method is alarming in the fact that it doesn't tend to kill a person immediately; it can take up to an hour sometimes for the brain to shut down,' Dr Park said.

Stam, Muller and Linda all stared at the doctor, a little taken aback.

'The more alarming thing about this method of killing someone is that it isn't the first time I've seen it.'

Chapter 15

Monica Stam's flight was almost ready to depart. She had left Bangkok airport twelve hours ago and had now made a stopover in Istanbul to catch a connecting flight to Munich. She was tired but also excited, as she hadn't been home for four years and she was looking forward to seeing her father. She had missed him. The passing of her mum years back, even though it had been devastating for them both, had brought them closer. She was also keen to see him after the latest media attention he had been involved in.

As the plane began taxiing down the runway, she took out her mobile phone and dialled her father's number. It rang for a minute before going to voicemail. She turned her phone off and gazed out of the window. The airport building was now a dot in the distance, with the midday sun towering high in the sky. She could see the high-rise buildings of Istanbul shimmering on the horizon.

She lowered the window shade and stared at the seat in front. She wasn't apprehensive about flying; she was thinking about her dad and the fact that he never picked up the phone. The reason she had tried to phone him and was now wondering why he never answered was that just before boarding the flight, she had seen a news report on her phone. It said that a body had been discovered late last night in a wooded area in Schwaberwegen, a town on the outskirts of Munich. She also knew what that meant when your dad was one of the best homicide detectives in Germany.

***

The police presence that had taken over the town of Schwaberwegen was now slowly being matched by the presence of local media vans and reporters. Head Inspector Klose was orchestrating his team to set up clear perimeters to keep them far enough away from the crime scene.

The statement regarding the discovery of the body had been made just after 10 p.m., and it had taken just thirty minutes before the first national news reporter was on the scene.

Inspector Schmidt had deliberately left before the official statement was made, to prevent anyone from following and discovering the location of Mr and Mrs Langer. He stopped outside the home they shared and waited as Philip and his wife got into their car, along with Poppy. They followed him down the small drive and out of town.

They drove south through the Ebersberger Forest and on to the village of Ebersberger itself, where they were to stay in a holiday lodge that was currently unoccupied and far enough from the main village of Ebersberger to be secluded.

Schmidt contacted Klose as soon as he had dropped them off, to be told of the media presence. He then tried calling Stam, but it rang out and went to voicemail.

He then turned the car and headed back to Schwaberwegen. The gloom cast by the snow-topped trees swallowed up his car as he re-entered the forest.

***

The forensic officer, Helen, who had briefed everyone late yesterday, had received a phone call from her head office in the Bavarian State Bureau in Eching, outside Munich. They had called to inform her that the results had come through for the piece of paper that had been sent to them late last night. They said they hadn't found anything that they thought would be of any great significance. Helen disagreed and said that the smallest of details could be important. They then told her that they currently had no staff to return the evidence to them, as they thought it wouldn't be required. After speaking to Head Inspector Klose, Lahm was dispatched to retrieve the paper and the file containing the results.

***

On the projection screen in the forensic lab were two images of the skull belonging to the man they now knew as Frank Mayer. The two images were side by side. In the first, you could make out that it was a skull; in the second, you couldn't. The second image looked like a small black dot on a piece of white paper that had been zoomed in on as much as possible.

'The part of the skull in which the hole has been made has been chosen specifically. The exact position, which I've determined from having seen this before, has not been chosen by chance. The small hole has punctured the external carotid artery that runs from the heart, passes over the skull, and supplies blood to the face, neck, and brain. If the artery is punctured, the brain cavity is flooded with blood, which can lead to a coma, and often, a slow death.'

'And this is the cause of death?' Muller asked.

'Correct. It was due to a bleed on the brain from a puncture made by a fine drill, a millimetre in diameter and two inches long.'

Muller looked across at Stam.

'And where exactly did you see this cause of death before?' Stam asked.

'It was on a case back in 2010. A body came in that we initially thought was an aneurysm. After a post-mortem, we noticed the hole in the side of the head, and when we checked it out further, we discovered the small hole was the cause of death.'

'Why was it so memorable?'

'Because we hadn't seen it before, but mainly because we had another three bodies come in over the space of the next six weeks that had the same hole on the same part of the skull. We believed it could be the work of a serial killer.'

'Was anyone ever caught?'

'No. Lots of people still discuss it today. Technically, the case is still open and being investigated by the Munich office.'

Stam knew that this was a lot of information to process, for everyone. He asked Dr Park for the file, thanked the local coroner, Linda, and asked if he could take Dr Park's report to read when he returned to Schwaberwegen. She agreed and told him to call her if he needed any assistance.

They all stood and shook hands. Stam began to leave, but Dr Park stopped him.

'The case from ten years ago, as I said, is still active. When I made my discovery, I had to contact my former boss to make him aware of the findings. He's promised to do what he can to assist us.'

'In what way can he assist?' asked Stam.

'He oversaw the forensic office in Munich when I

worked there and was heavily involved with the police in trying to track down the person responsible. He is now the security minister of Germany.'

'Karl Ballack?' Stam asked, with underlying aggression.

'That's correct.'

'Shit!' Stam said, before turning and leaving the office with Muller.

Muller left the office building after Stam and saw him leaning against her car smoking a cigarette. He looked deep in thought.

'What was all that about?' Muller asked, taking the keys from her pocket.

'Get in the car and I might tell you,' Stam said, throwing the half-smoked cigarette onto the ground.

They drove out of the small town and made for Schwaberwegen. They drove in silence for ten minutes before Stam finished processing the information he had just discovered.

'You remember a few months back, the case that went to court regarding the murder of the well-known defence lawyer? He was murdered in his apartment in Berlin.'

'Yes, I do.'

'And do you remember the murder of a child in Nuremberg that happened on the same day? A twelve-year-old who was kidnapped off the street in a rundown area east of the city.'

'I can't say that I do.'

'Exactly. Both cases happened within hours and fifty miles of each other.'

'And what does this have to do with Karl Ballack?'

'He's the security minister. I was working on the case

of the twelve-year-old boy. I strongly believed that it was the work of a child smuggling ring. I spoke with the head inspector of the case. He agreed and spoke to the police director, who took it to the security minister, Karl Ballack. He said that they didn't have the resources at the current time to pursue the possibility of the smuggling ring. They concentrated on using their resources to find the one responsible for the killing of the lawyer.'

Muller could remember the case; she also knew that the man who was brought to court was acquitted due to lack of evidence.

'The case lasted five weeks, and at the end, a verdict of not guilty was found.'

'I remember that.'

'What you won't remember is that in the five weeks of the trial, two more kids were kidnapped from two different towns around Nuremberg. Out of the three taken, one hasn't been found and two were found dead.'

'This is what the media publicity came from, I presume?'

'I said in a statement that the security minister should feel ashamed that he let the families of these children down and should resign from his post.'

Muller hadn't seen the articles in the newspapers, but she had heard stories regarding them.

'Is this going to be a problem for the case?'

'Probably. Unless he does his fucking job this time.'

***

Dr Park gathered up her things and headed out of the offices and back to town. She had seen a small hotel earlier where she planned to check the availability of rooms, for the next few nights at least. She thought that she might be required to help with the case and didn't want to have to travel back and forth from her home.

As she passed by the café that she had eaten breakfast in earlier, she took out her phone and dialled her ex-husband, for the second time in eight years.

Karl answered. 'Hi, everything okay?'

'As good as it can be.'

'You need anything?'

'Not just yet. We've identified the body with the hole in his skull.'

'What's their name?'

'Am I able to say?'

'I'm the security minister; I'm going to find out anyway.'

'Frank Mayer. He was a police officer.'

'I'll check it out. Was that the reason for your call?'

'No, I passed on your offer to assist on the case to the lead detective. He didn't seem too enamoured by it.'

'Why would that be?'

'I'm not sure exactly.'

'What's his name?'

'Oliver Stam.'

'Shit!' Karl replied and hung up the phone.

Chapter 16

As Stam and Muller neared Schwaberwegen, he remembered that his mobile phone had vibrated a few times in his pocket while he was in the forensic office. He took it out and clicked it open. Three missed calls from Inspector Schmidt and two from his daughter, two hours apart from each other. He had forgotten about her flight coming in today. His phone said it was 14:15. He tried to call her back, but it rang out three times before being disconnected.

'What is it?'

'My daughter's landing at Munich airport today, I forgot.'

'When?'

'Twenty minutes ago.'

They were interrupted by Stam's phone ringing. It was Inspector Schmidt.

'Stam, how did you get on?'

'We've got a lot to go over, let's just say,' Stam replied.

'We released the statement earlier and it's gone crazy with media here. Are you close by?'

'Ten minutes away. Is everyone there so that we can sit down?'

'Everyone except for Lahm. He's collecting the results from the note we found on the body.'

'Where from?'

'The Bavarian Institute.'

'Next to Munich airport?'

'Yes, why?'

'We'll see you in ten,' Stam said and hung up the phone.

Lahm had left Schwaberwegen and headed north for the A99. He hit the accelerator and took the old Golf up to 140kph on the autobahn before he thought he saw smoke rising from underneath the bonnet, then slowed and exited at the junction for Eching. The roads were busy as the lunchtime traffic was building.

He pulled his car into the office car park and parked near the front door. The building was old and grey and looked like an apartment block that had been built in the seventies, concrete grey with pokey windows.

After being told through an intercom speaker that all guests had to be signed in and wait in the holding room before entering, even if they were only collecting a file, he took a seat.

It took fifteen minutes before he was finally given the file and signed back out, and he was now sitting in his car as a plane roared by overhead, heading for Munich airport. He had put the car in gear and pulled out of the office car park when his mobile phone began ringing.

Stam arranged for Lahm to head to the airport to collect Monica, whom he had spoken to after she cleared security. He explained that he was in the middle of a case and had asked a detective he was working with to collect her. She was not surprised after seeing the news report before her flight departed that he wouldn't be there to collect her himself.

***

Inspector Klose had been accurate about the media presence that had descended on the town; there were now just as many news trucks as there were police vehicles.

This was exactly what Stam didn't want to happen, the case receiving more exposure than it needed. The media always wanted to feel like they were helping, when in fact they were doing the opposite.

Muller parked the car and they both got out and met up with Inspector Schmidt. They all spoke briefly before making their way to the church, where Inspector Klose was already standing at the entrance. He greeted them before they all headed inside and took a seat in the makeshift office that had been set up the night before.

'Okay. First, we're going to go over the information that Detective Stam gathered from the forensic examiner's office. Stam?'

'Okay, we've spoken with Dr Park regarding the cause of death, which has been concluded as a bleed on the brain from a puncture hole behind the left ear. This has been done with a fine drill, directly into the artery that supplies blood to the brain, and we believe that this was positioned deliberately. Dr Park has also seen this cause of death before.'

Muller was watching the two inspectors as Stam described the details. Inspector Schmidt's demeanour didn't change when he described the cause of death. Head Inspector Klose looked down when he heard that the weapon that had been used was a fine drill, however.

'Where?' Schmidt asked.

'It was from a series of killings that took place ten years ago in Munich. Four bodies in six weeks came in that had the same cause of death.'

'Was anyone charged with the murders?'

Stam was about to answer, but he didn't get the chance.

'No,' Klose interrupted.

Everyone turned to look at him.

'No one was caught. I know because I worked the case.'

Stam stared at him, now understanding where the serial killer question had come from earlier that morning.

***

Hans Fischer was inside his garage with the door pulled down. He knew that the police patrol car was still sitting in the lay-by across the street. When the detectives had left earlier, he had heard the car pull up, stop, and not start up again. Now he had a problem: he couldn't let them inside, not now anyway. If they began snooping around, they would find stuff he didn't want to be found, certain items that could be an issue. But he also knew he couldn't stop them forever. If they needed a warrant, they would get one by any means possible, he knew that. This meant his only option was to wait till nightfall and sneak out back with several items that could be incriminating, then head to his cabin up on the hill via the garage. From there he could dispose of the items out in the forest, hopefully where no one would find them. He had hidden things there before, some for a long time, without them being discovered.

He opened the garage door again and stepped outside, where the cold fog still hung low in the air. He looked at the car across the street. The young officer eyeballed him before he turned and lowered the garage door. When he had opened it, out of sight of the officer, he had kicked a small leather hold-all bag across the floor in front of the door. As he bent down to close the door, he grabbed it and kept it low and out of sight. He then headed around the side of the house and in through the side door. He set the bag on a cupboard next to the door. All he could do now was wait and pray that the detective didn't get a warrant before dark.

***

Lahm was waiting in the drop-off zone for Stam's daughter, Monica. When he took the call from Muller, he had just been leaving the car park of the bureau, which was only a five-minute drive from Munich airport.

The airport was loud and bright and filled with people heading for the sun. He sat waiting for ten minutes, watching the hustle of people exiting the front entrance and scurrying to the taxi and bus ranks. From the back, he saw who he thought could be Monica. She was short with shoulder-length blonde hair and a small face; she looked to be in her late twenties. Walking briskly towards the car, she looked confident.

She smiled at him as she approached the front of the car, and he smiled back as she passed by and opened the boot, dropping her bag inside. She then made her way to the passenger side and climbed in.

'You must be Detective Lahm?'

'And you must be Monica?'

'Correct.'

'You can call me Thomas,' he said as he pulled out of the airport and headed back onto the A99.

On the return to Schwaberwegen, Lahm drove at a steady pace. He didn't want to drive at excessive speeds with someone he didn't know.

'How was your trip? he asked.

'It was great, thanks. Glad to be back though, and to

see my dad.'

'I bet. How long were you away?'

'Four years.'

'Wow, that's more than a gap year!'

'You could say that.'

Lahm could see a slight resemblance between Monica and her father. Not so much with looks but with her directness; he liked that. She was also very good-looking. Must be from her mother's side, he thought.

When her dad had told her that a detective was picking her up, Monica had expected that it would be a middle-aged man in his fifties with receding hair and an out-of-fashion moustache, which was not the case. She thought Detective Lahm was maybe in his early thirties and she also thought he was attractive.

They drove on, chatting most of the way. Monica had asked him to take her to see her dad; she would figure out a plan when she got there.

Chapter 17

For the last fifteen minutes, Head Inspector Klose had brought everyone up to speed on the details of the case he had been involved in back in 2010: a serial killer was luring random people to an unknown destination, then drugging them before drilling into the sides of their heads with a drill only a millimetre in diameter. The killer had used the same method as Stam had just described with the body that had been found in Schwaberwegen.

'Were there any leads or suspects?' Stam asked.

'None. We established that whoever was carrying out the killings must have been doing so at a different location before dumping them in random places across the city, as there was never any blood found at the scenes. The body was never beaten or injured apart from the hole in the side of the head. And as far as any suspects were concerned, we were completely lost.'

'What about toxicology?' Stam asked.

'Only one of the victims was clean; the rest had all kinds of substances inside them. We never found anything consistent in all of them, though,' Klose replied.

'You think it could be the same person that's responsible?' Schmidt asked.

'I can't say with certainty that it's not.'

Stam was writing all the information down.

'The local forensic officer has managed to get an identification on the body from her examination. His name is Frank Mayer, and he was a police officer out of the Stuttgart office,' Muller said.

'Police officer? Did they find out when he went missing?' Schmidt asked.

'They said it was eight months ago,' Muller replied.

'We have to get more information on Frank Mayer. The coroner said she couldn't find any details regarding him or his disappearance. We need to look into that,' said Stam.

'I'll make a few calls and see what I can dig up,' Klose replied.

***

Detective Lahm entered the church and came into the meeting room. He told Stam that his daughter was outside. Stam excused himself before heading outside to greet her, which he did with a long-overdue cuddle. She looked different, he thought, and he was delighted to see her.

'You look younger than the last time I saw you,' he said.

'I wish I could say the same about you, Dad,' she replied with a smile.

He smiled in return.

'I'm guessing this is a big case. I saw it on the news before I left Istanbul. They said that a body had been discovered in the woods.'

'That's right. The media were told earlier today, and it's got a bit crazy.'

'I can see that.'

'Does that mean I'm not going to see much of you?'

'I'll admit it's not going to be easy for the next few days. But I will make time.'

'I know you will,' she replied.

Stam really had missed her. He cuddled her again.

'I'm going to find a place to sleep. Can we meet up

later for coffee?'

'Sure,' Stam replied. 'I'll call you this evening.'

Stam re-entered the meeting room. He took his seat and noticed Detective Lahm passing out the report from the forensics lab regarding the note from the mouth of the deceased.

Muller took out the file, which Stam asked her to read.

She quickly looked it over before she addressed the room.

'So, from the results, they have determined the paper is common stock, right enough, and produced in Germany. It's used for all kinds of purposes, as Helen said. Based on their analysis of the ink, they estimate that the note was written between six and eight months ago. There are no fingerprints or DNA on the note, which pretty much moves us on to the handwriting.'

Detective Lahm brought a chair across from the far wall and sat next to Muller.

She continued, 'The next report is from a specialist that they brought in to analyse the handwriting. I'll read out the report.'

'From my findings, I strongly believe that the person responsible for writing the note is left-handed; several indicators point to this.'

She paused and read to herself for a second, then continued.

'Although we have no legitimate process to confirm this, I do believe that the person responsible for writing the note is male.'

Everyone thought about what Muller had said for a second.

'Do you have a copy of the note?' Stam asked.

Muller fumbled through several pieces of paper before finding the copy and passing it to Stam. He ripped the piece of paper in half and stared at the four words on it. He could see the slant in the writing that made it look like the person who wrote it was left-handed. The writing in general was neat and clear, with no joined-up letters. He folded it and placed it in his notebook.

'We are now getting some faint outline of a profile; we have to work on this,' Schmidt said. 'What about the results from forensics?'

'Nothing new,' Stam replied. 'Dr Park found no DNA or evidence on the body regarding possible suspects. The only other thing in the report was a small fracture of the clavicle.'

'Her thoughts on this?'

'We've discussed it in person, but according to the report, it happened after death, maybe when the body was moved.'

'Can this be proven?'

'I will ask the question.'

'To sum up, then. The cause of death is the main artery in the brain being punctured by a small drill in the side of the skull. We have no DNA at the scene or on the body, and the only physical evidence we have is the note found in the mouth of the deceased, which we now know is clear of any DNA.'

Everyone looked around the room with the same look on their faces.

'We can only work with what we have, and what we have is Hans Fischer. Where are we on a warrant to search his lodge?'

'It will be through first thing in the morning,' said Klose.

'Not good enough. He's the only thing we currently have to go on; we need it sooner,' Stam replied.

'I'll apply some pressure,' Klose replied.

'Do we still have eyes on Hans's lodge?'

'We do,' replied Lahm. 'Officer Hunter and his partner are taking it in shifts along with myself. They're parked in the lay-by across from his drive.'

'Good. Any movement has to be monitored and relayed, understood?'

'Yes, boss.'

Stam looked at his watch: 16:48.

'Okay. For now, we have to wait on the warrant before we can proceed. Head Inspector Klose, can you arrange for the file regarding the original case to be sent to myself and Inspector Schmidt? I'd like to go through it and see what I can find.'

'I'll get on it straight away. Do you actually think it could be the same person responsible?'

'I don't, but I can't be sure,' replied Stam.

Everyone dispersed from the church. Klose got on the phone straight away with the Munich office and requested the file Stam was asking for. Lahm headed for the hunting lodge to relieve Officer Hunter for the night. Schmidt and Muller headed to a nearby hotel to grab some food, and Stam told Muller if the file arrived today, he wanted to go over it with her. She nodded before leaving.

Stam put on his coat and left the church. He messaged Monica and told her to meet him at a café in town in half an hour. She messaged him back a picture of a thumbs up that Stam's phone was too old to display, but he knew she had got the message, at least.

Instead of heading for the café, however, Stam turned left and walked toward the Victorian bridge. He crossed it and walked along the path to the point where the police tape forced him to turn right. There was no officer keeping watch. He stepped over the small path and across the snow to the scene. He tried to look at it from a different perspective, from the perspective of someone who knew that the body was there, from the perspective of Hans Fischer. Was it a coincidence that he had stumbled upon it that night? Or was it prior knowledge of where the body was that led him to approach it from the opposite side of the forest, a route that he knew would take much longer but also would prevent him from being seen? Whatever the case, Hans Fischer needed to be brought in.

Chapter 18

Detective Lahm had taken over from the young officer outside the hunting lodge. It was 17:52. The sky had now turned dark blue as the clouds began to gather high up in the sky before they descended. Lahm reclined his seat and got comfortable; he was on shift until 21:00, when Officer Hunter would take over and work through the night.

As far as he could see, nothing much had changed since his visit earlier today. The garage door was still closed, and no strip of light from beneath was visible, meaning the lights inside were off. The main house looked much the same, with no lights on in the main living room. The kitchen was not quite visible, and as far as his view showed, the house was in complete darkness. He had also noticed that the four-by-four was still sitting in the driveway, and no tyre marks in the snow meant that it hadn't moved from this morning either.

Lahm took out his mobile phone, opened and scrolled through the contacts in it and stopped at Monica Stam. She had given him her number before they entered the church, her reason being if she ever needed to be picked up at an airport again, she could call. Lahm knew the real reason – the connection – he had felt it too.

He clicked on the number and hesitated. He hadn't done this in a while, but he was positive that within only two hours of meeting someone, sending them a message was a little desperate, bordering on creepy. He started to type regardless and had only got a few words written when something caught his eye, a slight movement off in the distance, highlighted by the whiteness of the snow on the hill: a figure, dark green and moving fast. Lahm sat up and focused. It could be Hans Fischer heading up the hill behind the lodge; it was definitely a person stumbling in the snow and carrying some sort of bag in his right hand. Lahm got out of the car and raced up the side of the house, past the four-by-four and to the rear fence. The figure kept on going, a hundred feet ahead. Lahm would never catch him. He stood for another minute and watched as he disappeared over a rise in the hill.

Lahm knew he should have noticed him sooner; he was annoyed with himself but at the same time knew that if it was Hans Fischer, he had not left the house via the side door or the garage. He doubled back and headed up onto the porch. The kitchen window was huge, and he peered in to see nothing out of the ordinary. A dated kitchen with a living area beyond. No lights on or any activity, so he moved further along. Next to the barbecue area was an outside sitting area, and he passed by it to a window at the end of the building. He peered inside again; there were thin white curtains that hung from the ceiling to the floor. Through the curtains he could make out some sort of study, where there was a desk and a chair with some wall cabinets at both sides. There was a small couch to the right-hand side, and the area directly in front of the window was clear, like a walkway. He pushed at the window; it was solid. He took out his torch and shone it inside, but he couldn't make out any other details. He then checked the window frame; it was thicker than the kitchen window. He shone the torch inside again at an angle, and pointing downwards, he saw the chrome of a door handle. This was how Hans had got out; the door had been designed to look like a window.

Lahm was now positive that the figure was indeed Hans Fischer, but instead of taking out his phone to dial Inspector Schmidt or Stam, he walked back around the house. He wanted to have a look for himself. He reached the four-by-four and tried the handle: locked. He then walked to the side door: locked. Third time lucky, he thought, and made his way to the garage door. He grabbed at the handle and pulled it; it was also locked but didn't feel as sturdy as the car or house doors. He grabbed it with two hands and yanked at it. He felt something buckling or bending, a metal catch or lever inside, before the garage door opened. When it was opened, he stepped inside. No one was inside; the garage was empty. He took out his phone, brought up the number for Inspector Stam and dialled.

'Boss, it's Lahm.'

'I know, it says so on my phone when you call.'

Lahm didn't know what to say to that.

'I'm currently on shift at the hunting lodge and something has come up.'

'What?'

'I believe Hans Fischer has used a dummy door to leave the lodge. I think I may have just seen him heading over the hill to the rear of the house.'

'When was this?' Stam asked.

'A few minutes ago.'

'You still on site?'

'Yes.'

'Don't move. I'll be there in fifteen.'

Lahm put the phone in his pocket when Stam had hung up on him. Fifteen minutes to have a better look before he arrives, Lahm thought, before reaching up and pulling the rope that closed the garage door from the inside, slamming it shut in front of him, the same as Hans Fischer had done earlier.

***

Monica was sitting at the table inside the café where she had met her dad. He had left five minutes ago after receiving a phone call from another detective, and his coffee mug was still warm and half full. The café was still full even for such a late hour. She assumed that it was due to the influx of journalists and reporters that had descended on the small town. She noticed a few of them standing in line now, rushed expressions on their faces, their heads stuck in their phones.

After she had finished the last of her drink, she took out her phone and flicked through it. She checked for any news reports on the case he was working on; this was the only way she would find out anything, even with her dad being the lead detective on the case. Not finding anything new, she switched to her contact list and scrolled until she found the number of Detective Lahm. She clicked on it and hesitated. She was positive that after only two hours of meeting someone, sending them a message was a little desperate, bordering on creepy, but she did it anyway. The message was concise; it read, *Might be in need of a lift tomorrow, you free? xx*

She pressed the send button and got up from the table. She put on her coat and made for her hotel. She knew that she wasn't seeing her dad again tonight but that he might call later, regardless of the fact that she was still jet-lagged and needed to sleep.

She made her way down the back street that the café was on and out onto the main street, which was still busy.

It was a short walk from the café to her hotel, and upon entering, she noticed a woman standing at the reception. Monica overheard her asking if they had a room available, which they did. Monica smiled at the receptionist and then at the woman asking about the room, who smiled back. She was tall with brown hair that had a strip of pink dye running down it, and she was carrying a large bag.

After taking a shower, Monica changed and lay down on the bed. She could feel her eyes closing as she settled in. Just as she was about to fall asleep, her mobile phone pinged with the notification of a text message. She lifted the phone and checked it. It was from Lahm, and it read, *A bit creepy messaging so quick, guess it saved me from doing it lol. I will see what I can do xx.*

Monica smiled and put the phone back on the nightstand, falling asleep shortly afterwards.

Chapter 19

Muller picked up Stam from the café five minutes after he phoned her, and they made their way to the hunting lodge in Forstinning. Muller squeezed the car in front of Lahm's beat-up old Golf and they got out. Lahm was standing halfway up the drive as they approached.

'Hey, you got here quick!' Lahm said as they reached him.

'Winter tyres work a charm,' Muller replied.

'What have we got?' Stam asked, annoyed at the small talk.

'As I said on the phone, it looks like he got out using a hidden door at the rear of the property. I saw him halfway up the hill. I watched from the garden, but there was no way I could have caught up with him.'

'What about the house?'

'Looks the same as before: no lights on and all locked up, I've checked.'

'What about the garage?'

'Didn't try it,' Lahm replied. He knew he shouldn't have entered; he hadn't found anything that would help the case either.

Stam walked over to the garage door. He thought the handle looked like it would open, but he didn't want to jeopardise evidence by checking it.

'Muller, get Inspector Klose on the phone. We need this warrant as a matter of priority. Lahm, I need you to get your two officers here ASAP. I want this house surrounded with officers twenty-four hours a day until I tell you otherwise.'

'Yes, boss.'

Muller walked down the driveway, took out her phone and dialled Klose. Lahm sent a message to Officer Hunter, telling him he was required on shift earlier and to bring another two officers.

Stam walked around the house the same as he had the night before, only this time in the opposite direction, from the garage to the porch. He tried all the same handles as the night before; all were locked. After looking at the door that Lahm had told him about, the one that had been made to look like a window, he stepped off the porch and walked to the end of the garden. He looked out at the snow-covered hill. Even with the darkness, the white of the snow provided enough light to see.

'Hey, boss, I just spoke to Klose. Nothing can be done with the warrant until tomorrow morning. It's out of his hands,' Muller said as she came up beside him.

'Shit!' Stam replied. 'Where was it that he disappeared out of sight?' he asked Lahm, who had now walked over and was standing next to Muller.

Lahm raised his arm and pointed at nothing in particular. 'Over there, to the right of where we're facing now.'

That was of no help, Stam thought.

But just as he was ready to turn back to the house, something caught his eye further over on the right from where Lahm had pointed. It was a dark reflection, set within the hill and slightly hidden by the whiteness of the snow.

'What's that?' Stam said, now pointing himself.

'Where?' replied Lahm.

'Further to the right from where you pointed, a hundred yards up.'

Lahm focused and eventually saw what Stam was looking at.

'I'm not sure.'

'Looks like it could be a window. It's hard to see as it'll be reflecting the snow.'

'You might be right,' Lahm said as they turned back towards the house to find a way up the hill to investigate.

***

Hans Fischer had jumped over his rear fence when he thought it was clear to do so. The officer sitting in the old Golf across from his lodge hadn't seen him immediately as he was on his phone. Hans had climbed the hill as quickly as his old bones would allow him, which was still quick, considering. As he reached the top, he turned and checked the lodge. He couldn't see the police car from his position, which meant he couldn't see the officer either.

He opened the door to his small cabin. He thought about dumping the bag he had taken from his garage in the corner but decided it would be best to have it with him. He thought about taking his rifle but instead unlocked a small safe and took out a handgun. He closed the door and locked it before quickly checking down to the lodge: still no sign of anyone. He put the gun in one of his pockets and the key in the other and made his way down the other side of the hill and then south. He planned to skirt around the outskirts of the village. He reckoned that within thirty minutes he would be in the Ebersberger Forest.

***

Stam, Muller and Detective Lahm had got back in the Seat Leon, and Muller drove past the front of the lodge and took a right turn, past the lodge and up a tight side road. They passed the opening to a second road on the right that was not far enough up the hill for it to lead to what they thought they had seen. The road turned to the left before straightening up, which was when they saw what looked like the pointed edge of the roof of a small building of some sort. They got out of the car and headed over to it. It was a small wooden cabin with a door on the front and a large window on the side. Stam tried the handle, but it was locked.

'We'll have to wait for the warrant to get us inside,' Lahm said.

Muller was standing at one side of the cabin and Stam at the other, the side which had the large window in it. He stood facing back down the hill towards the lodge.

'This is where he fired the rifle at me last night,' Stam said.

Muller and Lahm walked around to where he was standing and looked down.

'We need this warrant,' Muller said as she and Lahm walked back around to the front of the cabin, with Stam a few feet behind.

'I'll have three officers here all night. If he returns, we'll catch him,' Lahm said.

Just as Muller was about to reply, she was interrupted by the sound of a loud crash, which ricocheted around the empty landscape. They both turned around to see Stam standing at the door of the cabin, which was now open thanks to Stam throwing a rock through a small glass window in its door.

'I'm done waiting. This guy is pissing me off,' he said

before putting his hand through the broken glass and opening the door.

Inside the cabin was a small table with an even smaller stool in front of it. In the corner was a wood burner with a dozen logs stacked neatly at the side. In another corner stood a rifle. It was inside a leather case that looked old and worn; they would take the gun and its case as evidence.

With all three detectives now inside, it showed how small the cabin was. Stam looked down at the lodge again from the same position he had on the outside. It was a good shot from this distance; he thought about a hundred yards, give or take, which required a certain degree of skill or training.

'Why does this guy have a small cabin a hundred yards from his house? Do you not find that strange?' asked Muller to no one in particular.

'I find the whole set-up strange,' replied Lahm.

'This is where he fired from; the angle is right for where the bullet bounced off the path in front of me, and then again with the one that hit the fence,' Stam said.

'You still think it was a warning shot?' asked Muller.

'I believe so. No one has that many rifles locked in their garage if they can't shoot. We need the file on him that you requested, Muller.'

'Yes, boss, first thing in the morning.'

'Bag the rifle and have someone keep an eye on this cabin. If he returns here tonight, I believe he'll come here before the lodge itself. Tell your men to stay out of sight; I don't want him getting spooked and fleeing.'

'Yes, boss.'

They left the cabin and walked the short distance to

the entrance of the road that they had passed on the way up the hill. The snow was deeper the further they walked as the road forked left and then right before opening into a small clearing. At the end of it was a dark green metal lockup, big enough for a car but too small for a van. The lockup was well concealed, set within large trees and tucked into the corner. Stam led the way. When they reached it, they could tell it was a well-built structure, much like the others. Muller circled it: no windows, just the one double door at the front. It had a bolt lock that was secured with a thick padlock.

Stam looked at Muller. 'Do we have any bolt cutters?' he asked.

'We've already broken into one of his premises,' replied Muller.

'Who's to say it belongs to him?' Stam replied. 'Besides, we've already broken into one. What's the harm in making it two?'

Lahm disappeared down the winding road and then reappeared five minutes later with bolt cutters: apparently, it was standard inventory for police vehicles these days.

Stam and Muller stood to the side as Lahm grabbed the cutters in both hands and cut the padlock. Stam then opened one of the doors and Lahm the other.

The first thing that came from the garage was the smell. A pungent smell that none of them could describe exactly; decay was the closest thing which they could think of.

Inside was a typical garage layout, with marks on the concrete floor from years of tyres running back and forth and stains from seeping brake fluid or oil. Along the far wall was another workbench, much like the one in the double garage. Again, several types of machinery and tools were hanging on the wall beyond the bench, all in their proper place.

Stam entered the lockup; the smell inside was even worse. He walked across to the far side. Behind him, he could sense Muller and Lahm following before stopping and staring at the same thing he was. The reason they were staring was that attached to the wall next to the workbench was some kind of wooden frame that had been bolted to the metal sheeting. It had straps at the top and bottom on both sides and one in the centre at the top. The three detectives stood motionless, staring at it.

'What the hell is this?' Muller asked.

'It looks like some kind of torture device,' said Lahm

'The kind you would use to tie someone down and drill into their skull,' Stam said.

Chapter 20

Karl Ballack was sitting in his office deep within the Reichstag government building in Berlin. It was a grand office in a grand building, in which he still, at times, felt an immense sense of duty.

The office had been renovated along with the main building towards the end of the Cold War and finally re-opened in 1999. Although it had been designed in keeping with the original plans, the office had modern technology which lent itself to functioning in the way it now was required to.

Karl had been the security minister of Germany for the past six years and had been regarded as the future of German politics when he was appointed. Coming from a working-class background, he had studied criminology and pathology at university before becoming a pathologist in Munich. After working in the field for twelve years, he had made the switch to politics, and with a lot of hard work and the best interests of his country at heart, he had quickly risen through the political ranks to the position he now found himself in.

The call that he had received yesterday from his now-estranged ex-wife, Angela, had thrown him. Not just because he hadn't heard her voice in so long, or at the mention of Oliver Stam, which was a name he had not wanted to hear again. But mostly it was due to her findings regarding the case she was working on. Being the lead forensic pathologist on the case in 2010, Karl had felt a huge sense of responsibility in helping the Munich police try to identify the killer. With his background in criminology, he had worked alongside them, trying to discover patterns or connections between not only the victims themselves but how they were killed. As it turned out, all four victims had the same cause of death: brain failure due to a hole drilled in the main artery of the skull. He had also determined that all the victims were alive when the hole was drilled and that the four victims had no connection to one another.

Karl pressed the intercom buzzer on his desk, and after a few seconds, his secretary buzzed him back.

'Sir?'

'I need access to an old file, an unsolved murder case in Munich from 2010. Can you find it and send it to my computer?'

'Sure thing,' was the reply.

Karl stood and walked over to the window. As far as jurisdiction was concerned, he knew it wasn't his place to be actively involved in such a case, but whether it was the fact that he had spoken to Angela again or the fact that the original case from 2010 had never been solved, he couldn't deny that he felt that surge of adrenalin rushing through his body once again, the way he used to when working an important case. The only thing that made him feel slightly apprehensive was Oliver Stam. On all counts, he had agreed with Stam on his rather public criticism of the German security system, and even though Karl was simply following orders from much higher up, the position he had found himself in meant that he was the one who had to shoulder the scrutiny. He was the one who had to speak to the media and deal with the backlash that came from it.

As he stood staring out of the large bay window of his office, he was interrupted by the sound of the intercom buzzing.

'Sir, the file has been sent.'

He headed back to his seat and brought the file up on his computer. He unlocked it with his security clearance password and began to scroll through. His secretary knocked on the door and set a cup of coffee on his desk. He looked at her and smiled a thank you.

After reading only a few lines, he was immediately thrown back into memories of the case. He remembered the media attention it had generated and the pressure from the German public to solve the case. Although he had not been a detective on the case, his input had become vital in providing a possible link to help find the person responsible. It also brought up memories of his relationship with Angela. They had been married a few years and were working in the same coroner's office, which would be challenging for most, but at the time they had cherished it.

He moved these thoughts to one side and concentrated on the file. Everything that was detailed in it hadn't been updated since March of 2011 when the case was filed. It had remained open but was now classed as an ongoing cold case.

Karl spent the next twenty minutes scrutinising it: the victims, the locations, and the possible leads that they had had, which, in truth, had not been very many. The case had baffled many detectives at the time.

When he had finished reading the file, he closed it and logged out. As he did, he saw a notification that he was tagged in that was also connected to the file. He clicked on it and a message appeared on his screen. It was from the Munich police office; someone had requested the file to assist on a case that was currently open regarding the discovery of a body in the Ebersberger Forest on the outskirts of Munich. The message and the request had been sent from Head Inspector Klose, a man Karl knew well. He had been the head inspector on the case back in 2010. Klose must be involved in the case in Schwaberwegen, he thought. He knew how hard Inspector Klose had worked back on the original case to find the killer; as it turned out, he might still have a chance too, more than ten years later.

Before Karl logged off, he clicked on the search button for all major crime files and typed in the name Frank Mayer. As far as the name was concerned, there were no personnel files regarding the name, but there appeared to be a file that the name Frank Mayer had a link to. Karl clicked on it, which brought up a second file that was named 'The Vier'.

The file itself was protected, but Karl noticed that this one was protected with the highest security clearance that the government used. Luckily, being the security minister meant he was one of them. Karl clicked on the file and entered his security details, username, and password, which in turn generated a random security key number which was sent to his phone. When he opened it, Karl noticed that since the file had been created at the end of 2010, only two people had accessed it. From the file's security log-in, he could see that the two men were the current prime minister and the previous security minister, Karl's old boss, a man named Mikael Schultz. Both men had accessed the file a few times shortly after it had been created, then nothing for almost twelve years, until eight months ago when Mikael Schultz had opened it but not amended it in any way. The strange thing about it now was that in the last two days, it had been opened again, once by Schultz, again, and once by the prime minister.

Karl scrolled down the page to see the information that the file contained but didn't get far. The file was made up of only eight words: forty-four letters making up four names. Four men's names, one under the other. The most alarming thing was that Karl recognised two of the names. Just as he was ready to save the file, the screen went blank, and he was kicked out of it. Someone must be monitoring the file.

***

The lockup that was situated near Hans Fischer's lodge was now awash with activity. Shortly after the discovery of the torture-like wooden frame inside, Stam had made a call to Inspector Schmidt. Schmidt had despatched the forensic team, who had now finished with the scene in Schwaberwegen. They arrived shortly afterwards and quickly began to comb the scene for any possible evidence. Inspector Schmidt also appeared and asked Stam and Muller to go over their findings at the small cabin up on the hill as well as the lockup. After a walk round, they all gathered on the driveway: Schmidt, Stam, Muller and Lahm.

'Where are we with the warrant on the lodge?' Schmidt asked.

'Inspector Klose told me earlier that it would be tomorrow morning before it's signed off,' Muller replied.

Schmidt looked at the garage. 'What the hell is the hold up with this,' he stated rather than asked.

'I'm not sure, but we have to get inside now. Hans must be caught and questioned. I should have done it yesterday when I had the chance,' said Stam.

'I agree. I'll speak with Klose and tell him to hell with

the warrant,' Schmidt replied with agitation in his voice.

After a brief phone call, everyone kicked into action. Lahm and Muller gained entry through the side door to the lodge. Schmidt followed and arranged for three officers to thoroughly search the premises with them. Stam found a set of keys hanging on a hook in the kitchen; he took them and made his way to the double garage.

The lodge was big on the inside and typical of the style of when it was built way back. Wood panelling covered most of the walls. There were wood-panelled doors throughout, and all the floors were carpeted with thick, expensive carpet. The smell inside the house wasn't foul, but it wasn't pleasant either. Muller started in the kitchen and Lahm in the living area.

It didn't take long for Muller to know that Hans Fischer lived alone. There was no woman's touch to be found, and everything was left as it lay. Dishes were piled up in the sink, and newspapers were piled up on the table that sat off to the left of the kitchen. There was also one solitary chair sitting at the table. She also determined that someone had been inside recently; the boiler light was turned on and she couldn't see a timer next to it, which meant it had to have been set manually. She could also see that the dinner plate sitting at the top of the dishes pile was relatively fresh looking. She made her way through to the living area to find Lahm, whose findings were the same.

'It has to be Hans that I saw climbing the hill; someone has been here very recently.'

'I agree,' replied Muller.

They combed through opened letters that were lying on a cabinet, all addressed to H. Fischer. Mostly bills and insurance forms, nothing of any significance. They then headed for the main bedroom, which was decorated like the rest of the house, with a bed and bedside cabinet from the seventies and a musky smell that hung in the air. Lahm checked the door that was disguised as a window. He pushed the handle and opened it before walking outside. He checked it from the outside again and wondered how anyone could get back inside, as there was no handle on the outside. He called Muller over and was about to ask her what she thought when Officer Hunter appeared on the patio.

'Detective Stam wants to see you both. He says he has something.'

Muller and Lahm closed the door from the outside and walked across the patio and down the steps. They headed down the driveway and turned right to the front of the house and the double garage, the same way Hans Fischer had yesterday when they went to see him.

Stam was inside and standing in the far corner of the garage. He had a small torch in one hand, shining it onto something that they couldn't see.

'Detective?' Stam said.

He turned and let go of whatever it was he had been holding in his other hand.

'Look at this,' he said.

They all met in the middle of the garage. Stam reached down and lifted one of the many deer skulls from the floor. He asked Lahm to hold it as he spun it around. He shone his torch against the side of the skull. The white of the bone was rough and scratched.

'You see that?'

Both Muller and Lahm squinted and concentrated on the spot where the torch was shining.

'What is it?' Lahm asked.

'It's a hole that I assume was made with a drill a millimetre in size, drilled just behind the left ear.'

Chapter 21

Hans Fischer was a clever man, a ruthless man, some who knew him might say, but as he stood in the middle of the forest in the dead of night, he couldn't rationally think of a way to get out of what he was now in the middle of.

The night air was crisp, and the wind was bitter. He had disposed of the bag that he had removed from the garage and tied up a few more loose ends, but ultimately, he saw no other option than to return to the lodge. The only thing that he could see being an issue was the lock-up, but he was clever enough to have it registered in someone else's name in no way connected to him. He was also confident that he had left the lodge without being seen by the officer sitting out front and that he could get back inside the same way as he left.

He decided to take the chance and make for the lodge. It was just over four miles; he could do it in ninety minutes, give or take.

***

The hooded figure had left his house for the second night in a row, along the same path he always took, and entered the wooded area that looked onto his house. It was unlike him; it was usually weeks in between the times he had to do this, but with recent events, his anxiety had got the better of him, and he saw no other choice.

From memory, he retraced the steps from the previous night, which he knew would bring him slightly south of the centre of the forest, less than a mile from the green metal hut that had been there for years.

After an hour he found the path, and shortly after that, he found the grave. The soil on top was still loose and he could see partial footprints, which he covered up and disturbed to make it less obvious looking. He set his rucksack down, removed the small shovel and got to work.

It took close to forty minutes before he had the body fully unearthed and out of the hole. He was now sweating and heaving. The good thing about this body was that it had only been buried yesterday, which meant the smell of decay and death hadn't had the chance to cling to it just yet. Once removed, the figure began his routine check of the body. First was the skull: all looked intact, no bullet holes or lacerations, and no deep compressions in the bone. Then down to the chest area: no visible puncture wounds or bullet holes. There were no clear signs of any strangulation marks either. After a final check of the lower part of the torso, all seemed clear, with no sign of any obvious injuries, and so began the painstaking task of burying the body for a second time. It would take slightly longer tonight than it had last night, however, mainly down to the sheer size of the man; he was well over six feet, with broad shoulders.

Eventually, with the grave filled in, the soil disturbed, and all visible footprints cleared, the figure packed his rucksack and made for home. He followed the same path back to his house. He was keen to return and be out of the forest, but then, out of the corner of his eye, he spotted movement, far off to his left, a brief glimpse of a man walking slowly. The hooded figure stopped and crouched next to a tree and watched. The man was standing motionless, a look of hesitation or contemplation on his face. The figure waited, only twenty feet from him now.

A whole minute went by before he eventually moved off, turning and heading east. Purposeful steps, not wasting any time. The figure crept forward, making sure the man had continued along the same path he had left on. When he was sure, he hurried through the woods and back to his house along the same route he had followed many times before, precisely, out of the view of any other lodges.

He entered through the rear door, and as always, removed his clothing and rinsed his boots in the utility room sink before placing his clothes in the washing machine and turning it on. He then started the shower and got in. Twenty minutes later he turned it off and got out, knowing no one else was home and that he was able to take this time. After drying himself, he unloaded the washing machine and hung the clean clothes on the dryer before making his way through the house and into the bedroom. He lay in bed and looked at the ceiling, going through the events of the last two hours over and over again, as well as the same nightly routine that he had followed every night for as long as he could remember, before eventually closing his eyes and falling asleep.

***

Detective Muller woke early the following morning, but unlike the previous morning, Stam was the one who had the coffee brewing and the croissants warming.

'Make yourself at home, why don't you!' she said as she entered the kitchen area.

Stam looked up at her and handed her a mug of coffee. She took it and sat at the small table, the same as Stam had the previous day.

'You sleep any better last night?' she asked him as she

took a drink of coffee.

'It's the same bed; what do you think?'

Muller smiled. Stam brought the plate with the croissants over to the table and sat across from her.

They sat in silence for a moment, chewing and sipping the hot coffee, before Stam spoke.

'You sure you're okay with me staying here?'

'Sure, it's not like you've got anywhere else to stay. As your daughter said, all the hotels are booked out with the journalists and reporters.'

'You not worried about your neighbours seeing me?'

'For what reason? Firstly, you're old enough to be my dad.'

'Thanks for that,' Stam replied.

'And secondly, I'm gay. You'd be quite the career switch.'

Stam smirked.

'So, what's the plan today? Did you get hold of Dr Park before we left the lodge last night?'

'She didn't answer, but she got my message. She's going to look at the deer skull today and try to compare the holes made by the drills if it's possible.'

'Surely it has to be. That's far too much of a coincidence, isn't it?'

'I would say so. We have to meet with Helen to see what forensics found at the scene last night. She's organising one of her team to transport the deer skulls up to the coroner's in Erding. But our main focus must be tracking down Hans Fischer. I'll speak to Schmidt when we get to Schwaberwegen. I have an idea.'

'Which is?'

'It's still brewing,' Stam replied.

Stam rinsed the mugs in the sink and heard the car

starting up again in the next lodge. He walked to the end of the hall, but again, he still couldn't see it. Eventually, he heard the car picking up speed and crunching over the freshly fallen snow. As he turned, he saw Muller entering the hall.

'You may have been up first and made breakfast, but you're still second in the shower.'

Stam headed back down the hall and past the bathroom door, which Muller had closed. He sat at the table again and thought back to last night. With the certainty that Hans Fischer knew that the police had an officer sitting outside the house and still making the decision to leave the lodge, that meant he must have had something important to do, or why take the risk? Stam had to find out what it could be, and quickly.

Just as he was about to get up, his mobile rang, and as it turned out, he didn't have to wait long to find out, or so he thought.

Muller opened the bathroom door. She stepped out in just a bathrobe and stood in the hall. Stam hung up the phone and looked at her.

'What is it?' Muller asked.

'That was Inspector Schmidt.'

'And?'

'He's just received a call regarding Philip Langer and his wife.'

'And?'

'They were found at the safe house this morning, each with a bullet in their heads.'

Chapter 22

It was 07:15 and Karl Ballack was sitting at the breakfast table in his apartment in a popular new development in the centre of Berlin. His wife had just left to take the kids to school, which was a ten-minute walk, before she went for her daily yoga session at a nearby fitness club.

Karl had told her he was working from home today, which in essence was true, but only because he was contemplating getting involved in something that he knew would have to be discussed far away from the government building. From what he had seen last night in the updates to the file, he knew that things would already be in motion, either to establish the possibility of a link between any of the names he had recognised or to escalate it. Whatever way it went, he would be involved.

He took out his mobile phone and brought up the number for his ex-wife, Angela, and paused for a second before pressing the dial button.

'Karl?' she answered.

Karl could tell from the line that she was driving. 'Angela, if this is a bad time, I can call later?'

'No, it's fine. I have five minutes. I'm on my way to another scene regarding the case I spoke to you about in Schwaberwegen.'

'Another drill to the skull?'

'No, not this time, but I need to speak with you regarding that.'

'That's why I called. I have some work that's just come up here in Berlin that I might have to deal with, but I plan to head out and meet with you soon.'

Angela wasn't quite sure how she felt about that but

understood it must be important for him to suggest it.

'Okay. Have you spoken with Detective Stam yet about the details of the case?'

'Not yet. I've discovered that Inspector Klose is in charge, whom I know from the original case back in 2010. Do you remember him?'

'I think so; the name rings a bell.'

'I'll make contact with him today and arrange for us to meet.'

'And Detective Stam?'

'We'll see about that.'

'From what I know of Oliver Stam, if anyone takes charge of this case, it will be him.'

Knowing she was probably right, Karl ended the call, lifted his jacket and briefcase from the counter and made his way down in the lift to his Mercedes. He started the car and had pulled out of the parking garage and onto Kottebusser Damm when his mobile phone rang through the Bluetooth in his car.

'Karl speaking.'

'Karl, it's Mikael Schultz. We need to speak.'

The meeting place Mikael had suggested was an upmarket bar in the centre of Berlin, not quite an exclusive club, but one trending in the right direction.

Karl parked his Mercedes and made his way towards the bar. He was greeted and his jacket was taken as he entered through a set of double glass doors. Inside was an array of muted tones, from the cloth on the seats to the curtains draped over the tinted windows. The inside was made up of two sides; on the right was the bar area, with tall stools neatly positioned around tall thin tables. On the left were rows of booths, each one tucked away for privacy. Mikael was sitting at the second to last one.

'Karl, how are you?' Mikael said, shaking Karl's hand before they both sat down.

'I'm good. How are you?' Karl replied.

Mikael Schultz was an important-looking man. Even though he was in his seventies, his eyes were still as sharp as the suit he was wearing.

'I've been better, and this business in Schwaberwegen is not helping matters.'

'I made myself familiar with the case last night. I've also been in contact with Dr Park regarding the investigation. She called yesterday.'

'Angela? Good woman, that. Shame it never worked with you two.'

Karl didn't reply.

'So, what's with the cloak and dagger, then?' he asked to break the awkwardness of the silence.

'That's the small talk taken care of, then,' Mikael said with a glare.

'The body that's been unearthed in Schwaberwegen has brought up some unwanted attention in certain circles within the German government. I am conscious of the fact that the security clearance for the file was bestowed upon you in your role as security minister, albeit the details were not made clear.'

'That is correct.'

'I'm here to make them clear. Clear in the fact that there is a possibility certain people may try and get access to that file, which cannot happen.'

'And how did you know I was aware of it? I'm guessing it notified you that I had opened it,' Karl responded.

Mikael didn't answer.

Karl continued, 'Are the people in the file in danger?'

'The persons involved in the file are relevant, and for that reason, I am warning you to leave it.'

'Frank Mayer was the man who was found half buried, and his name was on the file.'

Mikael looked around the bar. Karl wasn't quite sure why as they were the only people there.

'Yes, I know his name. But what we don't want is for the media to get wind of it. We've taken measures to keep it that way.'

'I'm a little confused as to why, though?'

'The file is top secret for a reason, and we want it to remain that way. In other words, we don't want you getting involved in the case.'

'I'm not sure this is sitting comfortably with me. If I'm not to talk about it or whom it's about, then why let me have access to it?' Karl replied.

'It comes with the job, I'm afraid, as strange as that may seem. And if it makes you feel any better, it doesn't sit all that well with me either.'

They both sat in silence for a minute as they sipped their ten-euro sparkling water.

Mikael stood after another minute.

'You're the right man for this job, Karl. No one's said it more than me.'

Karl looked up at him.

'Don't fuck it up now,' Mikael said before fastening his jacket and leaving the bar.

Karl sat and finished his drink, trying desperately to wrap his head around what he was, or was not, to do.

Mikael had left the bar and turned left towards the city centre. He reached into his jacket pocket and took out his mobile phone before reaching his car, then dialled a number that was saved to memory. The prime minister answered.

'Yes?'

'Sir, we might have a problem regarding Karl Ballack.'

***

The house in Ebersberger where Philip Langer and his wife had been placed was a bungalow that had been built in the early seventies. It was large, cream, and boring to look at, but its location was where its real beauty lay. It was one hundred yards shy of the Ebersberger Forest, with a garden that subtly blended into the trees. The closest neighbour was half a mile away, and the house itself was only used as a holiday home.

Detectives Stam and Muller had headed straight to the house after the call came in. Schmidt had arranged to meet them there, while Lahm had been sent to the hunting lodge, as Helen from the coroner's office had finished checking the garage for evidence and had now agreed to head to the house, even though she had been on shift for fifteen hours.

Schmidt greeted them at the gate after Muller had pulled onto the path and parked the car. He looked like his head was going to explode.

'What have we got?' asked Stam, not looking any calmer than Schmidt.

'We have a shitstorm about to hit us, that's what we've got,' Schmidt replied.

'We are aware of that; this is not the time to lose our heads. We have a job to do,' said Stam with a certain degree of control in his voice.

Schmidt took a breath and composed himself.

'When the media gets hold of this, we'll have a problem. We need this man in custody.'

'That's what we're trying to do,' Muller interjected, sensing the rising tension.

'We'll need to do it quicker,' Schmidt replied.

'I'm assuming you're talking about Hans Fischer?' Muller asked.

'You assume right. We have no one else.'

One of the officers who had come out of the house shouted to Schmidt that the coroner would be here in fifteen minutes if they wanted to have a look inside before she arrived.

They all headed down the path towards the door.

Stam stopped short of the door. 'We have two options regarding Hans Fischer.'

'Which are?' Schmidt asked.

'We release to the media that we have no suspects as of yet but are investigating various leads and avenues. Let him think that we haven't got anything on him and hope he returns to the lodge.'

'What's the other option?'

'The other option is the complete opposite: we light the bastard up.'

'How?' Muller now asked.

'We tell the media that the only suspect we have is a local man named Hans Fischer and we have to speak with him as soon as possible.'

Schmidt didn't reply. Instead, he opened the door and entered the hallway of the house. The house was neat inside but was altogether as dated-looking as the outside, with panelled wood on the walls and worn-out carpets throughout. Schmidt followed the officer through to the bedroom tucked away in the back corner. When they entered, it was clear that there hadn't been any kind of struggle. Mr and Mrs Langer were lying in bed, motionless, and apart from the copious amounts of blood now covering the top half of their bodies and most of the bed and carpet, they were still in the sleeping positions that they would have been in the previous night.

'What do we have?' Schmidt asked.

Stam walked around the side of the bed to where Philip was lying.

'Both have a single gunshot wound to the temple, close range, fired from a small handgun or pistol, as you can clearly see. I imagine they both died instantly and never heard the perpetrator. Either that or they've been repositioned,' said the officer.

'You think it was one person?' Muller asked.

'We're assuming so but can never be sure. Forensics will tell us better.'

'We need the type of gun identified as a priority; make sure forensics get on it straight away,' Stam said.

'Certainly.'

'Where did they enter the premises?'

'The bedroom window next to the back wall.'

All four of them looked over at the window as the officer continued.

'The lock was pried open. A check of the garden hasn't produced any evidence. The window was slightly ajar when we arrived.'

'Exited the same way?' Muller asked.

'Again, we assume so: no footprints on the carpet, and the front and rear doors were both locked when we arrived.'

'Who discovered the bodies?' Schmidt asked.

'A neighbour who was curious about the new guests in the house said that he walked past while walking his dog this morning and noticed that all the curtains were still drawn so decided to snoop around the back. When he noticed the window slightly ajar, he pushed at it, saw the blood on the carpet, and rang the police.'

'Has he been interviewed?'

'Yes. He's in his seventies and has lived in Ebersberger his whole life. Nosey neighbour is our initial thought.'

Stam didn't appear to be paying a great deal of attention to the officer, but Muller knew he was listening to his every word.

'What about their dog?'

'It was sitting at the front door when the neighbour pried it open, it's with a family friend of theirs now,' replied the officer.

Stam nodded as he walked back around to the other side of the bed and looked closely at Mrs Langer, eventually saying, 'I'm positive it's the one killer, but we will have Dr Park look at it. From what I can see, the bodies haven't been moved, which means they were killed as they slept.' He returned to the foot of the bed.

'What are you thinking?' asked Schmidt.

'I'm thinking we light this bastard up!'

Chapter 23

Over two hours had passed since Stam and Muller had left the house in Ebersberger. Schmidt had travelled back to Schwaberwegen in his car, followed by Muller and Stam in the Seat Leon.

On the way back, Stam called Dr Park and asked her if she would be available for a meeting in Schwaberwegen at 13:00, which she said she would be after she examined the deer skull she had been asked to check. She had also agreed to head to the lab straight after the meeting to examine the bodies of Philip Langer and his wife. Stam also called Helen, asking her to check the bullets that would be removed by Dr Park from the skulls of the couple.

The meeting room inside the old church was now full. Muller had brought in more chairs to accommodate the extra people. They sat in a semi-circle, facing the whiteboard.

Present at the meeting were detectives Stam, Muller and Lahm, along with Inspector Schmidt, Head Inspector Klose, Dr Angela Park, and Helen from the forensic lab.

Instead of the usual protocol of the previous meetings, Stam spoke first.

'First of all, I thank you all for attending. I know some of you have been working since yesterday morning, and I appreciate it.'

Stam looked over at Helen, who was holding a cup of coffee that was the only thing keeping her vertical at this point.

'I have brought everyone up to speed with the events

of this morning regarding Mr and Mrs Langer, which in my mind has moved the killer on from using meticulous planning to now feeling desperate and even threatened. Which, in my opinion, has now made them even more dangerous.'

Everyone was listening intently to Stam.

'My first question is, do we have a list of everyone aware of the safe house that had been used to house the couple?'

'I can answer that. Myself, Inspector Klose, and the officer in charge of logistics and communications were all that I believe were aware,' said Schmidt.

'And has this officer been questioned?' Stam replied.

'She has. She was here in Schwaberwegen last night and has been in the police force for twenty-one years. She's a good officer.'

'That doesn't always go for much,' Stam replied. 'That then leaves you and Inspector Klose,' he added.

An awkwardness began to descend over the room. Muller and Lahm glanced at each other in anticipation of what might come of Stam's statement.

Before any of them spoke, however, Stam continued.

'My thoughts are that the killer must have knowledge of the police presence or have been watching Mr Langer since he discovered the body in the Bluebell Woods.'

The room began to relax, just a little.

'Dr Park, can you tell us of your findings regarding the deer skull?' Stam asked.

'Yes, of course. The hole that was made in the skull was almost in the same location as the hole in the human skull, obviously not exactly, due to the skulls being different in shape, but in the general area that would suggest to me as being the same.'

'What about the size and depth of the hole?'

'Regarding that, my conclusion is that it was made with the same size of drill that was used on the human skull. Both are the same depth and width.'

'Okay, thank you,' Stam replied before turning to Helen, who was sitting to Dr Park's right.

'Helen, how did you get on with your examination of the lockup at the hunting lodge and the house where Philip Langer was found?'

Helen not only looked like she was half asleep but also a little annoyed, bordering on angry.

'The lockup in the hunting lodge was filled with a multitude of possible DNA, too much for us to analyse at such short notice. What I would say, however, is that there are eight different samples of blood from it being sent to the lab to be tested.'

Schmidt looked across at Stam, who in turn looked over at Muller.

'How quickly can you have the results from them?' Schmidt asked.

'I will need twenty-four hours to have them all tested. A little longer for the four-by-four, which I checked also. It's a smaller space but will have been cleaned a lot more, therefore more difficult to get samples from, but we're working on it,' she said.

'What about the bullets that killed Mr and Mrs Langer?'

'We have identified that they were fired from a Walther P-38, which, you will be aware, is the most common handgun used in Germany.'

'Thank you,' Schmidt replied.

Stam was about to ask that Helen and Dr Park leave them for now but realised that they would more than likely have further input regarding the case.

'Where are we on the file regarding Frank Mayer and the file from the original case from 2010?'

'I'm having bother retrieving either of them,' said Klose.

'Why would that be?' asked Schmidt.

'Most likely because someone doesn't want us to see them,' he replied.

They all thought about that possibility for a minute before Stam continued.

'The focus of this investigation now lies on the capture and arrest of Hans Fischer. Everyone clear on that?'

Everyone in the room nodded, including Dr Park and Helen.

'Okay, get to work.'

As everyone left the church, Dr Park waited at the entrance. She watched as Muller left, followed by Detective Lahm. He smiled as he passed, and she saw something familiar in his smile that made her think she had seen him before. As she stood wondering, Stam came out of the church and stopped next to her.

'What are you thinking about?' he asked her.

'I thought I recognised Detective Lahm, but I think he just looks like someone I know.'

Stam hid the fact that he wasn't particularly interested.

'I spoke with Karl Ballack earlier today. He says he wants to meet with me this evening.'

'Is that normal?' Stam replied.

'Not anymore.'

Stam didn't know what that meant.

'He says he knows Head Inspector Klose. He worked

with him on the original case and was intending to speak with him when he arrived.'

'That's fine with me.'

'What is it with you two?' Dr Park asked.

'Search it online, if you don't already know.'

Angela had no idea what he meant.

They walked out of the church grounds and across to the main square. As they reached one of the tents, they were approached by Inspector Klose, who had just ended a call on his mobile.

'Stam, I've just spoken with the security minister, Karl Ballack. He's made it clear that he wants to liaise regarding the case and says he has information that he would like to discuss with us. I've explained that the lead detective on the case is you and you will be free to speak with him later this evening.'

Stam didn't look particularly enamoured with the thought, but he understood that he was here to do a job.

'Okay. Did you get any further with the file from the original case?'

'I think that's what he wants to discuss. He believes certain people are trying to restrict access to the file.'

'Why would that be?'

'He doesn't know, but he managed to get a copy regardless and will bring it with him.'

'Good,' Stam said, still annoyed at the thought of meeting with Ballack.

'The reason he wants to come in person is to do with a second file that he knows with certainty that individuals within the German government are trying to hide.'

Inspector Klose made his back to the church as Stam and Dr Park headed down towards the Victorian bridge.

Stam looked at his watch: it had just gone 11:30.

'I'll speak to Karl and suggest we meet somewhere outside of Schwaberwegen if you like. What time will suit you?' Dr Park asked.

'Make it four p.m. Let me know where you decide to meet.'

'I will. I'm going to head back to the lab. The bodies of the gunshot victims will be arriving soon, and I'll bring my report tonight.'

'Thanks,' replied Stam.

They stood and watched as the water flowed past below, picking up ice from the banks and carrying it away.

'How is it you know Karl Ballack, if you don't mind me asking?' Stam said.

Dr Park continued staring into the river for a few seconds before answering.

'I worked with him for five years at the forensic lab in Munich. And was married to him for seven.'

Stam didn't respond.

***

Hans Fischer had spent the remainder of the previous night huddled up in a heavily wooded area just over half a mile from the lodge. Just before sunrise, he had got as close as one hundred yards to his cabin on the hill that overlooked the lodge. He saw at least two officers through his binoculars and noticed that the window in the door of the cabin had been broken, which meant that they hadn't bothered with a warrant.

He returned to the safety of the forest when he saw he had no way of getting back inside without being caught.

He knew he had to get back inside, even if it was only for a few minutes. All he needed to do was grab some money and his passport, which he had hidden in his study in case such a day ever came.

It was almost noon, and although the forest provided enough shelter to keep him hidden, he still felt exposed. He had stayed for days in the forest in the past while hunting, but it felt different now that he was the one being hunted.

As the hours ticked by, it gave him time to realise that even though he was confident he had removed any incriminating evidence from the lodge, he didn't plan to take the risk of walking straight into the arms of the police and the possibility of them finding something that might be used as evidence against him. So he decided to stay hidden until nightfall before trying to return to the lodge.

Chapter 24

Karl Ballack had left the bar in Berlin and made his way back to his office in the Reichstag building. The conversation with Mikael Shultz had left him a little annoyed but mostly curious. The secretive nature of the conversation and also the file that he had been given access to but told not to speak about made no sense.

On the short journey to the office, he dialled Inspector Klose and told him he had been informed of the case in Schwaberwegen and that with the obvious similarities to the case they had both previously been involved in, he wanted to help in any way he could. He didn't mention the conversation he had just had with Mikael. Klose had agreed and was happy that the security minister actually wanted to help, if that was what he intended to do. If not, Klose couldn't do much to stop him anyway, but he knew someone who could.

Karl parked his Mercedes, entered the building, and made his way up the grand staircase and onto the first floor where his office was. Seconds later, his secretary came in behind him.

'Sir, I have received several calls for you this morning, one of which was more important than the others.'

Karl got a strange feeling in his stomach, as if something had changed.

'From whom?'

'Three were from the head of the security police, but the most important one was from the prime minister.'

In all the years he had worked for the German government, he had never been contacted by the prime minister or any of his assistants. And now, after one meeting with Mikael regarding the case, he had missed a call from him.

'Can you dial his number and put him through, please.'

'Certainly.'

Karl sat at his desk and tried to think, again trying to make some sense of what could be going on. A few seconds later the intercom buzzed.

'The prime minister is busy but will be in touch shortly.'

Karl clicked the monitor on his computer and scrolled through until he found the file that he had checked that morning. He clicked on it, put in his username and

password, and then requested the security key. After a few seconds, the number came up and he typed it in. Nothing happened. He hit enter again. Still nothing. Then in red letters across the screen, it said ACCESS DENIED. Now he knew something was going on.

He grabbed the file from his desk regarding the case from 2010 and headed out of the office. As he passed his secretary, he stopped.

'Can you tell anyone who calls that I'm sick and will be working from home today?'

'The Prime Minister will be calling you back.'

'Tell him the same.'

'Are you sure?'

'Yes, but if he does call, let me know.'

Karl headed for the door, but before he reached it, the phone began to ring. His secretary paused and looked at Karl before answering. Karl waited.

'Karl Ballack's office.'

Silence as the person on the other end spoke.

'Yes. I've already explained that Mr Ballack is out of the office today, ill.'

Another silence.

'No, he won't be back in today, I'm afraid. Thank you, bye.'

'Was that the Prime Minister?'

'No, the head of security again. They're sending two men to the office.'

'You told them I wasn't in the office, though?'

'They said they're sending them anyway.'

Karl made his way down the hall and the grand staircase before reaching the front entrance. When he had entered, he had told the guard at the door that he had left his security card at home. The guard let him in regardless, knowing who he was, even though he shouldn't have. This meant that if anyone checked the computer, it would show that he was never here today.

He climbed into his car and dialled his wife's number; it rang out and he left a message telling her he wouldn't be home till late. He then put the car into drive and headed for Schwaberwegen.

***

Detective Lahm was standing outside of the lockup where the wooden torture frame had been found. Forensics had left shortly after he arrived, and the entrance was still cordoned off. Lahm crouched under the tape and entered; the smell of decay still lingered despite the doors lying open for hours now. He walked over to the frame, stared at it, and tried to imagine the fear someone would be going through if they were tied to it and the horror that must have taken place. Initially, specialists had been called in to try and remove it from the metal sheeting it was attached to, but it was decided that the best way was to take as many samples from it as they could rather than tampering with it in any way.

Just as he was about to leave, he heard footsteps behind him, and he turned to see Muller crouching under the police tape.

'This is some sick shit, isn't it?' she said.

'You got that right. What would it take for someone to tie another person to something like this and drill into their skull?'

'Someone pretty messed up, I would imagine,' Muller replied.

They both stood staring at it before turning and heading back out through the doors. The sun was beginning to fall, along with the temperature, as the afternoon dragged on. They both headed out of the lockup and turned left down the hill and back towards the lodge. Officer Hunter was standing at the entrance to the driveway as they reached it. He looked cold.

'What's the plan now? Have there been further instructions?' he asked neither of them in particular.

'We're waiting on orders coming through. I'm assuming the results of the samples forensics have taken may determine how to proceed,' Muller replied, knowing more than Lahm did.

'You honestly think that this Hans will return here now? From every direction, all you can see are police. If he has any sense, he'll be long gone.'

'We're hoping he doesn't have any other options. Or sense,' said Muller.

Muller thought about what the officer had said as she and Lahm continued up the driveway.

'I'm going to make a call,' she said to Lahm, who kept walking.

She took out her phone and dialled Stam. He answered on the first ring.

'Yes?' he answered.

'I know you said you wanted to light this bastard up, but I think your first option might be the better one.'

***

After he ended the call with Detective Muller, Stam discussed viable options with Inspector Schmidt and Head Inspector Klose. They discussed it in the meeting room inside the church and all came to the same conclusion.

First was to hold off telling the media anything until the following morning; Inspector Schmidt should be the one to do so. They also agreed that once they had the results of the samples taken from the lockup at the hunting lodge, and depending on the results, they would put their plan into motion. Until then they would wait. Schmidt told them he would speak to Muller and Lahm and let them know of the plan.

Stam said he was going to meet with Dr Park and Karl Ballack at a restaurant outside the village. Klose brought Schmidt up to date on the details regarding the files and the possible assistance from the security minister. Stam asked them to inform him of any information if and when it came in.

Chapter 25

Stam reached the restaurant earlier than planned and assumed the booking had been made under Park, which it was. He had driven one of the local unmarked police cars to the restaurant, which sat just off the main road between Schwaberwegen and Herdweg.

The place was nice enough and served traditional German cuisine, which Stam was more than happy with; he didn't much go for foreign foods. The young waiter led him through to a table, and he was surprised to see that Dr Park and Karl Ballack were already seated. The table was in the back corner of the restaurant and as far away from the small number of other diners as was possible.

Karl stood as Stam reached the table and put out his hand to shake it. Stam reluctantly took it. With everything that had taken place and with the media attention, he had never actually spoken with Karl Ballack directly. Stam knew that most of the time he could be a stubborn bastard, but for now, he decided to rise above it and focus on the case.

'I want to begin by saying that regardless of what's happened in the past, my focus here is purely as the security minister of this country. I want to assist on this case in any way I can. Whatever you feel towards me should be irrelevant.'

'You don't want to know how I feel towards you,' replied Stam.

Angela saw the direction that the meeting could go. 'Let's get one thing straight: I am now fully aware of the history between you two, and if this is going to encroach on this case, then I'm sorry, but as professionals, you are both going to have to set your differences aside and concentrate on the job in hand,' she said vehemently.

Stam knew she was right; Karl did too. They looked at each other across the table, and without saying anything, came to an understanding. Angela ordered for the three of them when the waiter arrived, and she began talking after he had left.

'I've brought Karl up to date on the findings from the deer skull I examined and how I believe them to be the same as the victim we found in Schwaberwegen. I waited for you to arrive before discussing what I discovered from the two bodies that were found in Ebersberger this morning with gunshots to the head.'

Stam looked at Karl and from his lack of reaction knew that he was already aware of the witness and that both he and his wife had been killed.

'The shots were fired from a Walther P-38 handgun; forensics retrieved the bullets. As you will both be aware, these guns are commonly used in Germany. The bullets have been sent to the lab for DNA, but I'm positive they will be clean, much like the scene was.'

The waiter arrived with the food and they sat impatiently waiting for him to serve them and leave.

'And the bodies themselves, did you find anything on them that might help?'

'From my examination, I can only confirm what it looked like to those who saw it, which was two innocent people being executed as they slept. Other than the bullets, there are no injuries or wounds on the victims.'

Karl looked over at Stam.

'Do you think it could be the same person who is responsible for both murders?'

Stam didn't like Karl Ballack, really didn't like him. From the second he had sat at the table, Stam had been trying to decide what his intentions were for being here. All the security ministers he had known while doing this job had never been as invested as Karl Ballack seemed to be, and Stam wasn't quite sure why. When he had discovered that he and Dr Park were once married, he thought it could have been that he wanted to be in contact with her again, but the body language from them both suggested otherwise.

'It could be a coincidence,' Karl added.

'I don't believe in coincidences; the two murders have to be connected. Maybe not as we think, but they will be connected,' Stam replied.

Stam knew he had to somehow find a way to work with Ballack; the case was more important than any feud they might have. For now, though, he would keep him at arm's length until he knew the real reason for him being here.

'I agree with Stam; they have to be connected,' said Angela. 'If the scene is still secured, I would like to process it myself, with the help of Helen, if that's possible?'

'Of course. I'll arrange for Helen to be there tomorrow morning to help you process the scene,' Stam replied.

The restaurant was beginning to fill, and more tables close to them were now being used. Karl was clearly conscious of being recognised and sat facing away from the front of the restaurant.

'I've managed to retrieve the file from the original case that Angela and I worked on back in 2010. Klose said I should pass it to you to read over. I will say that not much has been updated from back then. I read it over before I arrived.'

Stam lifted the file and quickly flipped through the pages. The file was big, with lots of notes from each victim, but evidently not with any real substance as far as suspects went.

'I assume I can keep this?' Stam asked.

'Of course,' Karl replied.

They all continued picking at their food, the rumbling of noise growing louder in the small restaurant and forcing them to talk a little louder now.

'This is not the only reason I wanted to come here in person,' Karl said with a hint of nervousness in his voice.

'I gathered that, as this file could have been sent by email,' Stam replied.

Angela heard the contempt in his voice.

'Yes, I know. The other reason is regarding a second file, although I am not completely sure of the details that it contains. I came across it by mistake, and it may have some connection with the case.'

'Did the access come with your position as security minister?'

'I believe it did. And as of this morning, when I first checked the file, I have been warned against discussing it.'

'By whom?'

'I'm not at liberty to say at present.'

'Any reason why you've been warned about it?' Angela asked.

'Not that I'm aware of. The file doesn't contain very many details. I tried to check it again before I left to meet you and have now been denied access to it.'

Stam was intrigued now.

'And what are these details?' Stam asked.

'I have to add that the warning I received came from as high up the chain as possible.'

'I understand that! What I don't understand is you driving three hours to be here to relay information that you're now reluctant to relay.'

'It isn't quite as easy as that.'

Stam now realised why he had come: he was scared.

'If you think it's worth telling and you think it can help, then you have to tell us,' Angela said, now feeling a little tense.

'Tell us or don't, just don't waste our time,' Stam added, growing more agitated.

Karl hesitated for a second before Stam noticed something change in him; maybe it was his conscience taking over.

'The file didn't contain any information or details; all it contained was four names.'

'Did you recognise any of the names?'

'I did,' Karl said, looking around cautiously.

'I'm guessing one of those names was Frank Mayer?' Stam said.

Angela looked at him.

'That name was on the list, but it wasn't the name I recognised. The name I recognised was Theo Schultz, the son of the previous security minister, Mikael Schultz.'

Chapter 26

Stam was in the police car he had borrowed to meet with Dr Park and Karl Ballack. He was now cruising back towards Schwaberwegen, going over everything. The cigarette he had lit as he was leaving, he flicked out of the open window before lighting up another.

The file that Karl had brought to the dinner was sitting on the passenger seat of the car. He had read over it as they drank coffee after the meal. Stam's first thought was that it seemed likely that it could be the same person responsible for the recent murders, but ten years in between was a great deal of time. The obvious second thought was that it could be a copycat killer, but Stam had discovered from the file that the cause of death in the original case had never been revealed. This meant that it either disproved the possibility or narrowed down the possible suspects if a copycat was responsible. This latest information, however, didn't change the plan that had been decided regarding Hans Fischer.

Stam dialled the number for Inspector Schmidt, who had agreed to the plan and said he would inform Klose, Muller and Lahm that it was to go ahead.

Stam slowed the car as he approached the junction on the road out of Herdweg. On the left was the road that led to Schwaberwegen, on the right was the road that headed north and away from it, towards Forstinning. Stam lit a third cigarette, knowing that it could be a long night. He indicated and turned right, away from Schwaberwegen, and cruised into the night.

Muller and Lahm had been informed that the plan was now in action and that they could finish for the night. Reluctantly, Lahm said that he could do with heading home to try and catch up on some sleep. Muller, on the other hand, said she wanted to remain in Schwaberwegen. She had some paperwork to catch up on and wanted to stay if she could assist in any way.

They left the hunting lodge in separate cars. Lahm had told Officer Hunter to pull back the police presence around the lodge but to keep the police car out front, with the three of them still working in shifts through the night, himself included. He said he would take the later shift and let Officer Graham know when he would be taking over.

***

Monica Stam was sitting in the restaurant of her hotel, eating alone and thinking about returning to Munich to see her friends. She had messaged her dad, who had texted back a single word reply, *sorry*, when she asked if he could join her for dinner. She had refrained from messaging Detective Lahm again, but it turned out she didn't have to. She was getting ready to call it a night when she heard her phone ping and saw Lahm's name was on the screen. She lifted the phone and clicked open the message.

Looks like I may have an evening off from work, how about that lift?

Not got anywhere to go, I'm afraid. Where do you suggest? Xx

Anywhere but here! Pick you up soon xx, Lahm replied.

The pub Lahm chose to eat in was quaint and smelled of spilt beer and smoke from the open fire in the corner, but its main appeal was it was quiet and cosy.

They sat in a booth next to the front window after ordering at the bar and instantly began chatting. Anyone inside the bar who was watching them would have assumed they were a couple. From the moment Monica had sat down in Lahm's car, for the second time, she knew that her first instinct regarding him was correct. There was something about him that she liked, and she could tell that he felt the same from the way he looked at her when there were small pauses in the conversation.

They spent the next two hours talking about nothing in particular. Just endless, roaming conversations, until they both became aware of the time.

'I've enjoyed seeing you tonight,' Monica said with a smile.

Lahm knew he was far too old to blush but thought that was exactly what he was doing.

'It hasn't been the worst night I've had,' he replied with a playful smile. 'We should do it again sometime.'

'We're still doing it now! Are you in a rush?'

'Not quite yet.' Lahm glanced down at his watch.

'Somewhere more important to be, then?' she said, smiling.

'Work, I'm afraid. I'm taking over from an officer at eleven.'

Monica looked at her watch: 22:25. She didn't want it to end, and she could tell he didn't either.

'I don't suppose we could do it again tomorrow?'

Lahm asked.

'I'm supposed to be spending time with my dad, but I doubt that's going to happen. I considered returning to Munich tonight.'

'What stopped you?' Lahm replied, half guessing it was his message. Monica smiled at him again and brushed her hand over his leg underneath the table. He took her hand and leaned in close. She felt a rush of adrenalin before he kissed her, softly but purposefully, and she could feel her cheeks reddening. They leaned back and stared at each other.

'I'll try to do what I can to get away from work tomorrow. Maybe we could have dinner together?'

'I'd like that,' replied Monica, wanting to kiss him again.

Lahm was just about to suggest picking her up after work tomorrow when his mobile rang. He looked at the screen: it was Officer Hunter.

'Hey, everything okay?' Lahm asked.

'Yeah, all quiet here, boss. I was just calling to say that if you want to take the time off, I can cover your shift tonight. I only started my shift a few hours ago, and Officer Graham will be taking over at midnight.'

'I'll have to okay it with Inspector Klose.'

'I already have. He says I'm fine to cover.'

Lahm looked over at Monica, who was applying lipstick.

'Sure, that's fine with me. If anything comes up, you call me. Okay?'

'Sure, boss. Enjoy your night.'

'Looks like I'm free tonight after all,' Lahm said to Monica with a smile.

'Excellent,' Monica replied. 'I might need a lift soon.'

'Where to?' Lahm asked playfully.

'My hotel, maybe. A nightcap could be in order.'

'My house is in the next town over if you prefer?'

Monica smiled. 'That sounds good to me,' she replied.

They grabbed their coats and headed for the door.

***

Angela had been dropped off by Karl. They had sat for another thirty minutes after Detective Stam had left the restaurant. They had eaten dessert and drunk coffee while speaking mostly about the case. On the awkward drive back to her hotel, they had agreed to update each other on any developments in the case and that Karl would continue to investigate what he could from his end. They smiled at each other as she got out and stood in front of the entrance to the hotel. As Karl drove away, she contemplated walking over to the bar for a nightcap but instead headed inside and up to her room. She threw her bag on the bed and took off her jacket. She stretched and turned on the TV to see that the case was still taking up most of the headlines of the local news. She poured herself a Scotch from the mini bar and was about to sit on the bed when she heard the noise of a car speeding away. Her window looked out onto the front street and the entrance to the hotel. Just as she reached it, she saw the back of an old VW Golf disappearing from view.

***

Officer Hunter ended the call with Detective Lahm and turned up the heater in the car. The temperature had risen slightly, but it was still freezing. Outside, the clouds had begun to gather and looked dark and menacing. He looked over at the lodge and then up at the hill beyond, but he couldn't make out the cabin. It was too dark.

He clicked the radio on, turned the volume low, and got comfortable. He had a long night ahead of him. Five minutes later he saw a small white speck land on the windscreen, and he leaned forward and looked up at the sky. A minute later the heavens opened, and the car was covered in snow.

***

Hans Fischer was now becoming desperate. He had stayed out in the forest many times, but not in these temperatures, and he wasn't quite prepared for the conditions. Now, as the snow started to fall, he knew he had to get back to the lodge, get what he needed, and flee.

He slowly crept to the brow of the hill and peered over. The cabin window was still broken, but the police cars and vans had left. Further down, he could see that the lodge looked empty. All the lights were off, and from what he could see, there was only the solitary patrol vehicle out front. Hans knew he could access the lodge without being seen by the car. The only problem he had was getting down the side of the hill without being seen, but he had to try.

The fresh snow that had fallen made descending the hill tricky. He also knew that his camouflage would make him stand out, so he kept low and moved fast, half running, half sliding. As he approached the cabin, he stayed back and cautiously rounded it from the rear. He glanced in the front window; no one was inside, but his rifle was gone. Not ideal, but he knew it was clean anyway. He looked down at the patrol car over a hundred yards away but couldn't make out anyone inside. The snow was heavy and had covered most of it, which didn't help. He continued down the hill with the patrol car in his sight, waiting for the driver's door to swing open, but it never did. Hans reached the bottom and then the back porch of the lodge and took shelter underneath it. He turned and looked back to where he had just come from: a wall of white. He caught his breath and walked to the fence that led to the drive and looked up: the patrol car was still parked, still no movement from it. The snow on the driveway was still fresh with no footprints, and the opposite side of the lodge was the same, no footprints. Hans reached into his pocket and brought out a small key as he placed his other hand against the kitchen window to see inside. Everything that he could remember was still where he had left it. No other signs of any disturbance, so he continued to the door of the bedroom that looked like a window, inserted the small key into the hidden lock, and opened it. The door creaked as it gently swung open, and Hans was still cautious of the fact that the officer might sneak up on him or be listening for movement.

The inside of the lodge was warm, and Hans considered staying to let his body heat up but knew that he couldn't take the risk; time was not on his side. He walked through the back to the hall that led into the kitchen, reached into a cupboard halfway along, and lifted a rucksack that he had already packed in case of such an emergency. He lifted it onto his back and headed back through to the study but stopped before he entered and peered into the living area. Some documents that he knew had been in one of the cabinets were lying open, and he suddenly became more apprehensive. He hurried to his study but refrained from turning on the light even though it was pitch black. The small bag he needed before he could flee was in the back of his desk drawer. He opened the drawer slowly, reached inside, grabbed it, put it inside his rucksack, and headed back to the door out to the porch. He opened it and slid back out, the cold hitting him as he closed the door and locked it. The porch was sheltering him from the snow that was still falling, heavier now. Hans reached the end, stepped down and stopped. The hill that was now on his left-hand side was fifteen minutes away over hard terrain, maybe longer, but he knew it was his best chance to get away. In front of him, however, in the snow that led to the gate out to the driveway, were footprints, fresh prints, not his own – those had been filled in with the snow – new prints. He looked up and over to the driveway, but the steps were heading towards the porch, not from it, and confused now, he spun and looked behind him. When he did, he was met with a Heckler and Koch pistol pointed at his face, and on the other end of the pistol was Detective Stam.

'How bad do you think my shot would need to be from here?' Stam said.

Hans turned, thinking he could run, but instead, he ran straight into the fist of Officer Graham, who had crept up the driveway and waited for him to run.

Chapter 27

Karl Ballack was driving back to Munich after dropping Angela off at her hotel and was contemplating his next move. He understood the position he had put himself in by discussing the file he had discovered and the warning that he was certain he had received. The fact that he had also mentioned the identity of the second name on the list, Theo Schultz, meant that there was no turning back now.

He dialled the number for his office and was redirected to his receptionist's mobile number.

'Hi, it's Karl.'

'Karl, where have you been? The two men who were on their way arrived shortly after you left and went through your office. They even took your computer! I couldn't stop them.'

'I wouldn't have expected you to. What did they say?'

'Nothing, they flashed their security badges and never spoke a word.'

'Okay. I'm going to be out of the office until I figure out what's going on. You should too; take some time off and stay home.'

'Is everything okay?' she asked, sounding worried.

'Yes, you don't need to worry. I just need to try and make sense of all this.'

'Okay. I downloaded everything you'd checked and sent it to your laptop before deleting it.'

'Thanks. I'll be in touch soon.'

Karl approached his apartment, but instead of pulling into the parking garage, he passed by and circled it once before parking further up the street. He got out of the car, crossed the road, and came round to the front of his building from the side entrance. He stopped and peered out and noticed a blacked-out Mercedes jeep parked two cars down on the other side. Two men were sitting in the front, both dressed in black and wearing hats, no doubt with his computer in the back seat.

Karl retreated into the lane that led to the side entrance and phoned his wife. He told her to pack a bag and wait thirty minutes, then use the spare key for his car, which was outside, and drive to her mother's house on the other side of the city. He told her not to worry and that he would be in touch.

When he ended the call, he returned to his car, took out his laptop, then locked the doors. He headed north on foot and made his way to the city centre. When he was on business, he had used the Mandarin Hotel on many occasions and thought this would be safe enough to use.

The luxurious hotel had his usual room available, so he booked it for two nights and made his way up to the top floor. He set his briefcase and laptop down, opened the patio doors and stood on the balcony. The view over the city was as impressive as always, but he couldn't appreciate it in the current circumstances. His phone vibrated with a notification from his wife to say she had made it to her mother's, and as far as she could tell, there was no one following her. He replied with a kiss and made his way inside. He took out his laptop, set it on the desk and took a beer from the fridge. He sat, opened the laptop, clicked on the file his receptionist had sent him and took a sip of his beer as it downloaded. The file he had been refused access to was the last thing on the computer; he entered his details and tried to open it, but again he was denied. He then opened his secure works email and brought up the address of the head of cyber security, a man named Sven, whom he had worked with for many years. He explained he needed help accessing a file. After a few minutes, he got a reply telling him it would take a while, at least a few hours, but that he should be able to get into it. Karl looked at his watch: 23:10. He just hoped that no one was monitoring his email.

***

Mikael Schultz was sitting in the office of his townhouse on the outskirts of Berlin and was still fretting over the current security minister accessing the file he had managed to keep hidden for so long. He had tried for years to have it deleted altogether, but this was something that was out of his control.

The phone on his desk finally rang and he answered it.

'Hey, sir, we're sitting outside the Mandarin Hotel. Our target has just arrived. How do you want us to proceed?' the voice on the other end said.

'I want you to make sure that he does not access any files. I don't care how you do it, just make sure you don't get caught,' Mikael said and slammed the phone down.

After a few seconds of thinking, he lifted the phone again and dialled the number for his son again. It rang out, and he left what was now the third message for him to get in touch as soon as possible.

***

Theo Schultz was sitting on his sofa in an affluent neighbourhood in the south of Salzburg. He was alone, and he had been for the last two days, as his fiancé was currently in Dubai with close friends for her bachelorette party before their wedding in three weeks.

He had spent the morning playing golf and the afternoon having lunch with friends. but now he was home, restless and looking for something to do.

The sun was setting, and he considered going to the gym, but the thought left his head a split second after it had entered it. Instead, he slumped down on the couch and remembered the messages he had received just over a week ago, an unknown number who said she had seen his profile online and liked what she had seen. His wife hadn't left for Dubai at that point, which meant he was wary of messaging, but now he needn't worry. He took out his phone; he had three missed calls from his father, which he ignored for now, and he searched through his history until he found the thread. According to the messages, Tania was a solicitor in her mid-thirties with a love of good food and wild nights. This wasn't the first time Theo had messaged this sort of woman, and for all his flaws, he wasn't naïve; he knew that Tania wouldn't be her real name.

He opened the thread and clicked on the last message. It read, *If you want to meet, you know what to do.* He did want to meet, and he knew what to do. He began typing. *Hey, if you feel like good food or a wild night, give me a message x.*

After pressing send, he felt a rush of excitement run through him. He got up and headed through to the bedroom and started to change. He thought of showering but knew he might not hear back from Tania, so instead, he pulled on a pair of shorts and an old t-shirt before wandering into the bathroom. It was dark outside; the sky was clear and the stars bright. As he looked at himself in the mirror and began to think back, the thoughts he had spent years in therapy learning to deal with began to resurface. The techniques that he had been taught instinctively kicked in and he shook the thoughts away. As he walked back to the living room, he heard a notification sound on his phone on the kitchen table. He excitedly walked over and lifted it; it was a picture from his wife of her and her friends standing in front of the Burj Khalifa hotel. Deflated, he set the phone down and made his way to the sofa, sitting down just as it pinged again. He headed back over and lifted it, expecting to see another drunken image from Dubai, but instead, it was a message from an unknown number. He clicked on it, and it read, *If I had to choose? A wild night it is!!!! Do you want to meet tonight? I'll be free later.* Theo looked at his watch: it was 19:05. He began typing a reply. *Sounds good, send me the location and I'll leave soon.*

After receiving the postcode, which was on the outskirts of Munich, close to the Ebersberger Forest, he typed it into his phone and saw he could be there before 11 p.m. He quickly jumped in the shower and changed, and fifteen minutes after replying to Tania he was sitting in his BMW X6 and heading for Munich and the exciting possibility of a wild night.

Chapter 28

Detective Muller was sitting in the temporary meeting room inside the church and had been since leaving the lodge. It was now past 8 p.m. The thought of travelling home and then having to return later if the plan that had been put in place worked seemed like a waste of time; the phone call she had received from Stam a few minutes ago telling her that Hans Fischer had been caught proved that her thinking was correct. Stam had also told her that he and she would be the ones to interview Hans and that Inspector Klose had been informed.

The snow was still falling when the car pulled up to the entrance to the church. Officer Graham was driving, and Stam was in the back alongside a crestfallen Hans Fischer. Muller opened the door as Officer Graham and Stam got out. She reached in, grabbed his handcuffs, and hauled him out. He shrugged and defiantly tried to walk at his own pace, but Stam grabbed him under the left arm and forced him in through the church doors, conscious of media cameras getting any pictures of their suspect.

Hans Fischer was taken to the makeshift meeting room and handcuffed for a second time, this time to the radiator that was attached to the back wall. He grumbled and protested but succumbed in the end. Stam stepped out of the office and was met by Inspector Schmidt and Head Inspector Klose, who had now joined them.

As was normal, Schmidt began. 'Firstly, great work on catching our suspect, and that goes to all of you, Muller particularly for realising that this would be the best option to catch him.'

Stam looked over at her, and she smiled briefly in response.

'Stam and Muller will be conducting the interview, and we need it to start as soon as we can before Hans requests a lawyer. I'm fairly sure he has been hiding out in the forest all night, and this might be the best opportunity to get information if he's tired.'

Stam lifted the bag that Hans had had on his back when they caught him and set it down on the table next to Schmidt. 'Check this for evidence; it belongs to Hans.'

Schmidt nodded. 'We'll get right on it.'

Muller opened the door of the meeting room and unlocked the second set of cuffs securing Hans to the radiator. He was silent as she grabbed at the remaining cuffs and pulled him up. He slumped down on the chair and rested his hands on the table that separated him and the now-seated Stam. Muller was directly across from him.

'And how are we doing tonight?' Stam asked sarcastically.

Hans Fischer was tired, but this didn't seem to have any effect on his attitude.

'Piss off.'

'That's not very nice, Mr Fischer.'

'I don't give a shit.'

'Where were you the night before last?' Muller asked, realising that the interview could become a no-comment situation if neither of them could be civil.

'In the lodge, same as I always am,' Hans replied while keeping his gaze on Detective Stam.

'You weren't at the lodge three nights ago when Mr Langer saw you in the Bluebell Woods.'

Hans switched his gaze to Muller now.

'That was one man's word against the other, and the last I heard, the other man has spoken his last words.'

'And what do you know about this other man?'

'As I said, he's spoken his last words.'

'You must see the facts in front of you, Hans. You were identified at the graveside of a half-buried body by a man who now has a bullet in his skull.'

'The facts I do see are that the only potential evidence you have was the sighting of me by a sixty-something-year-old man who is now no longer with us. Apart from that, I don't see any other evidence you can provide.'

Muller looked at Stam, who knew she was looking at him but didn't look back.

'Who says we don't have any other evidence?' he asked Hans.

'If you did, you'd be using it now,' Hans replied and leaned back in his chair.

Stam smirked at the overly confident attitude coming from him.

'Okay, so now we get to the part where we ask you again: where were you the night before last?' Muller asked again.

'I was in my lodge.'

'We know you weren't, Hans. What I think happened was that you started to feel the heat and you realised that your only option was to run away into the woods and hide, like the scared piece of shit you are. That sound about right?' Stam said.

Hans stared straight at Stam. His dark eyes filled with rage; he leaned forward and put his elbows on the table. 'I should have shot you when I had the chance,' he said through gritted teeth.

Muller almost reacted; she felt the anger in the words he spat out.

Stam was annoyed, but he quickly regained his composure. 'I will agree with you on that: you should have shot me when you had the chance because I guarantee you that you won't get the chance to again.'

Hans smiled a sarcastic smile, his smiling mouth spread across his face like a cartoon character's. 'I want to speak to my lawyer,' he said.

Stam was just about to reply when they were interrupted by a knock on the door.

'We might have something,' Inspector Schmidt said as he stuck his head through the open door.

Stam and Muller left Hans sitting as they left the room; they didn't bother handcuffing him to the radiator.

'What've you got?' asked Muller.

On the table in front of Schmidt were the contents of the bag that Stam had given him to search. There was a small torch, a waterproof base sheet, a water bottle, two protein bars, a hunting knife and a change of clothes stacked together: trousers, socks, pants and a shirt. They both looked up at Schmidt and wondered what it was that he had felt the need to interrupt them for; it turned out he was holding it in his right hand.

'Is that what I think it is?' Stam asked.

Schmidt nodded.

'A small handgun?' asked Muller.

'Better than that,' Stam replied.

'It's a Walther P-38 handgun, with two rounds missing from the chamber.'

Muller looked at it, then at Stam. 'We've got the bastard!' she said.

They all agreed that the best way to continue was to have forensics check the ballistics on the gun straight away and leave Hans to stew until morning when they got the results back. Hans would be taken to the local police station in Munich, which had a holding cell, until tomorrow at least.

Officer Graham hauled Hans to his feet, escorted him through the door, and headed for the church entrance. Schmidt had already made his way to the door. Hans still had a defiant look on his face as he approached Stam and Muller.

Stam stepped in front of him as he passed. 'Looks like asking for a lawyer might be the best decision you've made recently.'

'Fuck you!' Hans hissed as Officer Graham dragged him away.

Stam and Muller followed them out of the church and stood on the front step as the car was driven away. Stam took out a cigarette and lit it.

'He seemed to get very hostile very quickly,' Muller said. 'That's usually a sign of fear, but with Hans, I didn't get that impression. He seemed different.'

Stam didn't reply.

'What do you think?' she asked.

'I think we should have lit the bastard up!' he replied as he blew out a ring of smoke into the night sky.

Chapter 29

It had become clear that, even after such a brief period of time, it wasn't only a physical attraction that Monica and Lahm felt for each other. On the drive to Lahm's house, she gazed at him as he spoke. Nothing serious or personal, just two people talking and laughing.

When they reached the house, Monica stepped out of the car and waited for Lahm to open the front door. It was a nice-looking lodge, if maybe a little dated. The outside had been painted a dark grey colour a few years ago, by the looks of it, and needed to be freshened up. There was some outside furniture under the porch and a fire pit in the corner that was covered over for the winter. Parked in the grass on the opposite side of the driveway was an abandoned old car. She couldn't tell the make, but it was a faded yellow colour and looked like it hadn't turned a wheel in years.

Inside the lodge she was pleasantly surprised at the homely feel to it. The décor was fairly modern and overall clean looking. Compared to the homes of some of her old boyfriends, it was a palace.

Lahm opened the fridge, took out a bottle of wine, lifted two glasses from a cupboard and set them on the dining table. He opened the wine and poured two glasses, then handed one to Monica, who took it and smiled at him. He smiled back as they clinked glasses and took a sip.

'How long have you lived here?' she asked after swallowing the mouthful of wine.

'Just over twelve years,' he replied.

'It's nice. Not what I expected.'

'Do you not think I'm a little old for the bachelor pad now?' he said, smiling.

Monica smiled in return.

They held each other's gaze, both knowing that they were past small talk.

Monica stood and set her glass on the table and walked over to him, small steps, playful. Lahm sensed the mood change and set his own glass down. For the first time since meeting her, he felt nervous, and he knew that she had noticed it, but he also noticed her react to it and take the lead. She stopped and stood a few inches from him, her forehead in line with his chin. Her eyes peered up and her head followed. She stretched up on her tiptoes so their mouths were now almost touching. She made the first move. A gentle kiss on his bottom lip, teasing. She stretched up a little more and kissed him with a little more meaning. It didn't take long for Lahm's nervousness to disappear. He grabbed her around the waist and pulled her close and he kissed her this time, intense at first and then relenting slightly. She kissed back passionately. Lahm grabbed her and lifted her. She wrapped her legs around his waist, and he walked her to the bedroom, kissing her all the way there. They fell onto the bed, still kissing and wrapped in each other's arms. They only stopped briefly to remove each other's tops and then again as they slowly took off the rest of each other's clothes. Then they fell onto the bed, wrapped into each other, and made love.

Monica woke with a jump, her eyes fighting to focus. She wasn't sure how long she had been sleeping but had the feeling that it hadn't been for very long. She had been woken by the sound of what she thought was a door closing. She was disorientated, and it took her a second to remember where she was. When her eyes adjusted, she concentrated on the foot of the bed; did she see a shadow moving at the end of the bed? She looked over at Lahm, who was sleeping soundly. She switched back to the end of the bed; she was positive someone was standing there, and she suddenly felt frightened. She considered waking Lahm but didn't want to seem paranoid. She lay frozen in bed, listening for any more sounds, but all she could hear was water flowing off the hill behind the lodge, trundling towards the lake.

Reluctantly, she slid one foot out of the bed and placed it on the cold wooden floor, and then the other foot. She waited for another few seconds and got up. Now, standing in the dark, she felt vulnerable. A sliver of light was seeping in through a small gap in the curtains, but it wasn't helping her see. She took a step towards the end of the bed tentatively and stopped. She still couldn't see or hear anything, so she carried on to the door and reached out for the handle. The metal was cold against her palm. She opened it. A small creak broke the silence in the room, but it opened without any more noise. She stepped into the hall and looked toward the living area; the light from the moon lit it up in a yellowy dusk. The glasses were still on the table, half filled with wine. She turned right and looked down the hall towards the back of the lodge. At the bottom were three doors, one on each side and one facing her. She crept forward, the thick carpet dampening the sound of her steps now and the silence even more obvious. All three doors were closed, and the one facing her had a window. She could see outdoor clothes hanging on a drier, caked in mud and dripping wet. She stopped and looked behind her: still no one there, just the yellow light casting its glow. Turning back around, the door on her right was first. With a shaking hand she reached out and grabbed the handle, the coldness on her palm as she gripped it and began to turn, halfway, slowly. She was becoming more anxious. Just as it was about to open, a hand on her shoulder made her jump. Panicked, she turned, swinging her arms. It was Thomas.

'What are you doing?' he asked a little drowsily.

'I was woken up by a noise, then I thought someone was at the bottom of your bed,' Monica replied, her heart still racing.

'I never heard anything. Anyway, you can't go in there,' Lahm replied.

'Why not?'

'It's my brothers' room.'

Monica turned and looked at the door.

'You never told me you had a brother.'

'I don't tell many people I have a brother. Come back to bed.'

Monica reached out for the handle, but Lahm reached over and took her other hand. She desperately wanted to see inside the room, see if this brother she hadn't heard about was inside and if what Lahm was saying was true.

'He'll be sleeping inside; we shouldn't bother him.'

Monica paused for a second and then let go of the handle. Still shaken, she followed Lahm back to the bedroom, and he closed the door behind them.

***

Lahm's brother had heard him coming in through the front door and quickly realised he wasn't alone. He sat up in his bed and listened as his brother and whomever he had brought home talked for a bit before making their way towards the bedroom. He knew it was a woman. He listened to them making love: not that he enjoyed listening to this, but he had no option. After they had finished, he waited for another hour before leaving his room. At first, he put on his coat and headed outside, not liking the fact that someone else was in the house. He walked into the forest and paced for a while before giving into the urge and returning to the lodge. He stripped off his outdoor clothes and hung them up. He opened the utility room door and walked through, a gust from an open window somewhere catching the door and closing it a little more loudly than he wanted. He waited a few seconds, and when nothing came of it, he crept up the hall. Reaching his brother's bedroom door, he slowly turned the handle. He knew this door didn't creak after the initial creak when it was opened. He entered and walked to the foot of the bed and stood in the darkness, foreboding, spying on them. His brother was sleeping soundly, as he always did. The woman on the left of the bed was beautiful, with dark hair and a pale face. He stood watching them, mostly the woman. Her expression was calm and peaceful. He watched for twenty minutes and was prepared to watch for much longer when the woman made a sudden movement and began to stir. Lahm's brother reacted quickly and was able to move without being seen. He watched as the woman got out of bed before leaving the room. Soft delicate steps, cautious and quiet, minutes later followed by the more purposeful steps of his brother. It was only a minute before they both returned. He held his breath as their feet came into view and they sat at the end of the bed. The mattress above his head was now pressed against it. He stayed still and waited with short, quiet breaths. He knew it was just after 10 p.m., and he would wait for them to both fall asleep before sliding out from under the bed and watching them sleep again.

But he never got the chance.

Chapter 30

There wasn't any particular reason for Stam and Muller to wait at the church in Schwaberwegen to receive word that Hans Fischer was now in custody in Munich. They sat inside the meeting room in relative silence until Stam ended the call with Schmidt, and then, without discussion, they both got up and made their way out to Muller's car and headed for Herdweg.

'Is it still okay for me to stay at your place?' Stam asked, knowing that it didn't need asking but still wanting to be polite.

'Stop asking me that,' Muller replied, not annoyed, more tired than anything.

Stam didn't respond. He didn't need to, he understood.

They drove into the twilight. The stars appeared to grow ever closer the further they travelled. Stam took out his mobile phone, brought up the number for Monica and dialled. It rang for a whole minute, then cut off.

'Do you think Hans Fischer is stupid enough not to have known that coming back to the lodge meant he would be caught?' Muller asked.

'I think desperate men do desperate things, which distorts their decision making,' Stam replied.

They continued in silence before eventually arriving in Herdweg. Muller indicated and made the turn. Further up the road that they were travelling on, Stam saw the taillights of a car that had just come from where Muller was headed. But it was too far away to tell what model it was, never mind the registration.

They climbed out of the Seat and headed inside, but Muller hesitated at the door and awkwardly turned to face him.

'You want a beer?' she asked.

'Sure,' Stam replied sceptically.

'Stay here and I'll get us one,' she said before turning the key and entering the lodge.

Muller's lodge, like all the other lodges on the row, had a porch, which was not particularly big but spacious enough for two people.

He sat on one of the wooden chairs that were separated by a small table. After a minute, he heard the sound of electricity being turned on, a quiet clicking noise followed by a hum. Above him and to his right, he noticed the red glow of a patio heater as it kicked into life. Muller then appeared with two beers and set them on the table between them before taking a seat opposite Stam. They lifted their drinks and took a sip. The metallic blue from the night sky was reflected by the lake, and the moon glistened against the water, the same as it had for the last two nights. Both Muller and Stam appreciated the view and the calm as they sat drinking. The underlying sense of relief that they felt at the possibility of the man responsible for the recent murders being caught hadn't kicked in yet, and maybe it wouldn't any time soon. Stam was too old to let himself think that way until it was proven, and so far, the discovery of the small handgun, although it was good, wasn't enough. Not until the ballistics came back, at least. But he was glad Hans was off the street and knew it could be the gun that kept it that way.

'Why are we sitting out here?' Stam asked. 'Not that I'm complaining.'

Muller looked across at him. 'With everything that happened tonight, I think we would have both lain in bed trying to process it. Why not do it here? It's not like we would be sleeping anyway.'

'Fair point,' replied Stam. 'What do you think happened tonight?' he asked as he took another mouthful of beer.

'I think we managed to catch the only real suspect we have for a triple murder and now possibly have the evidence to back our theories up.'

'We can't count our chickens just yet.'

'I'm well aware. What I do know is that we're in a better position than we were yesterday.'

Stam nodded.

'That's not the only reason we're out here, though,' Muller said.

'It's not?'

'You've seemed different today, more in your head than usual.'

'You've only known me for three days. You don't have a lot to compare it to,' Stam said.

'You said it. I've had three days, and I pay attention to stuff like that.'

Stam knew she was right but was also amazed that she had noticed it this quickly. It was because of something Dr Park had said yesterday, and it had been playing on his mind ever since.

'So, what is it?' she asked him.

Stam didn't respond.

'You have something on your mind, I can tell.'

Stam finished the last of his beer and set it on the table. He leaned back in his chair, deep in thought. It's not that he didn't want to share his thoughts with Muller, it was more that he had never felt a need to share them with anybody before. He had spent a career working on his own and had done pretty well up till now. He also knew that Muller was smart and good at her job, just from the three days he had worked with her.

'Spit it out and we can both get some sleep.'

Stam waited for a few more seconds. Apart from knowing how smart and good at her job she was, he was now considering how loyal a person she was too. In the end, it was only a hunch, so he decided to leave it be.

'I'm just tired from sleeping on your shitty sofa bed,' he said with a smirk.

'I see the pleasantries are gone, then!' she said back with a smile.

She got up and returned to the lodge, knowing he was holding something back. She soon reappeared with two more beers. She opened them and sat. They both looked out at the lake and drank in silence.

***

Monica was more than freaked out by the goings on, and the last thing she could imagine doing was going back to sleep. She tossed and turned for a while before giving up, as she still felt like someone was watching her. She checked her phone: it was 00:48. Lahm hadn't managed to go back to sleep either. He could feel Monica beside him, unsettled. He didn't believe his brother had snuck into his room and watched over them, but he couldn't rule it out either. After another ten minutes, he saw Monica sit up.

'Look, I know you said you didn't hear anything, but I did, and it's freaked me out a little. I don't want to sound crazy, but I think I'm going to head back to my hotel if that's okay.'

Lahm sat on the edge of the bed and rubbed his eyes; he didn't want her to go, but he certainly didn't want her to feel uncomfortable.

'Just because I didn't hear anything doesn't mean that you didn't, and I understand if you feel a little shaken.'

Monica looked away from him, feeling a little awkward.

'I can drop you off at your hotel and head back to work for a bit. We're keeping a presence at one of the crime scenes that I should check in with anyway.'

They gathered their scattered clothes from the bedroom floor and then used the bathroom before making their way to the kitchen. Lahm had made some coffee and was pouring it when Monica got to the kitchen table.

'I'm sorry for not mentioning my brother. I guess it's just something that I'm still a little guarded with, and we hadn't got to that point yet,' Lahm said.

'It's fine. I know we only met a few days ago, and I don't expect to know everything. I just got a little spooked.'

Lahm took a sip of his coffee and looked at Monica. She looked beautiful, even at this hour. He didn't want to mess up whatever they had going on.

'Why don't I pick you up later tonight? We can have dinner here, and I'll tell you about my brother and maybe introduce you to him as well.'

Monica wanted to get back to her hotel to try and get some sleep, but she didn't want to end things this way and for it to be awkward.

'I would like that,' she said as she stood from the table and walked over to him. She reached up and kissed him on the lips. He grabbed her around the waist and pulled her closer, kissing back just as hard.

They left and Lahm closed the door. They walked along the small porch and down to the car. The cold engine fired up after a few tries, and Lahm backed the car out and then drove into the early morning mist and headed for Schwaberwegen.

Lahm's brother was waiting for the usual stillness of the house to return before moving from his position. He had lain as still and silent as he could under his brother's bed and heard the discussion between his brother and his friend. He watched as they both got dressed, the bottom of their legs visible as they hurried around the room, short, snappy steps in the darkness, fumbling for strewn clothes and shoes. He waited for the door to close and the lock to click before he slid out. He stopped at the door and looked down the hall towards the kitchen before he turned right and headed further up the hall. He passed by his own room on the left and then passed his brother's old room on the right. He had heard Thomas telling the woman it was his brother's room, which was a lie. He headed into the utility room and put on his old clothes from the drier and his hat and padded jacket, then exited the cabin through the back door and went out into the morning mist.

Monica smiled at Lahm before getting out of the car. They had agreed to meet that evening and that he would pick her up when he had finished work. She entered the hotel and passed through the empty lobby, heading for the stairs. She nodded to the woman at the reception, who smiled back.

Monica stripped off and took a long shower as soon she got to her room, trying her best to shake off the image of someone standing at the foot of the bed, watching over her. She reluctantly got out of the shower and dried herself before climbing into bed. She turned the bedside light off and lay in the dark, thinking, for a long time. She was tired but couldn't sleep. She couldn't get why Lahm was so adamant that she mustn't enter his brother's room.

Chapter 31

Theo Schultz had been driving for almost three hours and was now on a ring road skirting the south of Munich. His satellite navigation told him that his destination was nine minutes from his current location, and he could feel his adrenaline beginning to build.

The map told him he would be entering the Ebersberger Forest from the south, which meant he would pass through the town of Ebersberger before reaching it. Theo was familiar with the forest but hadn't driven through it or seen it before.

As the town faded away behind him, up ahead was the dark looming forest, creeping in on him from both sides. He checked the sat nav in the BMW: five minutes to his destination. As the darkness descended on the car, Theo suddenly became slightly apprehensive. The bursts of light from the sporadically positioned lampposts seemed like the heartbeat of the forest, but slow and laboured.

Theo slowed as his destination looked like it was around the next bend. The closer he got, he was convinced that it couldn't be the right postcode, as the screen showed that the forest continued for at least another two miles north. Theo pulled the car onto the side of the road, careful not to get stuck in the snow that had been ploughed into high banks, then lifted his phone from the passenger seat. He scrolled back to the message he had received from Tania and checked the postcode; it was correct. He thought about dialling her number but didn't want to come across as the kind of guy who was unable to follow directions.

He climbed out of the car, closed the door, and stood

in the cold night air. One of the lampposts was ten feet behind the car and lit up only a small area beneath it. He looked behind him: a whole lot of nothingness, an empty road surrounded by endless trees. He walked to the front of the car and stopped, opened his phone, and began to send a message to Tania. He noticed another voicemail from his dad, which he ignored. He was halfway through typing the message when he heard something off to his left, a small creaking noise like a footstep on a fallen branch. He straightened up, suddenly alert. He took a step closer to the snow on the side of the road and peered into the forest, but the denseness of the trees meant he couldn't see further than ten feet. He stepped back and pressed the call button for Tania instead of continuing with the text message. The phone struggled to connect in the remoteness of the location, but eventually he heard the dial tone and the clicking of the numbers being dialled. Another few seconds of silence, and then it rang, a sharp ring, loud in the silence, unusually loud. Theo was confused; he lowered the phone and listened. He could hear a different kind of ring, louder, even though his phone wasn't pressed directly to his ear. It took a third ring for him to realise that the reason for the loudness was that the phone he was dialling was the one that was making the ringing noise. He stepped to his right and heard the fourth ring of the phone, this time louder still. This turned out to be the last thing he heard as a hand grabbed him from behind. Theo kicked and struggled, but the hand that had grabbed him had some kind of rag in it that was doused in chloroform, and he could feel himself losing consciousness. He fought as hard as he could, but inevitably, it was of no use. Just before he went under, he felt the coldness of the fresh snow on his back as he was dragged down the embankment and into the seclusion of the forest.

The hooded figure had entered the forest not long ago. He wanted the hole that he would be using soon enough to be dug beforehand. He had worked fast but made sure it was deep enough. He didn't want anything to go wrong, not that anything had so far, apart from the first body, Frank Mayer, being dug up. But that hadn't been his fault, not really. Once the new hole was dug, he made his way to the metal shed deep inside the forest. He collected the chloroform and an old rag from a metal box that was bolted to the underside of the table and made his way to the road that split the forest in two. Staying hidden from any passing cars, he hunched behind a large tree a few metres from the road and waited patiently, the rush of adrenaline coursing through his veins. He resisted the urge to let himself feel like it might actually happen; after all these years, he could be minutes away from having his ultimate revenge.

After dragging the unconscious body of Theo Schultz along the untouched snow as far into the forest as was safe, the figure returned to the road and got in the car Theo had been driving. He drove it further up the main road and then down an access road on the right-hand side of the embankment, one he had used many times in the past. The access road led to a clearing that was positioned far enough off the road and wasn't known by very many people, especially with the snowfall that had now hidden it. After opening the gate, the figure eased the car down and around a sharp bend that eventually stopped at an opening hidden by the embankment on the right and an area of dense trees to the left. He threw a white tarpaulin over the car and made his way up and back along the road, the car now totally hidden from sight.

As he trudged back into the forest, he briefly allowed himself to acknowledge the feelings that were flowing through his veins.

He approached Theo, hauled him up onto his shoulders, and carried him the last hundred yards to the metal hut. One-handed, he undid the lock, entered, and laid the body down on the table. He fastened the straps on both the hands and feet before securing the head strap. He closed the door of the hut and locked it from the inside.

He looked at Theo Schultz lying on the bench in front of him. He was of average height and weight for his age. He had short black hair and the beginnings of a middle-age spread. The figure stood over Theo, excitement dancing in his eyes at the thought of what was to come. Ten years in the waiting, and now he had everything he had focused on all that time lying in front of him. Now he could begin.

He stepped over to the wall with the workbench and lifted the drill from it, then walked behind to the top of the table. He continued round to the side of it and started the drill spinning, the noise deafening in the close confines of the hut. Theo Schultz didn't deserve the small hole in the temple, not to begin with anyway. The figure placed his left hand on Theo's thigh to keep it steady, then found what he thought was the centre of his kneecap and pressed the tip of the drill into it. He gave the drill a tap and saw the metal tip bite into the skin, then stopped when he knew it was exactly where he intended. He pressed it again, this time for longer and with more force. A spurt of blood shot up and out, covering the table. The drill was loud in the small hut but was drowned out by the scream that was coming from the now fully awake Theo Schultz. The pain that coursed through him had made him conscious again.

The hooded figure watched for a bit; seeing the man he had waited so long to have under his control was satisfying but only fuelled his rage even more. He checked the straps to make sure they were secure. Two puddles of blood were now forming under the table.

Theo thrashed and screamed before passing out for a few seconds and then jumping back to life and letting out another scream. The figure resisted the temptation to drill into his temple; he could suffer a bit longer. He gagged him with a cloth before leaving. He turned the lights off in the hut and locked it from the outside. As he strolled back towards the path, he could still hear the mumbled screams echoing from the hut.

He trudged onwards through the snow, further away from the hut and the screams until all he could hear were his own thoughts.

Chapter 32

Karl Ballack looked at the digital clock next to the bed in his hotel room. It read 05:08. It had been a long night, and he hadn't slept. A few times, he thought about sending another email to Sven to see how he was doing but refrained. He would be doing all he could.

Karl stood and shook out his arms and legs and walked over to the balcony. The air was still, not warm and not cold but somewhere in between. The city was quiet, and to Karl, a sense of trepidation surrounded it. He was thinking about getting some sleep when the stillness of the night was abruptly broken by a ping from his email. He hurried back inside, sat at the desk, and clicked on the email. It was from Sven.

This file was locked up tighter than any file I've ever tried to access before, which was the reason it took so long. I've copied and encrypted it and sent it as an attachment. To be honest, there isn't much to it. Speak soon.

Karl opened the secure email and then clicked on the attachment. Sven was right, there wasn't much to it. Four names, just as he had seen earlier before he was kicked out of it. Two names he had heard of, two he hadn't. He took a picture of the screen with his mobile and then deleted the email. Just as he went to close his laptop, the phone on the table next to his bed rang, the hotel room phone. He answered it.

'Two men, heading upstairs. As you said, they look official.'

Then the phone went dead.

Karl had anticipated he might be followed, which was

partly why he had chosen this hotel, as it was one that he had stayed in many times, so he was friendly with most of the reception staff. When he had checked in late last night, he had booked his usual room. As a precaution, he had also booked the one next to it, which was the one he was currently in.

He knew time was now of the essence, so he quickly grabbed his bag and his laptop. He stepped through the balcony doors and launched the laptop off the edge just in case they managed to capture him. The height of his floor meant it would be smashed into tiny bits and hopefully thrown into a bin by a cleaner in the morning.

Just as he threw it, he heard the door of the adjacent room being kicked. It sounded like it had held, but then he heard a gunshot and a second kick before hearing the door crash off the inside wall of the room. He darted back in from the balcony and ran to the door. He opened it slowly and peered out, just a glance. No one outside the door of his usual room or further down the hall. He waited and took a breath, turned right, and headed for the stairs. He didn't hear any footsteps following behind him, only the piercing crack of a handgun. The bullet passed over his left shoulder and hit a pane of glass at the top of the staircase; the glass from it rained down on him. He carried on to the staircase and scrambled down it, the two men now chasing behind and moving fast. He could hear them in the stairwell as he reached the bottom. When he reached the lobby, he saw the receptionist who had called him and shouted at her to take cover. Karl turned towards the front entrance but changed course, ducked behind a seating area, and skirted around the back of the reception. To his right, he could see the two men exit the staircase and scan the room. They made the obvious decision and headed for the front entrance, allowing Karl to jump the reception desk, narrowly missing the receptionist who was hiding underneath.

'Have you called the police?' he asked quietly.

'Yes, they're en route.'

'Okay, great,' Karl replied, sucking in large gasps of air.

'Here are my car keys. It's a Mini. It's parked in the workers' car park.'

'Thanks again,' Karl said and scurried to the back of the reception and out of the employee door at the rear. As he closed the door, he could see the two men enter the hotel again and begin searching the reception. Karl came out into the night air and found the Mini three cars up. He climbed in and started it up, the small car ticking over once then sparking to life. He pulled away slowly and kept the revs of the car's engine low. He then turned onto the main road and accelerated steadily, not panicking. In his rear-view mirror, he could see the front of the hotel, quiet and still. Up ahead, he could see two police patrol cars and what looked like an armed response unit further back, lighting up the dark street like a fire in a tunnel.

He took out his mobile as he drove and dialled the number for Angela. He knew it was early but hoped she would be awake. She was.

***

Mikael Schultz was still sitting in his office when the call came through that the file he had tried for so many years to keep secret had been opened. His team couldn't determine who it was that had managed to hack into it, and they probably wouldn't ever find out.

Five minutes after being informed that it had been accessed, he phoned his two men who were sitting outside of the Mandarin hotel. He ordered them to find the laptop that belonged to Karl Ballack and shoot to kill if required.

Twenty minutes later, he received information that his men had been arrested and the security minister had somehow managed to escape injury.

He took out his mobile and called the prime minister to arrange a meeting.

Chapter 33

Stam was woken early the next morning by the sound of his mobile ringing. He grunted at first and then sat up on the joke of a mattress that he had now slept on for three nights. He stretched and yawned and then finally picked up his phone. It was Inspector Schmidt calling. He spoke loudly, with a combination of annoyance and anticipation in his voice.

'Morning, Stam. We've had some developments this morning.'

Stam looked at his watch: it was only 07:25. *How many developments could there be?* he thought.

'What's happened?' he asked.

'The ballistics have come back on the gun; we put a rush on them.'

'And?'

'They're not a match to the bullets that killed Mr and Mrs Langer.'

Stam lowered the phone and swore, which Muller heard as she came walking down the hall.

'What's wrong?' she asked.

Stam ignored her. 'How could that be?' he asked Schmidt.

'We have no idea. That's not all, though. Helen from forensics has called. She wants to meet with us as early as possible this morning.'

'Did she say what it was about?'

'No,' Schmidt replied, 'but she sounded adamant.'

'We're on our way.'

Stam explained to Muller over a rushed cup of strong

coffee about the gun not being a match to the bullets that had killed the Langers. She seemed as disappointed as him. But then he told her about Helen wanting to meet, which sounded encouraging.

Muller was quiet for a large part of the journey, thinking about last night, Stam thought, and how she sensed he was keeping something from her. He would tell her in time if he thought anything would come of it.

In the rush that had ensued after the call that morning from Schmidt, Stam hadn't realised until they were almost at the church that he had another two messages on his phone and one missed call. He read the two messages first before checking the voicemail. One was from his daughter, asking to meet today; she had something on her mind and wanted to talk it over. He felt bad that he hadn't managed to meet with her more since she had arrived, but in truth, he also had the feeling that she hadn't seemed overly concerned about meeting either. Regardless, he made sure to be available for her at some point today and messaged her back saying he would call to arrange a time soon. The second message coincided with the voicemail; they were both from Dr Park. Both seemed urgent and both were the same message: *Call me back asap*, they said.

Stam decided to call Angela back as they approached Schwaberwegen and the church.

'Detective.'

'Angela, everything okay?'

'That is still to be decided. We need to talk.'

'We are talking,' Stam replied, not realising how blunt it sounded.

'In person. Karl managed to get into the file he was speaking about last night.'

'That's good. What did he find?'

'Four names, two we already know of and two we don't.'

'Has he managed to look into the other two?'

'He was about to.'

'What stopped him?'

'Two government officials breaking into his hotel room and trying to kill him!'

'Okay, you know what this means?'

'What?'

'It means that whatever he's come across is something that they don't want him to know.'

'Who don't?' she asked.

'That's what we have to find out. When will he be here?'

'He's en route just now. As I said, we need to meet.'

Muller pulled the car over and took off her seatbelt. Stam gestured for her to stay in the car.

'How long till he arrives?' Stam asked.

'He said ninety minutes, give or take.'

'Tell him to make sure he isn't being followed and to meet at your hotel. We'll speak there, it might be safer. I'll make enquiries at my end,' said Stam.

'I was going to check over the Langer's house today,' Angela said.

'That can wait,' Stam replied. 'We may have other things more important. I'll be in touch.'

'Okay, bye.'

Stam hung up the phone and looked at Muller, who was still holding the steering wheel.

'This is more than a buried body in the woods,' Muller said, staring out.

'You got that right,' Stam replied before they got out and headed into the church.

Inside the church were Inspector Schmidt, Helen from forensics, and now Stam and Muller. Schmidt had brought them all coffees, and they sat in the makeshift interview room drinking them.

'Okay. First we have the report regarding the Walther P-38 handgun we found on Hans Fischer. And at the end of the day, it's not a match, not even close. This gun can use two distinct types of ammunition. The bullets we found were standard bullets for the gun. The ones we got from Hans's gun were a cheaper alternative, cheaper metal which reacts differently in the barrel when fired. The bullets we found never came from that gun, end of story.'

Everyone stayed quiet, with nothing to say in reply.

'The one positive we may have comes from Helen.' He gestured towards her to begin.

'Okay, so we received the DNA results back from the garage at the hunting lodge. As you will recall, we had eight different blood samples. Five of them came back as animal blood, probably deer, from what we found at the location. Two were undetermined, as the samples we had weren't good quality. One came back as a hit, and it was human.'

'Frank Mayer?' Muller asked.

'No. They have been identified as Felix Olson.'

'Do we know who Felix Olson is?' asked Schmidt.

The room was quiet for a few seconds. Then Stam spoke.

'He was one of the original victims from the old case back in Munich. He was the first person to be killed. I read the file,' answered Stam.

'We have also managed to get two samples from the four-by-four, which we will have tested in the next four hours,' Helen continued, but everyone was still shocked at the discovery of Felix Olson's blood.

'I have to call Dr Park,' Stam said before getting up and heading outside.

Chapter 34

Dr Park agreed to head over to the church. It was only a ten-minute walk, and knowing that Karl was still over an hour away, she knew she would be back in time to meet him.

Stam met her at the church entrance and asked her before they entered not to mention what they had discussed earlier on the phone.

'The fewer people who are aware of Karl Ballack's whereabouts means the less chance there is of him being discovered.'

'Does this mean you're warming to him?' she asked with a smirk.

'Not likely,' Stam replied.

Stam and Angela entered the makeshift interview room in the church and joined the others. When they had sat down, Stam asked Helen to tell her what she had discovered from the blood samples.

'Are you aware of the name Felix Olson?'

'Of course,' she replied. 'He was the first victim but the last one that we discovered had the hole drilled in his skull. He was an older man who worked as a delivery driver for the council. He was found behind a dry-cleaning store in the centre of Munich. No other injuries apart from the hole in his skull.'

'Was there any evidence on the body at all?' Schmidt asked.

'None whatsoever. Our findings regarding the time of death, compared to others, put him as the first victim. We tend to find with serial killers, the first time they kill, they're more aware of making mistakes. It's when they get used to it that they can start to slack and slip up.'

Everyone inside the office was writing down what Dr Park was saying. Stam knew the details and had already taken notes.

After they had all settled and finished scribbling, Stam began.

'With this latest evidence, we now have enough to hold Hans Fischer. I'm sure everyone is aware that we still need to find who killed Mr and Mrs Langer.'

'We also need to discover if the garage at the hunting lodge was where Frank Mayer was killed,' said Schmidt.

'Or if he has other premises that he could have used to kill him,' said Muller.

'Either way, we still have work to do,' said Stam.

Schmidt had arranged to question Hans at the station where he was being held. Stam said Muller should join him in the interview and that he had some enquiries to check up on here in Schwaberwegen and would leave it to them. Dr Park knew it was to meet with Karl Ballack and that he didn't want anyone else to know other than Muller.

Just as they were getting up to leave, Stam stopped. 'Where is Head Inspector Klose?' he asked.

'No idea. No one's heard from him since yesterday evening,' replied Schmidt.

***

Mikael Schultz was now sitting in the office of the prime minister of Germany. The two men were tense and anxious about the unearthing of what could come from the file being accessed, Mikael more so than the prime minister.

'We have to get a handle on this. You are clearly aware of the severity of the consequences if the details should be revealed,' the prime minister said while tapping a pen on his desk.

'It's that bloody Karl Ballack. I knew he shouldn't have been appointed as security minister,' replied Mikael.

'Don't start passing blame now. This should have been dealt with all those years ago. You knew what could happen if someone started digging.'

They both shuddered at the thought of the truth coming out. The prime minister could probably deny everything and squirm his way out of it. Unfortunately, Mikael could not; he would have to take the fall. Both of them understood this.

'Have you spoken with Theo?'

'No, he isn't answering his phone. I'll try him again now.'

Mikael took the phone and tried the number for his son. This time it didn't ring at all but went straight to voicemail.

'His phone's off now. Before, it rang a few times at least before I left him a message.'

'I don't like this.'

They sat in silence, both thinking and worrying.

'What about the other three names in that file?'

'As far as I know, Frank Mayer is the only one whom we couldn't contact. That was a few days ago.'

'I think it might be time to make contact and make sure they all know the script and stick to it. Or we use the alternative option.'

Mikael got up and headed out of the office and down to his car, wondering why his son's phone was now turned off.

Chapter 35

Stam was in the same patrol car as earlier, with Angela now in the passenger seat.

Stam knew the hotel wasn't far from the church, but he wanted to have the car with him just in case. It also meant he could park behind the hotel and gain access from the rear entrance.

Angela had said that she still didn't expect to see Karl for at least another half hour, which would allow Stam to contact Monica. Hopefully they could have breakfast together, if she hadn't already left. Just as they entered the reception from the rear entrance, Monica suddenly appeared at the foot of the stairs.

'Dad!' she said, a little surprised.

'Monica, I was just coming to see if you wanted to grab some breakfast.'

'Great!' she replied.

Now conscious of the slight awkwardness as the three of them stood together, Stam introduced them.

'This is Dr Park. She's a forensic pathologist who's working with us on the case.'

They shook hands. Angela recognised Monica from a few days ago when she had checked in, and she also noticed a slight change in Detective Stam's demeanour. His tone softened when he spoke with his daughter. Not that he was particularly harsh generally, but he spoke to his daughter more gently.

'You're free to join us,' Monica said to Angela.

Stam was surprised she had asked, but he knew his daughter was only being nice; she was like that.

'No thanks, I need to grab some stuff from my room.

Thanks, though,' Angela said before leaving them.

Monica headed over to the waiter who was standing in the dining room and asked him for a table for two. They sat at a window seat that looked out onto the icy high street through a partially frozen window.

'Were you really coming to have breakfast with me?'

'Of course! Your message seemed, shall I say, direct. Is everything okay?'

'Yes, I think so, at least,' Monica replied a little sheepishly.

'What's happened?' Stam asked, now slightly alarmed.

'Nothing really, nothing yet. I was just wanting to see how you were getting on with the case.'

'We may have a breakthrough. Not necessarily in this case, but we believe it could be connected.'

'Anything you can share?'

'Not really. We arrested someone we thought could be responsible for a double murder. Turns out we're not so sure now.'

The waiter approached the table with their food and coffee. Monica stared out of the window, thinking about the night before and what she had seen, or hadn't seen, as the case may be.

'Is the person you thought was responsible in custody?'

'Yes, and he will be for a while, until we prove it's him, or until we find out who did it.'

Monica seemed to relax a bit. Stam noticed it.

'There's something you're not telling me. What have you been doing while I've been working?'

She had known he would ask. She didn't want to reveal she was seeing someone he was working with just yet, although she had tried this in the past with boyfriends and he always figured it out. It was his job to detect.

'I've been seeing someone from around here. Nothing serious, someone I bumped into.'

'Is that what's on your mind?'

'No, it's all good. Just knew you had been worrying about me and wanted to check in.'

'Looking after your old man now after all these years, is that it?' Stam said with a smile and a mouthful of scrambled eggs. 'I'm not that old yet, am I?' he said after sipping his coffee.

Monica smiled in return and decided to wait and see what came from meeting Thomas's brother later tonight and if anything came up regarding last night. She was probably overthinking things and felt bad about the suspicions that were going through her mind.

***

Stam left his daughter after they finished breakfast. He kissed her on the cheek, then headed out of the hotel and turned right towards the centre of town, took a cigarette from his packet, lit it and took a long draw of it. He felt that something was going on with her. One thing he had known as she was growing up was that she didn't need anyone to look out for her, she was more than capable of doing that herself. He did feel that there was something she wanted to share, but for whatever reason, had stopped herself. He told himself to call her later today to see how she was.

Stam took the stairs up to the first floor of the hotel. Angela had told him her room number before breakfast, and Stam said he would come up when he had finished.

He knocked on the door and was faced with Karl

Ballack. He still had a heavy jacket on, which meant he must have just arrived. Stam entered the room without shaking his hand or even acknowledging that Karl was there. Angela was standing next to a large chest of drawers in the corner pouring coffee into two cups. She turned to say hi before lifting a third cup. The room was huge, more like a suite. It was extravagant in a traditional German way, decorated thirty years ago but still retaining a sense of modernity.

In the far corner was a double bed next to one window, and in front of the second window were two leather sofas facing each other. Behind that was a dining table with four chairs. A bathroom sat behind the sofas, opposite the chest of drawers Angela was standing at. A large TV was mounted on the far wall, with a local news channel playing.

'Stam,' Karl said, still a little uncertain.

'You made it, I see,' Stam replied.

'Just.'

Angela set the three cups down on the dining table and they all took a seat.

'Karl managed to take a picture of the file we spoke about.'

Karl had plugged his phone into Angela's laptop and enhanced the picture. The screen showed the only thing in the file: four names.

Frank Mayer
Daniel Smithe
Robert Ewing
Theo Schultz

From start to finish, that was it. Eight words, forty-four letters.

'Well, it's clear we know two of the names. We know one of the men on this list is dead and had been partially buried. Another name we know because of his father's position in the German government. The other two, though, who knows?' said Karl.

Stam was looking at the names, thinking.

'One of the men was a police officer. Another one of them is the son of the former security minister. I'm not sure how the two are connected, but the only way to connect them is by investigating the two names with which we aren't familiar.'

'How can we? From the events of last night, I'm quite sure my name will be on every police station desk.'

'You're the security minister,' Angela said, but she felt a little naïve after saying it.

'I was the security minister last night as well, and that didn't stop me being shot at.'

'He's right: if this is running high enough up the chain, then he won't get a word out of anyone. That doesn't mean someone else won't, though,' Stam said.

'Who?' asked Karl.

'I wanted to make sure I could trust you, and I believe now I can. We should keep the net on this one tight, however. Muller will be informed, but I need her to be part of the interview team that speaks with Hans Fischer later today, and she should get going soon. The only other one I trust with this is Inspector Schmidt.'

No one responded. They couldn't comment as they didn't know Inspector Schmidt. They didn't know Oliver Stam either, but they had to trust his instinct.

'Okay,' Karl said.

Angela nodded.

'I'll make arrangements for him to meet you both

here. Explain all the details you have and the incident from last night. He'll check the other two names out, under the radar.'

'Okay,' Karl said again.

'What are you going to do now?' Angela asked.

'I need to find out who else working this case uses a Walther P-38,' Stam replied and put on his coat.

'It's 10:30. You're going to have to stay here. No phone calls or messages. After what happened last night with you, Karl, I wouldn't be surprised if the German government's made an announcement saying you're missing, to try and flush you out.'

Karl and Angela both looked at Stam as he fastened his coat and left the room.

They turned to the TV on the wall. It was just coming through that a road traffic accident on the ST2080 was causing tailbacks and that locals should take other routes.

Chapter 36

Stam parked the patrol car in the same spot he had taken it from earlier. The police presence was beginning to die down from the previous night, he had noticed.

He stepped out of the car. The air felt crisp, no clouds in the sky, and the low morning sun seemed futile against the bitter cold.

He noticed Head Inspector Klose standing at the entrance to the church, milling around and typing on his phone. He started to make his way over to him but was stopped halfway by Muller. She had been waiting for him to return.

'How did you get on with Dr Park and ...'

Stam interrupted her. 'Keep that between us for now. I'm going to make Schmidt aware, but apart from that, it's only us who knows.'

Muller nodded in agreement.

'So, what the plan, boss?' she said.

'I need you to be part of the interview of Hans Fischer with me, but first I need to speak to Inspector Klose about the gun used to kill the Langers and how many officers use the same weapon.'

'Well, that's the reason I was waiting on you. Klose wants to be part of the interview of Hans as well,' she said.

'Well, I want you involved also,' Stam replied, annoyed.

'Well, that's the problem: so does he. He wants you here in Schwaberwegen while we conduct the interview.'

Now Stam was pissed off and sceptical.

Muller didn't speak.

'I'll speak with Schmidt. He's in charge, after all. I still need you there, though. But remember what I said about the other thing.'

'Sure, boss.'

Head Inspector Klose saw Detective Stam speaking with Muller, finished sending his message, and headed towards him. He explained pretty much what Muller had already told him. He wanted to be the one to conduct the interview but was happy enough for Muller to assist him. He then gave Stam some bullshit about Stam being here with Schmidt to keep a handle on what was going on. Klose also said they were starting to finish up with the scene and that he was convinced he had the man responsible for it. Stam nodded along without saying that he thought his head was up his arse and that it was too early to close the scene down. He thought he would have more sense speaking with Schmidt, however, and let Klose ramble on.

Stam then watched as Muller climbed into Klose's car and they made their way out of the town. Soon after, Schmidt appeared at Stam's side.

'You believe he's closing this scene down?' Schmidt asked with a little anger in his voice.

'I was about to tell him as much, but there wouldn't be any point.'

Schmidt nodded.

'And him doing the interview?'

'Don't get me started,' Stam snapped back.

They made their way over to the church but didn't enter. Stam lit up a cigarette and stood in the small courtyard. Schmidt could tell Stam wanted to talk.

'I found it strange a few days ago when he was unable

to get the file that we requested on Frank Mayer, but more significantly now with the original case from 2010, which I've managed to secure a copy of myself.'

'Why haven't you shared this information?' Schmidt replied.

'I had my reasons, and to be honest, I believe that it could lead to something bigger than this, which is why I need your help with it.'

'With what?' Schmidt asked, slightly annoyed.

As Stam smoked his cigarette, he laid everything out to Inspector Schmidt. The file on Frank Mayer. The second file that had been hacked into. The names that it contained. And lastly, Karl Ballack, which was the thing Schmidt found the most surprising of all of it. Stam then told him where they were holed up and that he wanted him to meet with them, and for Schmidt to use his contacts to try and find any information he could on the two names that they didn't recognise. He agreed and fully understood why Stam had been reluctant to divulge this information, but he was still a bit annoyed. What he didn't understand was why Stam had chosen to inform him specifically, but he decided to go along with it for now because he thought something seemed off with how Head Inspector Klose was leading this investigation.

Stam watched as Schmidt headed up Main Street towards the hotel. He checked his watch: 12:45. Three police cars and two support vehicles passed by him as he walked to one of the tents in the main square. He noticed Detective Lahm standing talking to a few officers, and he nodded as he passed. Stam found the assistant inspector in charge of operations. She was a young woman with brown hair and a serious face.

'Detective, how can I help you?' she asked.

'I'm looking to find out how many armed officers are working on this case, including detectives and patrol officers.'

The woman opened an iPad she had under her arm and started clicking and swiping. After a few seconds, she looked up at him.

'Altogether, there have been 52 armed officers involved.'

That was slightly more than Stam had expected.

'How many of these officers carry a Walther P-38?'

Again, she clicked and swiped before saying, 'Forty of them. The others are either armed response, who carry much more powerful firearms, and some of the detectives, who use much smaller guns.'

Much like the handgun that Stam carried himself.

'Thank you for your time, Inspector,' Stam said before leaving.

If the hunting lodge and its grounds had now been fully searched and no more weapons had been uncovered, then he would have to begin the process of inspecting every weapon of every officer involved.

Detective Lahm finished speaking with two patrol officers and made his way over to Detective Stam when he had saw that Stam had finished talking with the assistant inspector.

'Boss, did you hear about the accident on the ST2080 road?'

'No, what happened?'

'A car travelling north hit some ice and skidded off the road. The driver had to be cut out of his vehicle. I'm heading up to take a look with a few officers.'

'Okay. Anything significant about it?'

'Don't think so, but worth taking a look.'

'Okay,' Stam said again.

Lahm jumped in his old Golf and sped down towards the forest road. Stam turned and walked up Main Street, past the monument in the middle of the town, and further up past the hotel to the café he had met with Monica in a few days ago. It was lunchtime and he hadn't eaten yet.

He sat near the back, ordered eggs on toast with apple juice, and waited for it to be served. He took out his notebook and began checking back through details. He wasn't quite getting what was going on, but at the same time, he wasn't totally convinced that Hans Fischer was the answer to everything.

The waiter arrived with his food, and he put the notebook in his pocket and began eating with the growing sense that someone was lying, or at the very least, withholding information.

Chapter 37

Muller was sitting in the passenger seat of Inspector Klose's private vehicle, a BMW estate car that smelled new.

They were currently on their way to the police station in Munich that was holding Hans Fischer. The journey wasn't too long but longer than Muller would have wanted.

'So, what're your thoughts on the case, Detective?' Klose asked after they reached the edge of the city.

Muller was glad he was asking about the case and not attempting pointless small talk.

'I'm confident with the fact that we have Hans in custody. Whatever's going on, he's involved in one way or another.'

'How do you mean, whatever's going on?'

'Er' – she paused, thinking – 'just with the gun that killed the Langers. I thought we had him when we found the gun in his possession.'

Klose didn't reply, and she could tell he was thinking intently about her words.

'You think there are more people involved?' he asked.

'Surely not. There was no evidence of anyone else being there.'

Klose overtook on a side road and almost swerved into an oncoming car.

'Hans is the one behind it all. I know we didn't find Frank Mayer's blood at his house, but we got Felix's.'

'You could be right, sir.'

They drove on for a bit in silence. The lunchtime traffic was now starting to build. As they approached the station, Klose asked, 'What are your thoughts on Detective Stam?'

Muller was looking out of the passenger side window when he asked and didn't look round as she answered.

'I've heard everyone say he's a stubborn bastard but is also the best they've worked with. I'm starting to think they're correct on both counts.'

***

Schmidt was in Angela's hotel room. He was sitting at the dining table, in the chair that Stam had been sitting in earlier.

Over the last twenty minutes, Karl had explained in more detail what he had been involved in during the last 48 hours. Inspector Schmidt had listened intently; there were parts of the story he couldn't quite believe. Once Karl had finished, the inspector took numbers for them both and the names that were on the file that Karl had accessed.

Then, excusing himself, he sat on one of the leather sofas and made a call. His thoughts were that using at least two different people to make enquiries into the names could be safer.

His first call was to one of his old partners, now his closest friend, Franz. He was a senior analyst for internal intelligence in the German police. He had access to all manner of databases, criminal files, vehicle databases and the national census.

He explained the level of confidentiality involved and asked for nothing to be sent that could leave a paper trail: phone calls only. His friend agreed, knowing he wouldn't be asking unless it was of extreme importance. Franz said he would need at least until the end of the day but would gather as much information as he could before getting in contact.

When Schimdt returned to the dining table, he explained it would take a few hours before anything could be found out and they would have to hang tight.

'How long is it going to be before people start wondering where the security minister is?' Schmidt asked.

'I left word with my secretary that I'm taking a few days off to spend time with my family out of town. I have a further two days before I need to report to my seniors.'

'Good,' Schmidt replied.

After some small talk, Schmidt was getting ready to leave when the large TV on the wall, still on the local news channel, got their attention. There was an update on the accident on the ST2080, which Schmidt hadn't been aware of. The news reporter who was at the scene explained that a second car was now involved but was believed to be unoccupied. Within seconds, Schmidt's mobile phone started ringing; it was Detective Lahm calling him.

'Inspector, you may want to head over here. I think we have something.'

Chapter 38

Head Inspector Klose and Detective Muller had entered the Munich police station and been taken through to be fully de-briefed on Hans Fischer before interviewing him. They then entered the interview room to see Hans sitting in a small chair next to his lawyer, still with the same defiant look on his face as yesterday. Muller began the interview.

Thirty-five minutes later, they were sitting back in the BMW.

They had asked him question after question about the blood that had been found and him being identified at the crime scene that was discovered in Bluebell Woods, then regarding the person who had identified him being found dead in an undisclosed safe house. To every question he had been asked, his response had been *no comment*. At one point, Klose had to glare at Muller because of how restless and annoyed she was becoming at Hans as he sat there answering no comment before the questions were even put to him. She had wanted to lean over and smash his face into the table.

'I think we could have predicted that,' Klose said.

'He thinks that saying nothing will somehow help him. Let's see how that works out.'

They had pulled out of the car park and begun heading for Schwaberwegen when Klose's mobile rang through the Bluetooth in the car. It was Inspector Schmidt.

'I've been trying to reach you,' he said.

'We were interviewing.'

'How did that go?' Schmidt asked.

'Not great. What's up?'

'We may have something here. Head to the ST2080.'

'We're on our way,' Klose replied.

***

Stam, Lahm and Inspector Klose were standing at the bottom of a small access road that ran parallel to the main road through the Ebersberger Forest. The car that had been involved in the accident earlier, a VW Up, had hit some fresh ice and slid over to the other lane and then down the embankment. The snow that had been ploughed the previous night had taken some of the momentum out of the car but not enough. The small car had crashed through it, off the embankment and into the forest. The thing that the driver, a young man in his late teens who had a minor head injury and what looked at first to be a dislocated collar bone, hadn't expected, was that his car then smashed into the back of a BMW X6 that was parked and hidden under a white tarpaulin.

'Have you phoned in the registration of the BMW?' Stam asked.

'Yes, as soon as I got here,' replied Schmidt.

Lahm was helping one of the patrol officers to direct the recovery truck down the access road and round the tight bend to the main road.

'Do we have any ideas why this would be here?' Lahm asked as he joined the others.

'Maybe stolen and hidden here to see if anyone comes for it. Most cars like this have trackers in them that the owner or dealer can track if stolen. If no one comes for it in twenty-four hours, the thieves come back for it, thinking it has no tracker fitted.'

'I'm not so sure,' Stam said. 'It's positioning seems off

219

to me.'

'You think it's connected?' Schmidt asked, thinking about what Stam had said.

'Wouldn't be surprised.'

Just then, Schmidt's mobile started ringing. He stepped back and listened for a few seconds. The only words he said were thank you.

'Looks like you were right,' he said, staring at the two smashed cars in front of them. 'The BMW is registered to one Theodore Schultz.'

***

Mikael Schultz was still in his office. He didn't have anywhere else to go, not really. Since he had retired as the security minister six years ago, he had been brought in as an advisory director for a large security firm but had retired from that position last year, and now he found himself working out of his office in his four-storey townhouse.

He was now positive that his son, Theo, had dropped off the radar, and with the recent discovery of Frank Mayer's body, he feared the worst. Just as he was deciding what his next course of action would be, his mobile rang.

'Hi, Mikael, it's me. I'm using a burner phone.'

'Hi. Do you have any updates?'

'We've found Theo's car.'

'That's a start at least. No sign of Theo?'

'No. And it's not a good start either.'

'Go on.'

'His car was parked in the centre of the Ebersberger Forest, only a few miles from where they discovered the body of Frank Mayer.'

    'Fuck!' he said. 'I'm on my way.'

Chapter 39

As soon as the car was identified as being registered to Theo Schultz, Stam and Schmidt agreed that no one else needed to know about the file and what they were looking into. The immediate concerns were the whereabouts of Theo and if any harm had come to him.

Head Inspector Klose had now arrived on the scene with Detective Muller. They had both been brought up to speed on the latest information, and both Theo's mobile phone and his car registration were being tracked by the police communications department in Munich for any further details that could give them clues to his whereabouts.

After both cars had been recovered and the scene cleared, everyone made their way back to Schwaberwegen and let the local patrol officers get the road cleared of debris and the traffic flowing again.

The town centre was now all but cleared of a police presence as they arrived back in Schwaberwegen. A police van was still at the bottom of the town on the road that led to the bridge. The path into where the body had been discovered was still cordoned off, but they had pulled it forward to the end of the Victorian bridge.

They sat in the office inside the church and all came to the agreement that the possibility of Theo Schultz's being missing wasn't directly linked to the recent investigation for now, although it was strange that his car was found so close. Schmidt and Stam glanced at each other. Klose never lifted his head from his notepad.

'I've spoken with the prosecutor's office, and they've

received all the evidence we have at this point. They agree that the DNA that's been discovered inside the premises belonging to Hans Fischer is at least enough for us to hold him for another twenty-four hours after our initial forty-eight hours have passed, which will be in three hours' time,' Klose said as everyone settled down. He continued, 'They said they'll call when they've made a decision on the charges.'

'What about the crime scene here in Schwaberwegen? Do you think it's wise to pull out now?' Schmidt asked.

'We've had almost three days here, and I think we've got everything from it that we can,' Klose replied.

Stam chewed on the end of his pencil. He agreed that the scene had given them all they would get, but it was being cleared much earlier than was usual, and he wasn't sure why.

'This means we have to continue to find new evidence which links Hans to either Felix Olson or any of the other victims,' Klose said, summing up.

'I think I may be able to help with that,' said a voice from the door of the office.

Helen from the forensic office was standing behind them with a sheet of paper in her hand. She had arrived just as Head Inspector Klose began talking and hadn't wanted to interrupt.

'How's that?' Schmidt asked.

'We just got the results back from the four-by-four that belongs to Hans Fischer. We found three blood samples, two of which were identifiable.'

Everyone was now turned in their seats and staring at the piece of paper in Helen's hand.

'One of them was Felix Olson. The second was a woman named Lina Scholl.'

No one spoke for a few seconds.

'And who is Lina Scholl?' asked Muller eventually.

'The last victim who was found from the original case, outside a bar with a hole drilled in her skull,' answered Stam.

After Helen had explained the findings from the four-by-four, the rest of the meeting was pretty much Inspector Klose detailing how they were going to proceed. The scene was to be closed and the focus now on Hans Fischer and finding further evidence. He briefly left the room as his phone rang, and when he returned, he told them that the prosecutors had signed off on the current evidence to press charges against Hans Fischer.

He thanked everyone for their efforts and congratulated them on what would hopefully be a successful outcome.

'What about Frank Mayer? We still have no evidence to link Hans Fischer with his death,' asked Detective Muller.

'The prosecutor is confident of getting a conviction with the DNA from the two original victims.'

'That doesn't mean that he's responsible for the recent killing, though. It's been over ten years,' Muller replied.

Stam looked over at Schmidt and then at Muller. Muller looked over at Detective Lahm, who was already staring at her. Stam knew that the German police wanted to be able to put a name to the killer, but this didn't sit right with him. Before finishing up, Klose said that a statement would be made to the press regarding the capture of the suspected killer, Hans Fischer.

Stam stood and left the room before anyone else and was shortly followed by Inspector Schmidt and then Muller.

His cigarette was lit by the time they joined him on the front steps. The sky was turning dark as the afternoon gently approached evening. The cold air was now being blanketed by dark clouds that promised snow very soon.

'What are you thinking now, boss?' Muller asked. 'Tell me it's not the strip club?'

Stam looked around at her, seriousness in his eyes. 'We're a long way from that.'

He took out his phone and dialled Dr Park. It showed on the screen that the time was 16:45. The phone beeped and then rang five times before being answered.

'Angela, I have something. We found the DNA of Lina Scholl.'

Angela was quiet on the other end of the phone. Stam wondered what she might be thinking.

'Angela?' he said.

'Yes, I heard. That's great. I can't quite believe it.'

'I know. They have enough to go to trial.'

'You must be happy with that.'

'I'm not doing cartwheels, let's just say.'

They were both silent.

'Okay, we'll be finishing up here soon and I'll let you know if anything comes up with the other thing.'

'Okay,' Angela replied.

Stam took a long draw of his cigarette and blew the smoke out. Schmidt was still standing to his right-hand side. He had been on the phone at the same time as Stam. He put his phone back in his pocket and stepped forward to stand level with Stam.

'Tell me we have something?' Stam asked him.

'Oh, we definitely have something,' replied Schmidt.

Chapter 40

Directly after the phone call that Inspector Schmidt had taken, things began to move fast, which was in part down to the actions of Detective Stam.

Firstly, he informed Muller and Schmidt that he was not satisfied with the conclusion of the investigation and that he intended to continue looking for evidence; if they didn't want to assist him, he would be fine with that. They both agreed to assist him however they could.

He instructed them to finish with the crime scene in Schwaberwegen before he explained what he needed them to do, which at the moment was only the brief outline of a plan, and only to be carried out when Inspector Klose had instructed them to call it a night.

Stam took out his phone and called his daughter. She answered, and they arranged to meet for a quick bite. They agreed to meet in the café where they had met previously.

Angela Park and Karl Ballack were still holed up in the hotel room and were becoming increasingly restless as time went on. They had had lunch delivered to the room while Karl hid in the bathroom. They had also spoken about the early days of their relationship, which was strange in the fact that it was Karl who brought it up, but at the same time, it didn't feel uncomfortable to speak about.

Between lunch and reminiscing about the past, the news report regarding the accident on the ST2080 had taken up most of their attention as they waited on Detective Stam calling with any updates.

Detective Muller called Stam just as he was entering the hotel with Monica. After leaving the café, Monica said she needed to return to the hotel as she had to change clothes for plans that she had later that evening. They walked briskly along the high street before turning into the hotel reception. Stam answered the call from Muller, who said that she and the rest of the investigative team had been told to finish for the night and that Schwaberwegen had returned to the quiet to which it was accustomed. She also said that Inspector Schmidt was on his way to meet him and would be there in two minutes.

Schmidt met Stam at the door of the rear entrance to the hotel and they made their way up to the first floor and into Angela's room. They knocked quietly and were quickly greeted by a rather tired-looking Angela.

They all gathered at the dining table and took a seat. Schmidt took out a small speaker and set it in the centre of the table. Everyone else watched as he did so. He took out his phone, plugged a cable into it and sat down. A few seconds later the phone rang, and he reached over and pressed a button on the speaker. He adjusted the volume to be loud enough for them but not loud enough that any neighbouring hotel guests might overhear.

After some crackling on the line, an older-sounding man with a deep voice spoke. His accent was thick but clear through the speaker.

'Hi, Franz, it's Schmidt. I'm joined by Oliver Stam and two other detectives.'

Schmidt had decided to refrain from revealing the identity of Angela and Karl.

'Okay, great.'

'Could you start at the beginning of what you've

managed to discover?'

'Sure. So, first of all, we checked the four individuals' names that you gave me on all the databases we have access to, which is almost all of them. The first thing that we came across is that every one of these individuals has very little online footprint. Someone has gone to great lengths for these people to fly under the radar.'

'How do you mean?' asked Stam.

'Well, to begin with, none have had any kind of criminal convictions, no speeding tickets or parking tickets. They also have never been part of any census, never voted, or as far as we can tell, never even applied for a passport.'

'Surely that can't be right?' said Schmidt.

'I would highly doubt it. This is what I said at the beginning: someone is going to great lengths to keep these individuals hidden.'

'Does this mean you haven't managed to get any personal information on them?'

The voice on the other end of the speaker laughed briefly. 'You don't think for one second that I got to where I am by giving up that easily. You know me, Inspector.'

Schmidt smirked, a little relieved.

'The first of the names was Frank Mayer, whom you already know. The second was Daniel Smithe. He was born in a small town in Dortmund but moved to Munich in his teens. Not much else apart from that. I'll keep the personal details brief.' He continued, 'After what you discovered with Frank Mayer, we ran the details of Daniel through the missing persons database. Daniel Smithe was reported missing four weeks ago. In that time there have been no sightings, and what is more concerning is that there hasn't been a police report raised for him.'

Stam wrote everything down in his notebook.

'You okay for me to continue?' the deep voice said.

'Please,' replied Schmidt.

'The third man, Robert Ewing, is a 52-year-old business owner from Munich. He owns several garages and a warehouse. Again, we ran him through the missing persons database, again, he was reported missing two weeks ago, and again, we have no police report for him.'

'Three for three so far,' Schmidt said, annoyed.

'That then brings us to Theodore Schultz, who is better known to the public due to his father's political position of former security minister.'

Everyone subconsciously glanced at Karl.

'So far we have no hits on missing persons, but we did manage to get a licence plate for a company vehicle.'

'Wait, you have no missing person report?' asked Stam.

'No, why?'

'His vehicle was found just outside of Schwaberwegen three hours ago. He's missing.'

'If it hasn't been twenty-four hours, then it wouldn't be on the system.'

'Can you check if a police report has been raised for it?'

They could all hear tapping through the speaker.

'No report either, which is strange. I got a company mobile number as well, which we ran a trace on. It made several calls last night from a network tower southeast of Munich. As of 23:02 last night, it's been turned off. The last location was just off the ST2080 road in the middle of the Ebersberger Forest.'

Everyone had been taking in the details, some of which they were already aware of.

'So, what we have is a file containing the names of four people that have all gone missing in the last eight months. The last three in the last four weeks. Each of them, as far as we can tell, are not connected,' Schmidt said.

'Surely there must be something that connects them all. Why would they all be in a file that someone is going to such lengths to keep hidden?' Karl said.

They all sat in silence, thinking hard.

A crackling sound cut in from the speaker, interrupting the silence.

'I might not have the answer, but I've just found something that might help.'

'What is it?'

'Twelve years ago, around the time of the original case, all four of these men were police officers in the Munich police force and worked out of the same station.'

***

Mikael Schultz was now approaching Schwaberwegen, and he wasn't quite sure what the best course of action was to take. On the one hand, at least one of the four men from the file was dead, and he had just been told by a former colleague that Robert Ewing had also been reported missing. Now, with his son going off the radar, it only left Daniel Smithe, and with the way things were going, he wouldn't be surprised if he were also missing.

He had tried to make this file go away for many years and to erase all traces of it, but now he felt someone might be doing it for him. Of course, the root of the problem was his son, but the blowback he, and possibly the Prime Minister, would face would be insurmountable.

He slowed and approached the turning for Main Street. With the police presence now gone, it looked very different from what he had seen in the media coverage for the last three days. The small, sleepy town looked picturesque.

As he drove by a Gothic church on the left, his mobile phone started ringing through the car's Bluetooth. He answered.

'Hey, it's me.'

'Any luck?' Schultz asked.

'No, nothing. The scene in Schwaberwegen has been closed.'

'I know, I'm in the middle of it.'

'Why?' the caller asked, surprised.

'The official reason will be that my son has disappeared and I'm here to help search for him.'

'And what's the unofficial reason?'

'The unofficial reason is that I'm cleaning up his mess. The same as I've been doing ever since that night in Karlsfeld.'

After hanging up the phone, Mikael decided the best place to stay would be a hotel close by, so after turning his car, he drove back up towards Main Street. He found a hotel soon enough in the middle of town and went in to check availability. He was checked in and given a room on the first floor by a young blonde receptionist. He took the stairs and walked along the elegant corridor to the second room on the right. He sat on the edge of the bed and took off his shoes. He reached back into his pocket, took out his phone, and dialled the number for one of the men he had used at the Mandarin Hotel in Berlin.

'Sir?'

'I'm at the last location that Theo's mobile phone was traced to. In Schwaberwegen. I need you both here straight away.'

'Okay, sir. We're on our way.'

***

Monica Stam had left her father and gone to the hotel bar for a drink before she had to get changed to meet Thomas, who was picking her up.

She had stopped in the bar of the hotel and was halfway through her second cosmopolitan as she flicked through her phone. She was half dreaming about returning to her travels but also thinking about the talk with her dad in the café. He seemed a little more concerned than normal. He hadn't asked directly what she was doing later tonight, but he had certainly skirted around the subject. She knew he was tired and should take a break, but she also knew better than to tell him as much.

After she finished her drink, she got up and headed to the reception area and then to the stairs before walking up to her room. As she passed the reception, she noticed an older man checking in. She saw the side of his face as he thanked the receptionist and followed behind her. When she reached her room and closed the door, she took out her phone and dialled her father's number, which he answered eventually.

'Hey, you okay?'

'Yeah, I'm just getting ready to go out shortly, as I said.'

'Okay. Why are you calling?'

'Do you know the old security minister – Schultz, I think was his name?'

'Yes, why?'

'He just checked into my hotel. He's in the room next to Angela's.'

Chapter 41

Detective Muller was standing on the outskirts of the ST2080, far enough into the shadows so as not to be seen by any passing cars that might be looking out for any signs of the accident. She was cold but well wrapped up in two layers, a thick jacket and a hat that covered her ears. She wasn't the only one who was freezing in the forest, though. There were at least another five officers, all of whom had been involved with the scene and the grave of Frank Mayer, all out there somewhere, all cold, but all armed.

Muller looked at her watch: it was 18:24. She hadn't been given an exact time by Stam for how long she had to stay. His words were, 'Either I'll hear from you, or you'll hear from me. Just stay alert.'

She agreed with his reasoning for wanting her there, and his plan, at least the part he was willing to reveal. But he was still keeping some of it from her, she knew that. The main thing was that she agreed he was definitely onto something. And neither of them believed that this was solely down to Hans Fischer.

The wind picked up and the trees creaked and howled. She stepped further into the forest and waited and watched. Three minutes later she saw three sharp flashes of a torch deep in the forest. She took out her phone and dialled the number that she and all five officers in the forest had been given.

'I think we saw something further into the woods. You want me to send two guys in to check it out?'

'What was it?' Muller asked.

'One of the officers saw a dark figure, he thinks. It

was moving fast; he believed they had a hood up. He's not sure.'

'Okay, but send three officers. And be careful,' Muller said.

Muller walked back nearer the road. She hauled herself up and took out her phone again. She brought up Stam's number. She was going to dial it but stopped herself; did she really have anything to tell him? She didn't think so. She put her phone away, carefully edged down the snowy embankment, and began to blend into the shadows again.

***

Stam relayed what his daughter, Monica, had told him on the phone. Mikael Schultz, the predecessor to Karl Ballack, was now staying in the room next to Angela's.

'Surely they don't know I'm here?' said Karl with worry in his eyes.

'If they do, someone has tipped them off.'

'But who?' he asked.

'I have my suspicions,' Stam replied.

Angela put her hand on Karl's arm, showing her concern.

'Look, this doesn't change anything. For all we know, they have no idea we're here. And that's how we continue for now. We have to look into the four names from this file and their connection to it all. Schmidt, can you call your colleague back and have them check all major cases in Munich around the time that these men worked together, more specifically around the time that they were transferred to other stations.'

'Sure, what you are thinking?' Schmidt replied.

'I'm not exactly sure myself. But four police officers don't end up in a file that's protected by the German government without being involved in something.'

'I can reach out to my secretary; she's good at researching and finding information. She could help,' Karl said.

'No, don't. I guarantee you that they will be watching her and her computer,' replied Stam.

Schmidt chose to call Franz again but not via the speaker on the table. He disconnected his phone, walked over to one of the large windows, and when Franz answered, relayed to him what Detective Stam had requested. Franz said he would need at least thirty minutes but would call them back.

'He needs thirty minutes to check it out,' Schmidt said as he sat at the table again.

'Okay, good,' Stam said. 'I'm going for a walk.'

***

Deep in the middle of the forest, the hooded figure didn't have the luxury of time. He felt a shift and knew that officers were patrolling the outskirts of the forest. Since the discovery of the car that belonged to his latest victim, he had hung around. The police seemed to be closing in, but he was positive that they didn't know what they were looking for. Either way, the magnificent ending he had dreamed of for years for the last of the four names couldn't be played out just as he had wished. The last thing he wanted was for the final body to be found, alive anyway, and for his daddy to get him out of another hole he might find himself in, literally.

The figure quietly took the key from his coat pocket and undid the lock to the metal hut. He stepped into the relative warmth and was immediately hit with the distinct smell of blood. The figure lowered his hood and walked slowly to the head of the table. Theo Schultz was conscious, but only just. Large pools of blood from the holes in his kneecaps had formed and now congealed under the wooden table. His face was ashen and his eyes red from crying or panic, or both. The figure took it in for a minute, staring deep into Theo's eyes. He wished he could take his time, try and beat his record for keeping someone alive, which was nine days, whilst inflicting the most horrendous pain on them. But now he had to finish it.

The piece of paper was already sitting on the workbench as the figure took a pen from the drawer and carefully wrote four words on it. Same as all the others, the words that meant so much to him. *You have no idea.* He took the piece of paper and placed it on Theo's chest, the air filling his lungs making his chest rise just a little. The figure returned to the workbench, but instead of the drill, he reached up to the board that was screwed to the wall and lifted a hunting knife from it. The knife was well used but razor sharp; he had made sure to sharpen it. It had a wooden handle stained dark brown and had been made forty years ago from good quality wood. It felt good in his hands. The figure pulled up his hood and returned to the top of the table, holding the knife by his side, in his left hand. He used his right hand to gently touch the right shoulder of the barely conscious Theo, whose eyes shot wide open, drowning in terror. The figure lowered his head so it was only two inches from Theo's, whose terrified eyes were now fixed on the hooded figure, praying for some kind of intervention. For reality to return. But it didn't happen.

'You knew this day would come; you knew in your heart that I would find you. You also knew deep down that you deserved this. You have been living a lie ever since that day.'

Theo began to scream, but the cloth in his mouth muffled it. The figure removed the gag with his right hand and then held Theo's head in the same movement as his left hand came up, the knife shining in the light above the table. The figure didn't hesitate. He pressed the knife to the right-hand side of Theo's neck, the blade sliding into the skin, a trickle of blood seeping out. Then he used one steady movement and ran the knife from one side of Theo's neck to the other. Six inches long and half an inch deep. He could feel cartilage snapping and muscles slicing open. The blood bubbled and then flowed down both sides of the neck and onto the concrete floor.

It took no more than three seconds, start to finish, for the knife to slice the neck wide open. And for those three seconds, the figure watched with satisfaction as the life finally drained out of Theo Schultz.

Once the blood had stopped, the figure took the note with four words on it and prised opened the now lifeless Theo's mouth, placing it inside before closing it back over. The next step was to bury the body in the grave that had already been dug, but the figure was well aware that the location of the grave was in the general direction of where the accident had taken place earlier, and he knew the police presence was not too far from it. Instead of risking moving the body and being seen, he turned out the lights and exited the hut, locking it behind him. He waited and watched to make sure no one was close by before he made his way through the forest. He kept away from the paths and headed towards the location of the grave. After five minutes of walking, he approached the site and hid behind a large tree. He listened hard and thought he heard something off in the distance which sounded like a voice. He waited until he was sure he couldn't hear anything and stepped from behind the tree, only to see the light from a torch a hundred yards to the left, flickering between the trees, silhouetting him. He didn't bother trying to hide again; the person holding the torch had seen him. The figure took off, not towards the hut but away from it, southeast. Behind him, at first, he could see the sporadic flash of the torch pointing in his direction, then darkness, before it lit up the surrounding area. He hustled left, his large jacket slowing him down. He reached a rise in the forest floor and could see the hill on the other side. He checked behind him: no light shining. He took a breath and was ready to carry on when a shout echoed in the forest. He spun to see the torchlight only fifteen yards from him.

'Stop! Don't move!' a man's voice screamed.

The figure turned and took off down the hill, rushed and panicked. He slipped and skidded downward; the terrain was icy in parts and in others thick with muck. As the ground levelled out, the hooded figure stopped again, sweat on his forehead and in his eyes. How could he have been so careless after everything he had accomplished, almost getting caught? Just as he was ready to continue, the light of the torch shone on the floor directly in front of him. He tried to run, but the loose ground under his feet made him slip. He turned and looked behind him. The man with the torch was now almost on top of him.

'Don't move!' the man shouted as he swung the torch

he was holding. It missed the figure by inches. As it flew past, it gave the figure a chance to throw a punch to the man's stomach. The man folded in two and fell to the floor. The figure hovered above him; he could see now he was a police officer. He was wearing a uniform, now covered in dirt. The figure leaned down and lifted the torch. The man spun round, holding his stomach.

'You don't have to do this,' the man said.

The figure leaned down close to him, his face still covered by his hood. The man froze. The figure picked up the torch from the ground and stood up again. The thought crossed his mind to smash the man's head in with the torch. But instead, he opened the bottom clip and let the batteries drop out. Then he threw the torch as far as he could into the woods and took off again.

Fifteen minutes later, breathing hard and still drenched in sweat, he reached the edge of the tree line. He leaned against a large tree and looked out over the hills in the distance and began to cry. Tears he had held in for more than ten years, and now he could let them all out. Every tear that rolled down his face was filled with a mixture of satisfaction and relief.

He raised his hood and left the forest, maybe for the last time.

Chapter 42

Monica had showered, changed, and was putting on some make-up before heading downstairs.

She was still wondering why her father had been keen to meet with her earlier, but she liked the fact that he had made the time. Not that they had spoken about anything interesting; he had seemed preoccupied, no doubt with the case.

As she left her room, she checked the mirror behind the door. She looked smart without being too fancy. She closed the door and walked down the hallway, then down the staircase and past reception. The restaurant was busy, she noticed, as she headed towards the front entrance. She stepped out into what was a bitterly cold night. Luckily enough, Thomas was waiting right out front in his VW Golf. She climbed in, thankful for the heating inside the vehicle, and leaned over and kissed his cheek. He put the car in gear, pulled away from the kerb, and headed for Herdweg.

Angela was standing at the window and saw Monica as she left the front entrance of the hotel and climbed into a car before it pulled away. She was feeling claustrophobic in this room and needed to get out. Stam had re-entered the room twenty minutes ago but didn't say where he had been, and Inspector Schmidt had spent the time scrolling through his phone, checking records.

Karl had anxiously paced back and forth, briefly stopping to watch the news on the TV, although she knew he wasn't taking it in.

Just as Angela returned to the table, Schmidt's phone

began ringing. He quickly ushered everyone to sit at the table as he reconnected his phone to the speaker. After some crackling on the line, Franz's voice could be heard.

'Is everyone there?' he said.

'Yes,' replied Schmidt. 'What did you find?'

'Okay. So, from running checks on all major cases around the time that the four officers worked together, I've found two. One had to do with a major drug bust in the city, and I mean major. Dozens of officers were involved in an undercover operation to bring down two of the biggest dealers in Munich.'

'Are any of the officers in the file involved?' asked Schmidt.

'Only one, Robert Ewing. He oversaw the tactical division.'

'Could it be connected?' Schmidt asked.

'I don't see how,' said Stam.

'What was the result of the operation?' Schmidt asked anyway.

'The result was cocaine and heroin with a street value of 86 million euros being seized.'

'I remember that case,' said Karl. 'It was in the news for weeks afterwards.'

Stam nodded.

'I don't see how the drug investigation could be connected to our investigation. What was the other case?' Stam asked.

'The second was nowhere near as high profile as the drugs bust, but it was in the news as well. As far as I can tell, it hasn't been solved either.'

'What was it?'

'It was back during the serial killer case, the one you're dealing with now. A young woman who lived and worked in Munich, who was only twenty-two years old, was travelling home from work late one night but never made it. Her car was found the next day, abandoned in the empty car park of a hotel that had been closed months before, on the outskirts of a town called Karlsfeld. The following day, her body was discovered in a field a mile away from the car. The body was in quite a mess as well. There was evidence of sexual assault as well as blunt force trauma to the head.'

The room was quiet for a second.

'What was the cause of death?'

'Strangulation. They said it was with a metal wire, and it was so bad that she was almost decapitated.'

'Were these details ever revealed to the media?'

'No, not the strangulation. At first, everyone thought it was the serial killer, and when the police couldn't find who was responsible, they said that they believed that it was most likely the work of the serial killer as well, and eventually, the case went cold.'

'What was the victim's name?' Stam asked Franz. But it wasn't Franz who answered, it was Angela.

'I knew her.'

Everyone turned to Angela.

'I worked with her at the coroner's office in Munich during the original case.'

'Who was she?' Stam asked.

***

Detective Lahm pulled into the driveway of his lodge and parked the car. He was happy to be introducing Monica to his brother Max, and not just for Monica, but for Max also. After everything that had happened in the past, he wanted his brother to begin living some kind of life that involved meeting people and getting out of the house, which he had managed less and less of late.

They stepped onto the porch, and Lahm took out his keys and unlocked the front door. A single light over by the couch was the only one that was turned on; the rest of the lodge was in relative darkness. Over by the kitchen sat the dining table, which had been set for three people, all neat and organised. Soft music was playing, and a pleasant smell was coming from the kitchen. Monica thought it smelled like lamb.

'Did you do all this?' she asked Lahm as he took their coats and hung them on a coat hook in the hallway.

'Not all of it. I prepared the food this morning and put a timer on the slow cooker. The table, I asked Max to set for me.'

'It looks and smells nice.'

'I agree,' Lahm replied, a little surprised himself.

Monica sat at the table, took out her lipstick and glanced up the hallway. Lahm's bedroom door was closed, as was the room beyond that he said was Max's room. The utility room at the back was slightly ajar, and the bathroom door on the left was also closed. She was now a little nervous about meeting Max, almost apprehensive, but she wasn't quite sure why: maybe the feeling she had from last night.

'You want some wine?' Lahm asked as he appeared from the kitchen.

'Sure,' she replied.

'Dinner will be ready in ten.'

'Is Max home?'

'He'll be in the back. He gets quite nervous meeting new people.'

'Okay,' Monica replied as Lahm poured her some wine.

Lahm set the wine bottle on the table after pouring some for himself.

'I'm going to see if he's all right and tell him dinner will be ready soon.'

Monica smiled at him.

Lahm headed up the hallway and passed Max's room door. Instead, he went through the utility room door, which he closed behind him.

Monica sat and sipped her wine. After a few minutes, she took out her phone. She scrolled for a bit and then put it away, not wanting to come across as rude. She checked her watch; it had been nearly five minutes since Lahm had left. She stood and skirted the dining table and peered into the kitchen. The hob was on, with three rings burning. Different vegetables in each pot were coming to the boil. She then entered the hallway and walked slowly up it. She passed Lahm's bedroom door and carried on the same as she had the following night to the door further up, Max's room. She stopped and waited. She couldn't hear any talking from the utility room, and the frosted glass meant she couldn't see anything either. She reached out her hand, again knowing she shouldn't be prying but again unable to stop herself. Her hand slowly made for the handle; it was only a few inches away. Why could she not stop herself? The tip of her index finger touched the cold handle, and then she heard a bang from the utility room that made her jump. She stepped backwards, and at the same time, the door of the utility room opened. She tried not to look startled as Lahm came through it.

'Hey, what are you doing?' he asked.

'Just nipping to the bathroom. I think your vegetables will be boiling over by now,' she said and turned left into the bathroom. Lahm looked at her curiously before heading for the kitchen to take the vegetables off the boil.

When Monica had finished in the bathroom and got back to the table, Lahm was sitting on his seat again. He looked different, like he was contemplating something, or many things, maybe.

'Is everything okay with Max?' Monica asked, a little unsure how to read him.

'He'll be through in a bit.' He paused after saying it. A long pause that became awkward.

'There are some things you need to know about Max before you meet him.'

'Okay,' said Monica.

Lahm sat up straight in his chair, nervous. Monica suddenly noticed how dark it seemed inside the lodge. And now the mood was becoming just as dark.

'Max has been through a lot; he's still going through it now. Well, the effects from it, at least.'

Monica wasn't sure what to say, so she nodded sympathetically instead. Lahm took this as a cue to continue.

'We lost our parents when we were young. Max was only eleven and I was fifteen.'

'What happened, if you don't mind me asking?'

'They were killed in an accident while on holiday. Their bus was in a crash and they both died.'

'I'm so sorry.'

'It was hard on us both but mostly on Max. He already had some issues before.'

'Like what?'

'He was anxious growing up, from an early age.

Always kept to himself in school and eventually became isolated. Then the anxiety got worse, and he developed obsessive-compulsive disorder.'

'I've heard of that,' she replied.

'Not the kind where you constantly wash your hands or bleach your bathroom every day so you know it's free from germs. His disorder was more intrusive. I remember when we shared a room when it first began. He was standing at our bedroom light switch; it was the early hours of the morning. He was turning the switch on and off, on and off, for four hours, and all the time, my dad was standing next to him, screaming in his face to stop, but he couldn't. He said if he did, we would all die. My parents couldn't understand it. Neither could I, but I knew he couldn't stop it. He was constantly double-checking things to make sure they were turned off or closed over, even after he knew he had done it already and triple-checked it. It was hard on him, and it only got worse when our parents died.'

'That sounds terrible.'

'It was. But that wasn't the worst part. That came after what he witnessed ten years ago. Someone close to him was attacked and killed. He saw it all happen and couldn't help.'

Monica didn't know what to say.

'After that, he developed PTSD and his mental health suffered further. Along with the OCD, everything just became difficult for him. I was all he had left, and he was scared something would happen to me too.'

'Has he got better since?'

'We finally got the right medication, which has helped, after fighting for a diagnosis for long enough. But he rarely goes out: only at night when no one is around.'

'Are you sure it's okay for us to meet now?'

'He says it is. He just needed a minute.'

Monica hesitated before her next question. She knew it could be sensitive, but she was curious.

'The killing that he witnessed, do you know who it was and what happened?'

Lahm looked straight at her. He was thinking, she thought. Deciding whether to reveal whatever it was that his brother had witnessed that had caused him so much pain. A moral dilemma. Then she saw his eyes change slightly as he made the decision to tell her.

Chapter 43

'As I said, it was ten years ago, and Max was only twenty at the time. Don't get me wrong, he still had his problems, but counselling was really starting to help with the disorder, and his mental health was improving, allowing him to begin socialising more. This weekend in particular, he had been in the city and had caught a lift home from a friend who worked late and often drove him home when she could.'

Monica wasn't sure if she was ready to hear whatever Lahm was going to say, but now she had no choice.

'They were on the outskirts of the city when Max asked his friend to pull over so he could pee. It was late and everywhere was closed for the night. So his friend pulled into the car park of an old hotel that had closed months before. Max got out and had headed into a wooded area when he heard a car pull into the car park. After he had finished, he headed back to see a BMW had pulled up next to his friend's car and that there were four men inside, three of whom had got out. Max was fifty feet away, and as he approached, he could see that the three men were clearly intoxicated. They staggered from side to side, and one of them even fell as he rounded the car. Max then saw the shortest of the men tap on the driver's window. His friend, alone in the car, in the middle of nowhere and in the middle of the night, had her door locked. Max approached slowly, drunk and a little unsteady himself. The man tapping on the window got louder and angrier at being ignored. Max then knew he had to do something, but against three of them who were clearly drunk and a fourth who was still in the car, he knew he had no chance. But he tried all the same. He came out from the trees and walked over to the car. The man closest to him, who had fallen, turned after hearing Max's steps and came towards him. Beyond him, Max saw the man who was tapping on the window take out a gun. Max, now terrified, grabbed at the man who had approached him and wrestled him to the ground. He kicked him in the face as he heard the man with the gun shout, 'Police, get out of the car,' before hearing the smash of glass. Max ran for the car, but at this point, his friend had been dragged by the hair out through the driver's window and was screaming in panic. Max came round from the rear side of the car; the engine was still running, and the headlights were on and illuminating the trees in front. A second man came from behind him and punched the side of his head. Max stayed up, but he was dizzy. He steadied himself and turned. The guy came at him again, but this time Max threw a punch first that caught him in the jaw. His head flopped back, and he fell to the ground, unconscious. The man with the gun, who was still holding his friend, retreated, waving the gun at him as he lifted his friend around the waist with one arm and threw her to the ground behind him. His friend screamed and cried at Max to help, but he was still dazed and staggering himself from the impact of the blow to the head. Max carried on towards him, now ten feet away. He could see the glint of evil in the man's eyes. He looked right at the car the men had arrived in. The fourth man was sleeping in the back seat. He turned back, facing the man with the gun. He took a breath and decided that even with a gun, he had to try and stop him. He lunged at him but didn't reach him. The man who he'd wrestled to the ground and kicked in the head had snuck up behind him and grabbed him around the neck. Max said he fought with all his strength, but eventually, he lost consciousness. He said the last thing he saw before passing out was his friend being dragged into the woods by the man with the gun, with the other two men following after them.'

Monica was not only speechless but was almost in tears.

'This is horrendous. I don't know what to say.'

Lahm lowered his head. His eyes were filled with tears as well.

'How do you know all this?'

'Max. He told me the story over and over again. Repeatedly, exact word for word.'

'Did you go to the police?'

'Of course.'

'We tried everything, but nothing ever came of it. I tried when I joined the force as well, but there was no evidence, and Max couldn't recall what the men looked like.'

'Do you think they were actually police?'

'I'm not sure. They might have just said that to get his friend out of the car.'

They both sat in silence with their wine glasses in their hands.

'Do you know who the friend was?' she said after a while.

'Her name was …' He hesitated. 'Her name was …'

Just as he was about to say the name, the door of the utility room opened, and Max, looking hesitant, walked down the hall towards them. He didn't look at Monica or his brother directly, he just pulled out a chair and sat. After a few seconds, he began tapping at the side of his plate over and over again until Lahm spoke.

Chapter 44

'Her name was Heidi Winter. She was a university student who was doing her work placement with Karl and myself at the coroner's office in Munich,' Angela said.

Karl lowered his head as Angela spoke. He could remember her. A friendly and polite young woman who worked with them for well over a year, if he remembered correctly, during the case of the serial killer. He remembered how fascinated she had been with everything. Always asking questions and writing notes down constantly, all the intricate details.

'I remember the night she went missing. We had worked most of the day and late into the night. I believe the last body had turned up with the drilled hole and we had spent hours examining it. It was late, and I told her she could stay at mine and Karl's flat in the city, but she insisted she wanted to get home as she was picking someone up. I believe it was her fiancé.'

'Her fiancé?'

'Yeah, she had recently got engaged and they had moved into a lodge together.'

'You know his name?'

'No. We were close at work but not socially. She was young, and I could tell she was in love, but she never spoke much about personal stuff.'

'Did you speak to the police regarding her disappearance?'

'Yes, both of us did,' Karl answered.

'Did she pick up her fiancé after she left?'

'The police said there was no proof that she had. He wasn't found at the scene.'

'Franz, are there any other details in the case file?' Schmidt asked into the speaker on the table.

'That's the thing. Since they concluded it to be the work of the serial killer, the file hasn't been updated, or at least for us to see.'

'Was there anyone else interviewed?'

'That's the thing. As soon as they made their decision, the file was closed. No details in it apart from the victim's name, the location, and a description of the vehicle.'

'Was there a registration number or make?'

'No, only that it was a four-door Volkswagen,' Franz replied.

'There have to be more details of the car,' said Schmidt.

'I'm confident there will be, but I'm also confident that they'll be hidden or security protected the same as the file with the four names was,' Stam said.

'Could this all be connected?' Angela asked.

'It has to be,' replied Stam.

'But how?'

Stam was quiet as he looked through his notepad.

'Franz, is there any way you can dig deeper and find more details of the case regarding Heidi Winter?'

'I can try, but my suggestion is if you want to find out details regarding the case, you have to start with Mikael Schultz, or at least what he has access to,' Franz replied.

'I think what we have to concentrate on is the fact that the last name in the hidden file, Theo Schultz, is missing and his car has been found not far from the Ebersberger Forest. That seems too much of a coincidence,' Karl said.

Stam looked over at Schmidt.

'And the fact that his father is in the room next to us,'

Karl continued.

'I may have a way to access Mikael Schultz's files, but I'll need your help, Karl,' Stam said.

'In what way?' Karl replied.

'Franz, is there any way of getting Karl into Mikael's room if he should vacate it?'

'Not that I know of,' Franz replied.

'I have a colleague that could help with that. He can hack into anything,' Karl replied.

'Okay, see what he can do.'

'I think we have to focus on finding Theo,' Schmidt said, just as Stam's mobile phone started buzzing on the table in front of him. Everyone looked at it.

He walked over to the window and answered. It was Muller. After a brief conversation, he returned to the table.

'We've found Theo Schultz.'

Chapter 45

Stam was in the passenger seat of Inspector Schmidt's car as he drove towards the ST2080 road where Theo Schultz's car had been found earlier that day. He was driving fast for the conditions but not as fast as Muller would be, he thought.

Muller had called to say that she had just discovered a metal shed in the middle of the Ebersberger Forest, just over half a mile from where the car was found and close to where Detective Stam had said to keep watch. She said that one of the officers had given chase to a figure they had seen in the forest, but after catching up with them, they had managed to escape. She said they then combed the surrounding area and eventually came across the metal shed, which was locked. Upon opening it, they discovered the mutilated body of Theo Schultz. That was when she had made her way back towards the road and called Stam.

Schmidt parked his car at the side of the ST2080 for the second time that day. He and Stam got out and were greeted by a cold-looking Detective Muller and a young officer. The officer was also frozen looking and covered in dirt.

'Good work,' Stam said as they convened in the middle of the road.

'Not us: it was you who had the idea.'

Stam looked into the forest.

'How did you think that this might have worked anyway?' Muller asked.

Stam thought about it for a few seconds before speaking.

'On the first night, after we had the meeting in the church, I followed the path that led to the hunting lodge. As I reached the road that we're standing on now, a car passed by. I didn't want to be spotted, so I hid on the embankment on the other side of the road.'

Schmidt looked to where he thought Stam was talking about.

'After it passed, I came back up from the verge, and I thought I saw someone on the other side, hidden by the trees, or so they thought.'

'You think it was the killer?' Muller asked.

'At the time I wasn't sure what it was exactly, but then when Theo's car turned up, well, I have said I don't believe in coincidences.'

Everyone stood quietly, not sure what to say.

'We have to see the body.'

'Okay, but I'll warn you, it isn't a pretty sight,' Muller replied.

The walk through the forest was long and arduous due to the terrain. They all walked in single file, with the young officer leading. He described to Stam what had happened and how, when he finally caught up with the figure and he was on the ground, they had the chance to kill him, but for some reason, they left him in the dirt and fled. Stam found this strange.

They turned off the path that had been made in the snow and headed through heavier snow until they reached a dark metal shed. A second officer was standing at the door, which was slightly ajar and letting out some light.

'Has anyone touched the body?' Stam asked.

'No. As soon as we found that Theo was inside, we stopped and called you.'

'Okay,' Stam replied.

Stam entered the metal shed first and was immediately hit with the smell of fresh blood. It was everywhere. Mostly on the concrete floor, a large deep-red puddle that almost looked like a hole.

Stam carefully walked around the blood and saw the sight at the top of the table. Theo Schultz had been savagely beaten. His knees had blood pouring from them, which Stam assumed was from holes being drilled in them. He carried on to the top of the table and saw where the majority of the blood had come from. The cut on Theo Schultz's neck was so deep it made Inspector Schmidt flinch, which took a lot after so many years as a crime scene inspector. Stam could see all kinds of tendons inside the cut and what he thought were vocal cords as well.

'And no one has been in here?' Stam said, looking at the body.

'No, only me, as I said.'

Stam moved across to the wall that had tools hanging from it.

'We need to get Dr Park to examine the body. If the time of death is within the last 36 hours, then this will rule out Hans Fischer as the killer,' he said as he made his way to the door.

'It looks to me like it was carried out recently,' Muller said.

'Me too,' added Schmidt.

'That's why we need Dr Park here as soon as possible,' Stam said.

The four of them made their way back the same way they had come. Their original footprints were still visible in the compressed snow. When they reached the road again, Stam took out his phone and dialled Dr Park. After a brief call telling her that he needed her at the crime scene as soon as possible, he hung up the phone and walked back over to where Schmidt and Muller were standing.

'She's on her way,' he said.

'Okay,' Schmidt replied.

'Now make the call,' Stam said.

Schmidt nodded, took out his phone, walked to the edge of the road, and dialled the number for his boss.

'So, what do we do now?' Muller asked as she hopped from foot to foot as if somehow it could help with the cold.

'Now we wait,' he replied, hoping his hunch was correct.

***

Monica couldn't eat, not after what she had heard. Her mind was racing. She couldn't believe what Max had been through and witnessed. No wonder he was struggling mentally.

She looked over the table at him as he picked at his food. He was a little taller than his brother with lighter hair, blonde almost, bright blue eyes and a square jaw. He was stronger looking too. His complexion was pale, and he had worry in his eyes, an anxiousness that looked like it was desperate to get out. He was handsome despite the clear anguish, she thought.

'How's the food, Max?' Thomas asked.

Max began tapping his fork on the table. He looked over at his brother. 'It's good.'

He had a deep voice.

'I like your hair,' Max then said.

Monica looked up at him. He was looking straight at her.

'Thanks, I like yours too. Blonde hair suits you.'

Max didn't show any expression. He just lowered his head and picked at his food again.

Thomas looked over at Monica, and she looked back at him and smiled. Thomas was happy to see his brother speaking to her.

'Anyone for dessert?' Thomas asked, noticing that no one was eating anymore, just being polite.

'Sure,' replied Monica.

Thomas stood and was lifting the plates from the table when his mobile phone started ringing in his pocket.

He set the plates down and answered.

'Hey,' he said. After that, he listened. Monica and Max were also listening. Eventually, he said. 'I'll be there in fifteen.'

Just as Thomas ended the call, Max stood up from the table and hurriedly walked back up the hall. He passed his bedroom door and went through the utility room door but didn't close it completely.

'What's up?' Monica asked.

'They've found another body in the woods.'

Monica looked worried.

'I have to go.'

'Okay.'

She heard the utility room door close at the end of the hall.

'I can drop you off in town, but we have to leave now.'

'You're going in the opposite direction.'

'If we're quick, I can drop you off. It was your dad on

the phone. He's called in all detectives.'

Monica looked up the hall. She thought she could hear another door closing.

'Max usually goes for a walk in the woods after dinner.'

'I can stay here.'

'I could be away for a while, maybe all night. It would be better if you headed back to town.'

Thomas's mobile rang again. 'Hi. Okay, I'm on my way now.'

'You should go.'

'I can't leave you here.'

'You can't take me with you either.'

'I'll call you a taxi.'

Monica, in all honesty, didn't want to stay here. Not that she was afraid, not of Max. She had seen a softness in his eyes that she liked even though she was maybe a little wary of him.

'Okay. That's fine.'

Thomas grabbed his jacket from the coat hook in the hall and walked up to the utility room. He went in for a few seconds before heading back to the table.

'Max has gone out. I'll call a taxi from the car.'

'Okay.'

He leaned down and kissed her on the forehead. She smiled and told him to be careful. Thomas closed the door and headed out to the car. Monica heard it starting up and reversing out of the driveway. The car then headed down the road before turning left and onto the main road to Ebersberger.

***

After Angela had finished the call with Detective Stam, she relayed what Stam had told her and what he wanted Karl to do next. He agreed and thought it would work, so he took Angela's phone and called his secretary on her husband's mobile phone. He knew his number as they had become good friends since she had begun working with Karl. He told her what he needed her to do, that he believed all communication between them would be monitored and that she was not to contact him or anyone in Parliament directly. She agreed and said she would make the call straight away.

After he had given Angela the phone, they looked at each other awkwardly before she hugged him and told him to be careful.

She left the room and headed for the hotel entrance. Karl watched and waited as Angela got into the patrol car that was sitting outside and was driven away. He returned to the table and sat facing the TV. He just hoped that Detective Stam's intuition was correct and that this hell could be over soon.

Chapter 46

Stam lit a cigarette and inhaled the smoke. He let it sit in his lungs for as long as he could before blowing the smoke out and watching as it floated into the night.

The sky above his head was clear and black, and the temperature had dropped once again. It was easily minus four, he thought. He took another draw of his cigarette and looked down the long empty road, and he realised that he was standing almost in the exact position he was on that first night when he thought he had seen a figure lurking in the trees. He closed his eyes and thought back, trying to remember, focusing on the image, but nothing came. It was merely a silhouette or a shadow at best. But he had seen something. He opened his eyes again to see that Inspector Schmidt was standing right in front of him.

'I've made the call,' Schmidt said.

'And?' Stam replied.

'And we'll see.'

***

Karl was still sitting at the dining table thinking how badly he wanted to speak with his wife and kid. He was also thinking about the involvement that the man sitting in the next room to him had in all of this and the lengths he was going to in order to conceal what they now suspected his son was involved in. He also knew that his family could wait until this was over. He stood up from the table and walked over to the window. Couples strolled past hand in hand, hunched together against the cold as they scurried to their destinations. Karl could see the frost forming on the outside of the window. He was about to pour some more coffee when he heard the muffled ring of a mobile phone. He quickly walked to the far wall and pressed his ear against it. He could hear the muffled half of a conversation and the deep drone of Mikael Schultz's voice. On the other end of the call would be the person Detective Stam suspected, telling him about the discovery of his son. The conversation lasted thirty seconds, maybe a little more. The next thing Karl heard was the opening of Mikael's room door, then the thud of it closing seconds later. Karl waited another two minutes, took a deep breath, and picked up the key card. After contacting Sven, he would be able to gain access to Mikael's room; all he needed was his room number and the hotel's Wi-Fi code. Karl opened his room door and peered out; the corridor was clear. He took a step and turned left, making his way quickly towards Mikael Schultz's door. He tapped the key card on the sensor, hoping that whatever Sven had done would work. It did. The mechanism released and the door opened slightly. Karl pushed it open a little further and stepped inside. The room was identical to the room he had been holed up in all day. He checked the bathroom and the cupboard to make sure the coast was clear, and when he knew it was, he began searching for a laptop or briefcase belonging to Schultz. As Stam had predicted, he had left in a hurry, leaving his laptop sitting on the bed.

He lifted it, headed over to the door, secured the latch from the inside and sat at the dining table. He opened the laptop and clicked on the tab; it was protected with a password. He took out his phone, a burner phone that Inspector Schmidt had given him before he left. He opened it and typed Sven's email address, which he knew from memory, and sent the email. He then sat anxiously in his seat and waited, hoping for a quick reply, which he got, but not as an email; it was his phone that began ringing.

'Hey, Sven, thanks for replying so quickly.'

'Sure, are you inside the room?'

'Yes, I've located the laptop that we believe the files are on. We need access to it.'

'I'm guessing it's locked?'

'Correct. We're short on time on this as well.'

'Okay. Is this a smartphone you're calling from?'

'Yes.'

'Good. I need you to connect it to the Bluetooth of the laptop. Even with it being secured, it should still let you connect.'

Karl lowered the phone and scrolled through it, making sure the Bluetooth was visible, and clicked on the connectivity icon on the bottom right of the laptop. It buffered and then a small pop-up screen appeared, and the make of the mobile phone he was using appeared. He clicked on it, and the phone buffered again before the tab on the screen changed from *available* to *connected*.

'That's it connected,' he said into the phone.

Sven didn't reply. Karl could hear tapping and clicking through the phone, and within fifteen seconds, the screen of the laptop jumped to life and the cursor began to scurry across it, opening a page before minimising it and then opening another, all in the blink of an eye. Karl watched the screen for a minute until he saw what he presumed was a file that looked like it had been deleted and placed in a recycle bin. Sven restored the file and opened it, then Karl had two attempts at opening the file, which were denied, before he heard Sven's voice.

'I have to run a program to get the password. It'll take at least ten minutes.'

'I don't know that we have ten minutes.'

'Nothing I can do.'

Karl was distracted by a noise from the corridor, which sounded close to the hotel room door. He stood up from the table with the phone still pressed to his ear and headed towards it. He was only a few feet from it when he heard a creak coming from just outside. He stopped and waited. Then he saw the handle shake, gently at first, and then it lowered. Someone on the outside was trying to get in.

'We definitely don't have ten minutes.'

Sven started typing even quicker; Karl could hear him through the phone.

***

Monica finished the last of the wine in her glass. The house was quiet and felt cold now it was empty. She didn't want to be here now that she was alone. She stood up from the table and made her way towards the hall, where her jacket was hanging on the hook, but instead of lifting it, she continued down the hallway. The floor creaked beneath the cheap red carpet. She walked slowly, cautious for reasons she wasn't quite sure of. Thomas's door was on the right, closed. She passed it as she had earlier. Max's bedroom came next, on the right. She walked past it until she reached the utility room. She opened it slowly and walked inside. It smelt damp and dirty. She took a step in and stopped. On the near side wall was a counter with a washing machine and a drier beneath it. A clothes stand was near the back door. On the left were cupboards and another countertop. In the far corner was an area that had had heavy outdoor clothes stored in it, boots and jackets. This led to a shower room.

Monica stepped back through the door to the hallway and closed the door behind her. She took a few steps and stopped at Max's room. She faced it and glanced back down the hall to the dining table. Dark and still. She faced the door again. The handle was cold in her hand, the same as it had been last night. She turned it slowly, and it creaked. She pushed gently and it led into darkness.

Her first step was tentative, her second the same. There was a light switch on the wall, which she flicked upwards, but it didn't work. Reluctantly, she took another step. She was now in the room, but she still couldn't see anything. A sliver of light was coming through the curtain but wasn't helping. She could make out a bed in the far corner, but that was it. She fumbled forward, awkward in her movements, feeling with her feet more than her hands. She checked her pockets for her phone so she could use the torch to see, but when she checked, she realised it was in her coat pocket. She headed for the window and the sliver of light. She passed the bed and came to the window; she pulled open the curtains fully, which did generate more light but not enough. She turned and could tell that the room was big, with what appeared to be a brick fireplace on the far wall. On the opposite side of her, she thought she could make out a lamp, so she headed towards it. Again, cautious in her steps, small tentative ones. When she reached the table where the lamp was, she felt along the cord to find the switch; she flicked it and a dull yellow light popped on. She stood and turned. The room was big and the carpet red, the same as the hall. Only half of it was lit up by the dull light, however. She walked across to the bedside table, which had another light on it. She turned it on and the whole room was lit up this time. What she could see was not what she had expected. She stood motionless. On the wall between the window and the fireplace was a large pinboard, the same size as the wall. On it were newspaper cuttings, dozens of them. Pieces of string were tied at one end and then pulled to the other side, like a detective's evidence board. Along with the newspaper clippings, there were photographs: some large and some smaller ones, like holiday snaps. They looked older, like they had been taken years ago, maybe ten years or so. Almost all of them were of the same person, a young woman with brown hair and a friendly smile. She was wearing a lab coat in some of the pictures. On the floor at the edge of the fireplace were dozens and dozens of cards: birthday and anniversary cards, mostly, all set out, all with images of puppies or teddy bears on them. Monica couldn't take it all in, but then she noticed that in the top corner of the wall was another picture. It was of two people, and it had been taken more recently. The picture was clearer than the rest, and it sent a shiver down her spine.

***

Dr Park arrived at the scene. The officer who was driving her parked the patrol car as instructed, on the edge of the ST2080 road. There were only a few police vehicles parked on either side of the road, which she thought was strange considering the possible discovery.

She was met by Stam as she collected her case from the boot of the patrol car. He looked a little stressed and smelt of smoke when he greeted her.

'Thanks for coming so quickly.'

'Sure. What've we got?'

'Another disturbing crime scene, I'm afraid.'

'And is it Theo Schultz?'

'It is. His face is still recognisable, but the rest of him isn't too clever looking.'

'I assume you need a rough time of death to know if Hans Fischer is the killer?'

'You should be a detective,' Stam replied.

Stam led Angela down the embankment and into the woods. They followed the same path that Stam had taken there and back not long ago. A police tape had since been put up to show the way to the shed, almost a mile of it attached to the trees along the way.

They eventually reached the metal shed, and Stam nodded to the officer standing at the door; it was the same one he had met on the first night when he made his way through the forest to the lodge.

Stam entered first, followed by Angela. She had seen enough murder victims to have seen everything, but even Stam noticed a little shock in her eyes. Stam gave her a look, stepped back nearer the workbench, and allowed Angela space to do her work. As he knew she would be, she was thorough and precise. She laid out her case and took different instruments from it before putting on gloves and setting a plastic cover over parts of the body she might come in contact with, then she got to work. Stam watched and didn't speak.

After only ten minutes, Angela removed her gloves and wrote a few sentences in a notepad before turning to face Stam.

'So,' she said, wiping some hair from her forehead, 'this is not the best environment to conduct such an examination, but from the wound on the neck and the blood that has now formed, combined with the rigor mortis, I would estimate the time of death to be anywhere within the last 4 to 6 hours.'

Stam looked at her and then at the mutilated body of Theo Schultz. His mind was racing, but his eyes never wavered. His theory on Hans Fischer not being the one responsible for these two deaths appeared to be correct. But that didn't make him feel any better.

'Thank you, Angela,' he finally replied.

'That's not what you wanted to hear, is it?'

'Not exactly, no. But I expected as much. I have to get back to inform Inspector Schmidt, but you can stay if you need more time.'

'Better letting forensics in to do their job.'

'Okay,' Stam replied before turning and exiting the shed.

Angela followed closely behind as Stam marched through the snow, following the police tape back to the road. As he did, he constantly checked his phone, but he had no reception this deep in the forest. He wanted to speak with Muller and send in the forensics team.

Eventually, the light from the streetlights on the road became visible and Stam and Angela emerged from the trees. Stam had given up on the phone signal and was just about to tell Muller, who was standing waiting on them, about what they had discovered when a phone rang behind him. Angela fished in her coat pocket and took out her mobile. She answered and then quickly handed the phone to Stam.

'It's Karl. I think he has a problem.'

Chapter 47

'Karl?' Stam said as he took the phone.

'We have a problem.'

'Yes, Angela said. What kind of problem?'

'I managed to gain access to Mikael's room and got the laptop which you suggested he might leave behind.'

'Good.'

'I contacted Sven also. He managed to hack into the laptop, but the file we're looking for is proving slightly more difficult to access. He's running a program that may take up to ten minutes.'

'Okay. That doesn't seem like a problem to me so far.'

'That's not the problem. The problem is someone is trying to kick in the hotel room door.'

'Shit! Stam replied. 'I was correct, then. Whatever's on that file will lead us to what's going on.'

'What should I do?'

'You're going to have to barricade the door and wait for that program to run.'

'With what?'

'Anything and everything. You're a smart guy – think!'

Karl ran over to the drawers nearest the window and threw the vase and coffee machine on the bed. He grabbed the wooden cabinet and dragged it across the room. It was heavy and awkward to move. He kept at it until he reached the door and jammed it as close as he could get to it. He leaned on it and breathed hard as the hotel door right next to him shuddered and creaked with every kick it was taking. Surely someone had heard the noise and phoned reception by now.

He grabbed the phone from the bedside table. When he lifted it, though, the line was dead. *Is this a setup?* he thought. *On Mikael's part? Has he planned this?* Surely not. More likely, he had disconnected the phone for security reasons when he checked in. Either way, Karl didn't like it.

He hurried back to the dining table and picked up the mobile phone. Stam was still on the line.

'Okay, that seems secure now. What should I do?'

'Just hope to God they don't get through that door. An officer is on his way,' Stam said and hung up the phone.

***

Mikael Schultz was sitting in the back of one of his men's blacked-out BMWs en route to the Ebersberger Forest after receiving a call from his friend. It was a call that he had half been expecting, if he was being honest with himself. After the disappearance of the other three men in the file, he had known Theo would be next, but it didn't make the news any easier to hear. On the one hand, his son was a massive fuck-up – everyone close to him knew it – but at the end of the day, he was his only son, and Mikael had tried everything he could to get him on the right path. Certainly, after that night in Karlsfeld, he knew the best thing he could do for him was set up a trust fund, buy him a house as far away from Munich as he could while still close enough to keep an eye on him, and hope to God he never fucked up again. But in the end, it hadn't been far enough.

The BMW had just entered Schwaberwegen when Mikael's mobile phone pinged with a notification. He opened his phone and scrolled through to the message. It was from a security application he had on his phone telling him that someone had accessed his personal email.

'Shit!' he said out loud. He had left his laptop in the hotel when he heard the news. He dialled one of his security team who was travelling in a car behind.

'I've left my laptop at the hotel, and someone has just got access to it. I can't go back now, but I need you to go. Find out who and make sure they don't see anything they shouldn't.'

'Okay, boss.'

Mikael stepped out of the car at the edge of the forest, where most of the police activity was. He was approached by an annoyed-looking Detective Muller, who had recognised him as the car he was travelling in approached.

'Excuse me, can I help you?' she said sternly, trying to appear as though she was unaware of who he was.

Just as he was about to answer, they were interrupted by an angry-looking Inspector Klose, who had abruptly parked his car and raced over to meet with the former security minister.

'I'll take this from here, and I'll speak to you soon regarding what's gone on here.'

'Sure thing,' she replied.

Klose stared at her before he asked, 'And where is Stam?'

'I'm pretty sure he's somewhere close by, doing his job, I would imagine.'

Klose looked rather pissed off at her comment. He glared at her before heading into the forest with Mikael.

Detective Schmidt had heard the conversation and

approached Muller when they had left.

He smiled at her when she finally took her eyes off the back of Klose's head.

'You do know you're going to pay for that, don't you?' he said.

'It was worth it,' she replied.

Stam met with them after passing the phone back to Angela, who was sitting in a patrol car filling in paperwork for the examination she had done on Theo Schultz.

'Is it right enough, then?' he asked.

'One hundred percent,' Muller replied. 'He even arrived at the scene before Klose did.'

'So, Klose has been the one who's been filling in Mikael Schultz about the case, and he's obviously connected in some way to the attempts to track and stop Karl from accessing the file.'

'But why?' asked Muller.

'We'll find out soon enough,' Stam replied.

'What was Karl's problem?' Schmidt asked.

'He's managed to access the laptop but is waiting on a program to run that will hack into the secured file.'

'Is that not a good thing?' asked Muller.

'It is, but he also has someone trying to kick in the door of the hotel room. I've sent officers over there now, but I'd rather one of you went as well.'

'I'll go,' said Schmidt.

'I want to go with him,' said Angela, who had got out of the patrol car and was now standing next to them.

'Okay, but be careful,' Stam replied.

***

Head Inspector Klose followed behind a local officer through the woods, with Mikael Schultz following close behind. The forest felt dark and cold as they waded through the snow in silence, both of them thinking of what they were about to witness when they reached the crime scene. Klose, being in the position he was, had seen many horrific crime scenes and was prepared for it. Schultz, on the other hand, was not.

As they entered the shed, two forensic investigators were in the process of examining the body. Schultz, at the sight of his dead, mutilated son, left the shed and was sick twice. He regained his composure and re-entered to see what, at that moment, was the most difficult thing he had ever had to witness. The state of the body and the surroundings instantly replaced his feeling of anxiety with fury. He leaned on the table next to the body and cried in anger. After a few minutes, the investigators apologised and said they had to remove the body now that the scene had been examined. Klose thanked them as they hauled the body bag onto a stretcher and left the shed.

Mikael Schultz had looked broken when he came in; now he looked vengeful.

'Do they know when this happened?'

'From the discovery of his car late last night, I'd say it was within the last twenty-four hours.'

'That means Hans Fischer couldn't have done this. Impossible.'

Klose lowered his head.

'That means we have someone else who's aware of the original case, and obviously, the file.'

Klose looked up at him.

'It has to be the witness from that night,' Schultz said.

'After all this time, why now?'

'I don't know.' He paused. 'I'm assuming we still haven't tracked him down?'

'No. We checked at the time, and for years after. We concluded that he'd moved away or changed his name. Either way, we haven't managed to trace him.'

'Well, you're going to have to now. Because it has to be him who's responsible for my son's death.'

They left the shed and entered into the darkness and the unknown.

Chapter 48

Monica stood staring at the picture that was pinned to the wall in front of her. The hairs on her neck stood up. The picture was of herself and her father. It had been taken a few days ago; she knew from what she was wearing. The picture had been taken from across the street from the café with a good-quality camera. She backed out of the room, hurried up the hallway to her coat hanging on the coat hook, and took out her phone. But instead of fleeing out of the front door as she should have done, she headed back down the hallway. The house was still quiet and now felt sinister, but she had to know who or why someone was taking her photo. She entered the room and crept over to the shrine on the far side. The light from the lamp was still shining and flickering a dull yellow. She kneeled next to the cards and took a picture with her phone. She also took a picture of the photo of her and her dad. She reached out to a pile of what looked like more photographs stacked in a bundle on the floor. With one hand, she lifted them and flicked through them. A few of the images were blurry and out of focus, and some were of what looked like the lake out front. She flicked through them until she came to one that at first looked out of focus, but something caught her eye. It looked like a grave; the image was dark, but what caught her eye was what she believed could be a skull sticking out from the grave.

She lifted her phone. She hadn't realised until then that her hand was trembling uncontrollably, but she managed to scroll to her father's number and hit dial. The phone was silent for longer than normal, as though it could be out of service. She breathed hard. It felt like minutes she had been waiting when the dial tone buzzed and she could hear the ringtone. She stood. Her legs were now trembling nearly as badly as her hand.

'Dad, Dad!' she shouted into the phone.

'Monica, can you hear me? Are you okay?'

'Dad, something isn't right here! I found pictures, something isn't right!'

'What pictures, Monica? Where are you?'

Stam knew she was panicked and had never heard her speak this way.

'Monica, take a breath and speak slowly. Where are you? What's going on?'

'I'm at the lodge. The guy I'm seeing. They have our picture. Dad, something isn't right here.'

'Okay. Tell me where you are, and I'll come get you.'

'I ... I don't know,' she replied, realising she wasn't exactly sure where she was.

'Monica, you have to listen to me. Tell me where you are!'

'Dad, I don't know.'

'Who is it that you've been seeing?'

'It has to be him that took the pictures!'

'What pictures?' Stam was becoming angrier the more panicked his daughter was sounding.

'There are pictures of us, and of graves dug in the snow. Loads of pictures.'

'Whose house are you at?'

'It has to be Max; it has to be!'

'Did you say Max?'

'I have to get out of here!'

Monica stood and was ready to leave when the lamp went out. She screamed in fear.

'Monica, you have to listen to me. Tell me something that will tell me where you are. Like I taught you when you were young. I need something.'

'I … The lights just went out. I … I have to leave.'

'Tell me where you are, Monica!'

'It's dark. I don't know, there's a yellow Bug outside. Like the old days.'

She was incoherent.

'I don't know what you mean, Monica. What's yellow, a butterfly?'

Subconsciously, while having the conversation, Stam had begun heading towards his car. He was unaware Muller was standing next to him, growing increasingly worried at how he was sounding.

'Monica, tell me more!'

'Dad. I need you. Da…'

Stam listened closely. His daughter had stopped talking. He could hear scraping and muffled tones through the line. It was like someone was holding her mouth as she tried to speak.

'Monica, where are you?!' Stam shouted into the phone.

There was no reply. Just the muffled sound. He listened hard. Nothing for a whole minute except the scuffling noise, and then he heard a scream that turned his blood cold. It was more than a scream; it was the sound of absolute terror.

'Dad, I can't! No! Dad, you have to help!'

The next thing he heard was a thud. Then the line went dead.

***

279

Inspector Schmidt was driving faster than Angela thought was possible with the current conditions. But she was reluctant to say anything with the possibility that Karl could be in danger. She was worried about him, more worried than she thought she would have been.

They entered Schwaberwegen, where Schmidt turned right and headed for Main Street. They pulled up at the hotel entrance and the car skidded to a halt on the icy road out front. Schmidt got out as a young couple exited the front door of the hotel. He yelled at Angela to stay in the car as he ran through the door that the couple had left ajar. Inside, he told the young man standing at the reception desk he was police before making for the stairs. When he had reached the top stair of the first floor, he unholstered his gun and stopped. There was no banging, no thud of a heavy boot kicking at the room door. There was no noise at all.

He crept onward. The hotel was quiet, with no nosy guests peeking out at the commotion. That could be a good thing or a bad thing, considering they might have seen a madman kicking down a door, presumably with a gun in his hand.

He passed the room he had been in earlier. It was locked, so he continued to the next. From ten feet away, he could see splinters of wood sticking out from the frame. He quickened his pace and saw that the door was not currently attached to the frame. It was lying a few feet inside the room. He drew his gun and held it out in front of him. He stood on the broken door and leaned in. As he turned to face the dining table, he noticed that the room was the same as the one he had been in earlier, identical, in fact. The TV was on the wall, the dining table on the far side with the large bed and two windows. He didn't see anything else, only felt the shock of pain on the back of his head.

What felt like hours later but was only a few minutes, Schmidt came around. His head was pounding as if someone was jumping on it.

He checked the room; it was basically the same. The only difference was the body lying in the middle of the floor, covered in blood.

Chapter 49

Karl was now more than positive that the person who was kicking the door was definitely going to get through it, and very soon at that. He had called Sven again to see how long the program was going to take to finish and was told another five minutes. Instead of hanging up the phone, he placed it on loudspeaker and set it on the table. With every thud on the door, his anxiety grew. He checked his watch: it had been eleven minutes since he had spoken with Detective Stam, and he knew it wouldn't be much longer until the police were here.

'It's finished,' Sven said.

'You have to be quick, Sven, please!'

He heard Sven tapping away. He knew he didn't have long.

'Okay, I have access to the file. Wait.'

'What is it?'

'It's bigger than I thought and even more protected than the first file I hacked into.'

'What does it say? Be quick!'

'It's very detailed.'

'Sven, hurry!' Karl replied as out of the corner of his eye he saw the wooden cabinet he had barricaded the door with move slightly. Not much, but enough.

'Sven, what does it say?'

'It says …'

Karl didn't hear the rest of what Sven said. The man who had been kicking the hotel room door had managed to get through. Karl turned at the last moment to see the butt of a handgun smashing into the side of his head. He fell off his chair and onto the floor. He wasn't unconscious but wasn't far from it. His head was woozy and his eyes cloudy. He touched his head and felt blood on it, lots of blood. He tried to stand but couldn't. So instead, he dragged himself up onto the chair and pulled at the table. The person in front of him was big and dressed all in black, even bigger from Karl's position on the floor. He couldn't see their face but knew it was one of Mikael's security team. Karl steadied himself and reached over for the laptop, but the man grabbed it before he could. Then he walked over to Karl and pointed the gun at him. He was towering over him. Karl knew what was coming and expected it any second. But what he didn't expect was the figure who suddenly appeared behind the man in front of him, who had the gun now at his left-hand side. They were a lot smaller, and he couldn't make them out, but he saw them sneak up behind, slowly at first, and then faster, lunging.

Karl focused his eyes and shook the blood from his forehead. He saw the man in front of him more clearly now: a tower of a man with a square jaw and eyes that were deep-set and close together. The person behind was someone he didn't expect to see, especially with a piece of splintered wood in their hand, which they stabbed into the neck of the man holding the gun.

***

Angela sat in the car for a few minutes after Schmidt told her to stay where she was before she decided she couldn't sit and do nothing. If Karl were in danger, then so was Inspector Schmidt.

She got out of the car and went in through the front entrance. The man at the hotel reception was on the phone, more than likely to the police, Angela thought. She climbed the stairs tentatively. The sitting area of the hotel was busy, but the lobby and stairs were quiet. When she reached the top of the stairs, she turned and looked along the hallway. She could see the back of Inspector Schmidt. He was creeping towards the door to the room next to hers. He had his gun drawn and looked tense. She hung back and watched, her heart starting to beat louder in her chest. From behind her, she could hear a commotion from the reception area. She had a quick look, but there was no one on the stairs. When she turned back to the hallway, she could see Schmidt entering the room. He stepped over some wood on the floor that she thought must have been from the door frame being kicked in. She watched from a distance as Schmidt entered the room. She took a step forward and listened hard. She couldn't hear anything, so she carried on slowly and then heard a thud. She rushed for the door and saw that the door *had* been smashed in. Silently, she made her way in, lifting one of the pieces of splintered wood and gripping it tightly in her right hand.

Inspector Schmidt was lying face down on the floor to her right. There was blood seeping from a small wound on the back of his head and dripping on the floor. He looked unconscious. In the corner, next to the table, Karl was sitting on the floor. He looked dazed and frightened as he looked up at the giant of a man standing over him. Angela gripped the piece of wood in her hand a little tighter and realised that the man who had his back to her was holding a gun. At that point, she knew her options were limited. The man raised the gun and pointed it at Karl's head. She didn't hesitate after that; she took two quick steps and swung her arm. The piece of wood punctured the man's neck. She let go as the blood squirted out. The man tried to turn, but all he did was swivel his head and fall onto one knee. A few seconds later, he fell to the floor with blood flowing from the hole in his neck.

Chapter 50

Monica could feel that she was going under. The cloth that was covering her mouth and nose was doused in what she assumed was chloroform; whatever it was, it was stinging her throat and nostrils. Whoever had grabbed her was strong, but they were also panicked. The darkness meant she couldn't see who it was, and when she looked up, they had a hood on, which was covering their face. She reached up and tried to grab at their face, but she couldn't reach. She grabbed at the hand that was around her neck, but she couldn't release it, it was too strong, and her strength was waning because of the chloroform. She kicked her feet as she was being dragged from the room out into the hall. She kicked at the walls and the floor, but nothing was working. She could feel her head spinning and was aware that she was close to losing consciousness when she threw both her hands around the legs of her abductor. The figure stumbled and then steadied themselves before falling. Monica took the chance to stretch her leg out and push against the cupboard door with all her remaining strength. This time the figure stumbled and went down, their head hitting the edge of the door to the shower room, making the cloth fall to the floor.

Monica took in a huge breath of oxygen and coughed it straight back out. She lay face down for a minute, filling her lungs in preparation to run. She stood unsteadily and looked over at the figure on the floor. They were sprawled out and facing down, but their head was lying to one side, with the hood of their jacket still covering their face. Still shaken, she stepped closer to them, then another step. Every fibre in her body was screaming at her to run, but she wanted to know who the person was, she needed to. She took a third step and was now standing over the body. She was trembling again, but despite the fear, she leaned down slowly and reached out with a shaking hand. She touched the damp hood; it felt smooth and cold and sent a shiver through her body. She gripped it tightly and was ready to pull it down to reveal their identity when she felt something on her leg. Looking down at her ankle, she couldn't see anything; the room was still dark. She tilted her head to the side and saw an outstretched arm with a long pale hand right next to her. She began to slide her leg away and had started to pull the hood down when the pale hand suddenly opened and grabbed at her leg.

Monica screamed, let go of the hood, and ran for the back door to the lodge. She pulled the door open and was hit with the bitter coldness and then the black wall that was the edge of the Ebersberger Forest. She scrambled across the decking area and fell onto the snow-covered ground. She didn't bother looking behind her; she didn't want to know if the figure had got back up. She just climbed the small mound at the rear of the garden, entered the forest, and ran as fast as her legs and lungs would allow her.

The hooded figure came round. He could feel the pain in his head, but he was instantly aware that Monica had fled the lodge. He knew that there was no way he could let her get away; she had seen too much. The figure got to his feet and wiped some blood from his eye that had run down from the gash on his head. He reached down, grabbed the cloth from the floor and headed out into the darkness.

'Why is no one answering?' Stam raged as he sped through a poorly lit back road en route to Schwaberwegen. After hearing the desperate pleas from his daughter, his head was in overdrive. She had mentioned the name Max, but it didn't register with him.

'Where are we going?' Muller asked.

'We need to find her! Nothing can happen to her – nothing had better happen to her!' he yelled.

'It won't. We'll find her.'

Stam took an upcoming bend too fast and almost slid into a ditch. The rear-wheel drive and the ABS were both working hard to keep the car on the road.

'If we can get Schmidt's colleague in cyber security to track her phone, he could maybe find her location.'

'Did she not say where she was?'

'She was scared out of her mind. She did say, 'It must be Max', though. At least I think it was Max.'

Muller looked at him, thinking. Then the silence was broken by Muller's phone.

'Who is it?' Stam asked.

'It's Schmidt.'

'Hey, everything okay?' Muller asked when she answered.

'It is now.' Schmidt began to explain but was cut off by Muller.

'We have a problem. Is Sven still available?'

'Yes, why?'

Muller told Schmidt about the phone call that Detective Stam had received from his daughter and that they needed Sven to track the phone if possible. Halfway through the call, Schmidt put the call on loudspeaker so that a rather dazed Karl, Angela, and Sven, who was still on the line with Karl, could hear. As they spoke, Sven got the number for Monica from Muller and ran it through the program he had on his computer to try and triangulate the device.

'Is the number getting a hit?' Stam shouted.

'It's coming through now.'

Everyone was quiet. Almost a minute passed before Sven said, 'The phone is turned off; it can't locate it.'

'Fuck!' Stam shouted as he punched the steering wheel.

'What can we do now?' Muller asked.

'We managed to access the file,' Karl said. 'It might help.'

'What does it say?' asked Muller.

'Sven, can you read out what it says?'

'There was an original file from the case regarding Heidi Winter. It had been hidden and protected, even more than the file with the four names. It mentioned more details and explained how four local police officers were involved in the incident, as well as a chief detective who was in charge.'

Stam was thinking hard, so much so that he wasn't concentrating on the road. He was thinking about Heidi Winter and his daughter, along with the original case from 2010 and the recent case. Everything was linked, he knew it, but he couldn't figure out what the thread was.

'Heidi Winter was raped and beaten before being strangled that night. The four officers' names aren't on it, but I think we know who they were.'

'Is the chief detective named in it?' Schmidt asked.

'No,' Sven replied.

Stam was thinking about Philip Langer and the gun that had been used to kill him, and how his killing may not have been what it was made to look like. Instead of trying to get rid of a witness, had it been done to try and implicate someone further? Stam thought about the first night after the body was found, his walk through the woods. Details flowed through his mind. Everything he had written in his notebook, everything he had seen. Tiny details, something someone said or done. He zoned out from the conversation that was going on.

'Stam!'

'What?'

'The file says that there was a witness that night. It says they never found out who. They fled the scene.'

'It could have been her fiancé,' Muller said.

Stam slowed the car.

'What are you doing?' Muller asked.

Stam was quiet, still thinking.

'What is it, Stam?' Schmidt said.

'A yellow bug!'

'A what?' replied Schmidt.

'Sven, does the new file have a registration number of the car Heidi owned?'

'Yes.'

'Can you find the make and model?'

'Sure,' Sven replied and began tapping on his computer.

Everyone else was quiet.

'It's a 2003 Volkswagen.'

'What model and colour?'

'It's a Volkswagen Beetle.'

'What colour?'

'Yellow.'

'Shit!' Stam said as he pulled on the handbrake and slid the car across the other side of the road.

'What is it?' asked Muller.

'A yellow bug! I know where she is.'

'Where?'

'The lodge that's next to yours has an old VW Beetle in the drive. A yellow one.'

'Shit, so it has! How do you know it's where she is?'

'When was the last time you saw a yellow VW Beetle?'

'Shit!' she said again.

'I'm assuming you know who lives there?'

'Of course. It's Thomas.'

'Thomas who?'

'Thomas Lahm!'

Stam took his eyes off the road for a second to look at Muller, who looked somewhere between shocked and angry.

'Does he live alone?'

'No. He lives with his brother.'

Stam sped up in the direction of Herdweg.

'His brother's name is Max,' Muller said.

Chapter 51

Monica had been scrambling frantically through the forest for what felt like an hour but in fact was only a few minutes. Her chest was heaving from taking in huge breaths of freezing air, and her clothes were wet from falling in the snow.

She hadn't turned around to check if the figure who had grabbed her in the lodge was following her, and she didn't want to. She wanted to keep running until she reached the other side of the forest and safety, but she wasn't a dreamer; her father hadn't allowed her to be. He was practical and resourceful, and she had to be the same or she may not survive.

Up ahead in the darkness, she could see a large tree that lay in a small dip in the forest floor. She scurried behind it and tried to control her breathing, but it was difficult. She now dared a glance around the tree from where she had come. She couldn't see the hooded figure, but she couldn't see much at all. Thick black trees were visible against the light of the moon, which was low in the sky. Beyond that, she could see mountains in the dark, and she had the fear that she hadn't managed to run far enough.

She put her hand in her trouser pocket to get her phone, but it wasn't there. She checked all the pockets: no phone. It must have fallen out when she was being dragged. She took in another deep breath and could still smell the chloroform in her nostrils. She couldn't stay put. She could hear her dad's voice ringing in her ear: *if in doubt, run*, he would say.

After a second check around the tree, she took off

running. She struggled to keep upright but kept on going, slipping and falling but always getting back up and carrying on. After another minute she reached a small valley that had a steep drop to the bottom. Knowing it was her only path, she fell back onto the snow and slid down, leading with her feet. It was maybe twenty feet down, and at the bottom was a small stream that trickled through the forest. Monica landed in it and stopped. She looked back up the hill, but still, no one was there. She stood and crossed over the stream, but when she reached the opposite side of the valley, she stopped. A noise had caught her ear. She looked up, but there was still no figure. She turned to head up the other side of the valley but was stopped in her tracks. Standing in front of her was the hooded figure she had tried desperately to escape from. Their face was only inches from her own, and the cold breath coming from their gaping mouth passed over her face.

Her next thought only lasted a split second, and it was something that her father had told her many years ago. He said when people are in a situation of panic, fear, or terror, the average person's brain can't process what it is they are presented with. The fear takes hold and they freeze. Their eyes get wider and their mouths open, and they lose that second that they have before whatever may be coming, comes. Monica wouldn't let this happen to her. In the split second she had when everyone else froze, she would make it count. But what she chose to do in that split second happened simultaneously with a dark metal object coming towards her and hitting her on the side of her head, resulting in her body hitting the forest floor and everything going black.

Stam approached the left turn into the small town of Herdweg and took the corner at speed. Muller was gripping the door handle as the car straightened and Stam hit the accelerator again.

'Where is Detective Lahm?!' Stam shouted at Muller.

'I called him when we found Theo Schultz and told him to attend the scene. He said he was leaving straight away.'

'Call him! Tell him we're at his lodge and to make his way there.'

Muller nodded as she took out her phone and dialled Lahm's number. It rang for a long time before being answered.

'Muller, what's up?'

'Where are you?'

'I'm on patrol at the entrance to the ST2080. Everything okay?'

'No. We may have a possible suspect; we're in pursuit.'

'Where are you?'

'In Herdweg.'

'Herdweg!' he replied, surprised.

'Yes. We're heading to your lodge.'

There was a delay on the phone before Lahm replied. 'I'll be there in fifteen minutes.'

Muller hung up the phone.

'Did he sound surprised?' Stam asked as he turned at speed onto the road that led to Muller's lodge.

'Very.'

'He might put two and two together,' Stam said.

'It's his brother. Would you?'

'I don't have a brother,' Stam replied.

Muller said nothing.

Stam skidded to a halt. They jumped out of the car and ran to the front door of Lahm's lodge. It was locked. Stam was ready to smash the window next to the front door when Muller shouted at him to follow her around to the rear of the property. Muller led as Stam followed, both with their guns drawn and moving cautiously.

The lodge had no windows on the side they were on, which meant they had no visuals. Muller signalled to Stam to stay close as they approached the end of the lodge. She slowly looked around, her gun cocked and ready, but no one was there. They carried on slowly. When they got to the rear of the lodge, Muller could see the back door was open. Stam came alongside now and stepped up onto the rear porch. The wood creaked, which made him stop: no noises from inside, so he carried on. The door opened onto a utility room. He could see there had been a struggle. Cupboards were lying open, and he noticed blood on the floor. He turned and told Muller to wait and cover him. He took another step into the utility room and was getting ready to open the door that he assumed would lead to a hallway when a noise made him stop. It was a high-pitched noise, far off in the distance but piercing. It sounded like a scream. More worryingly, it sounded like it could have come from his daughter.

***

Inspector Schmidt was desperately trying to get Stam or Muller on the phone. He needed to know where to send officers to assist, but as soon as Stam said that he knew where she was, he had hung up the phone, and both their phones were now going straight to voicemail.

'Can you trace their phones?' Schmidt asked Sven, who was still on loudspeaker, as he threw his own phone down in frustration.

'Not if they don't have a signal. I can make a call to the cell providers to triangulate the phone numbers, but that kind of thing can take hours, if not days.'

'Can't you hack it?'

'It'll still take hours and doesn't always work.'

'Shit!' he replied. 'There has to be something we can do!'

The phone Schmidt had thrown across the room, which had landed on the bed, started ringing. Schmidt ran over to it, hoping it would be Stam or Muller, but it wasn't. It was Head Inspector Klose.

'Schmidt, what's going on?'

'What do you mean?'

'Don't give me that. Detectives Stam and Muller raced out of here ten minutes ago and neither one is answering their phone. So, what's going on?'

Schmidt didn't want to disobey his boss, but he was now convinced Klose was involved in this. And he wasn't going to let him make things harder.

'I don't know sir, I'm at home with my feet up. I'll try Stam myself.'

'If you're lying to me, then you will be …'

Schmidt hung the phone up and cut Klose off. He decided he had more important things to worry about.

'I may have something,' Sven said through the crackle of the speaker.

'What?'

'The yellow VW Beetle that Stam was asking about.

I've just managed to get into the vehicle records for it. It was owned by Heidi Winter from 2007 until her death. The car was checked for evidence and months later released to her family. Shortly after that, it was registered in the name of Lahm. The address it's registered to is in Herdweg.'

'It's too coincidental that it's so close. Sven, send me the address. I'm heading there now. When the police arrive, tell them what happened. We also need to find and arrest Mikael Schultz. He has got something to do with this.'

'I've already contacted someone in government that I can trust and explained what's been going on with the hidden files, the attempts on my life and my suspicion of the involvement of Mikael Schultz. They have just recently released a federal warrant for his arrest,' said Karl, who was sitting at the table but was still clearly shaken up.

Schmidt nodded at him before grabbing his keys and heading for the hotel entrance.

Chapter 52

Monica woke with a sharp intake of breath. She opened her eyes, but they wouldn't open fully. She was cold, her head hurt badly, and she felt disorientated. She tried to wriggle her arms free, but she couldn't move them, not fully anyway. They were being restrained, but by what, she couldn't figure out. She looked upwards but something wasn't right. The last moments before she was knocked unconscious flooded her thoughts. The object had come towards her and then hit her, and after that, it went dark. And it was all still dark, worryingly. She blinked and tried to focus on what was in front of her, but she couldn't see anything. Everything was black, but it didn't feel like she was blindfolded. She couldn't understand. She tried to scream and felt something in her mouth, something foreign that shouldn't be there. The blow to the head must have done damage as she couldn't think clearly. It felt like a piece of paper that was in her mouth. She flicked at it with her tongue; it felt like it was beginning to soften with the saliva. She turned it over with her tongue and managed to fish it to the front of her mouth. She pushed it to her lips and tried to spit it out, but it didn't go anywhere. It just stopped as soon as she opened her mouth. She didn't understand. The darkness, the cold. She tried to blink again, but all she could see was blackness. No lights, no stars in the sky, no anything. It was then that she realised what was happening to her, that she was living everyone's worst nightmare. The terror and panic began to build up inside her and her body went rigid. She couldn't see anything or move her body. And the realisation now engulfed her: she had been buried alive.

***

Stam had taken off into the forest in the general direction of where he had heard the scream before it had even stopped. Muller, a little fitter and obviously younger, followed after him. They both realised immediately that it wasn't just the scream of someone scared; it was the scream of someone fearing for their life.

The ground was still laden with icy patches and the terrain was difficult to navigate. Rises in the forest floor were hard to see due to the snow, but they both ran as fast as possible and prayed for another scream to guide them. Muller had decided that following directly behind Stam was not the best option. She knew the size of these woods and knew that what they were hoping to find was harder than trying to find a needle in a haystack. So she filtered out to the right and tried to stay parallel with Stam, covering more ground but still in the same general direction.

Stam's mind was racing, along with his heart. He tried to think of his first night in the forest again: the figure he was sure he had seen as he crossed the ST2080 road and the route he had taken that night, the lake on his left and the three paths that were carved out by the tree line. He tried to get a sense of where that would be in relation to his current location. If a person roamed these woods at night to torture and kill, they would have at the very least some vague route that they would use. Stam worked out that he was heading towards the ST2080, which would be a long way ahead. He also figured out that the path he had followed that first night, to his mind, was maybe a hundred yards southwest of it, and he thought that if the killer was using the woods at night to stalk and kill, then he would use this corridor of the forest.

As he careered down a small embankment, he thought he saw something off in the distance, maybe a shadow, fleeting but definite. He quickened his pace to where he had seen it and stopped. He was breathing hard, but his breaths were all he could hear. He walked on slowly and stopped near a large tree. He listened again, but apart from his breath, the forest was silent. Then he heard footsteps behind and to his right. It was Muller. He had forgotten she was even with him.

'What is it?' she asked, panting.

'I saw a shadow, over there by the valley. It was only for a split second, but it was something.'

Muller scanned the dark forest in front of her and could see plenty of shadows.

'Monica!' Stam shouted at the top of his lungs.

They both listened but heard nothing.

'Monica!' he roared again, this time even louder. The echoes reverberated through the forest. They listened again when the echo died, and two things happened simultaneously.

One of the things that happened was a sound, a scream. Not a loud shrieking scream like before; it was muffled but not by distance, Stam thought, by an obstruction. Stam began walking towards where he thought it had come from, but the other thing that happened a split second after the muffled scream was the opposite of a muffled scream. It was the intense and abrupt explosion of a bullet being fired from a handgun.

The bullet passed them both just above but in front of their faces. It was closer to Muller, and she flinched at the noise and fell backwards to the ground. Instinct kicked in, however, and she quickly got to her feet to see that Stam had not reacted to the gunshot at all. He was already five feet in front of her, trying to locate the sound of the scream. Another bullet was fired and only added to the ringing noise from the first shot. This one was directed at Stam. She saw the flash of the muzzle from the corner of her eye and saw the bullet hit a tree a few feet from Stam's head, pieces of wood bursting from the impact. Muller did not flinch; instead, she raised her gun and fired in the direction of where she had seen the flash. Nothing happened, no return fire or movement. She fired again and caught a glimpse of something moving in the trees not far from them. She began walking towards it, her gun still drawn, but then she stopped. She heard the muffled scream again. Stam was looking at her when she turned towards him. He looked at her as if to say, *you heard that too?* Muller hurried towards him, and they both knelt and listened. Then came another scream, muffled but getting louder. Stam took a step and saw on the forest floor what he had seen that first night with the first body. It was an area in the snow that was black, a hole that had been filled in. Dark soil was visible where snow should have been. They both dropped their weapons and began scraping at the soil frantically. Surely his daughter hadn't been buried alive? His heart was racing at the thought.

They dug as fast as they could until Muller felt what she knew wasn't soil. It was soft and warm.

'Here, I've found something!'

Stam moved to where Muller was digging and began clawing at the soil. Eventually, he saw an arm and pulled at it. It moved a little and he cleared more of the soil to reveal a hand. He clasped it, and it clasped back. It was

Monica, he knew it was. They both began digging furiously where they assumed her head would be, and finally, they saw it. They continued digging until they cleared her mouth and saw her gasp for air as quickly as her lungs would let her. Then another breath, before she let out a scream which wasn't muffled. This time it was so loud that it shook the whole forest.

Chapter 53

When Monica was out of the grave and Muller knew she was okay, even though she was scared out of her mind, she turned to where she had seen the shadow before. She walked towards it but couldn't see anything. Behind her, Stam had dragged his daughter free of the grave and was holding her in his arms. Muller continued, gun drawn, moving slowly, when she heard something off to her left. She turned to see what it was, but what it was became clear instantly. It was the noise of someone moving as they fired a gun. The bullet hit her in the leg, high up on the thigh. She went down fast, as though someone had stolen the body from her clothes. The pain was immediate. It didn't wait for the adrenaline to wear off; all she felt was pain.

As she lay in agony, she could see from her angle that Stam had got up and was ushering his daughter towards her. He told Muller to apply pressure to the wound with one hand and to hold her gun in the other. He grabbed her under the arms and propped her up against Monica so she had the best sight of anyone approaching. Stam took out his mobile to call for backup but knew the chances were slim regarding phone signal. He put it back in his pocket and looked out into the darkness, and he saw it. The same shadowy figure he had seen that first night. They were thirty feet in front of him, and they saw him too. Stam took off, straight towards them. They hesitated and then took off running themselves.

Stam was running even faster than he had before; he had rage coursing through his veins. The figure was younger than Stam and was moving a lot faster than he was. It appeared that they knew the layout of the forest better as well. Stam, old but determined, which he had heard many times before, was not going to give up easily, though. He approached a small clearing in the trees and saw the figure up ahead. They took the opportunity to glance back to see where their pursuer was. Stam saw the outline of the face, but with the hood still up and the darkness, he couldn't make out who it was. The figure then darted west, through an overgrown path and away. Stam followed twenty feet behind, and it took all his strength to stay upright as he slipped on the icy snow beneath. Ahead he noticed mountains coming into view above the tree line and realised that they were heading back to Herdweg. Stam took out his phone as he ran and checked the signal on his phone: still no reception. He had to contact Schmidt for backup in case the figure got away. He carried on, now closer to the outskirts of the forest, and he recognised the route from earlier. He stopped at the top of a small embankment. He couldn't see the figure now, only hear the rustling of their clothes as they ran. Through the trees, he could see lights from distant lodges; Herdweg was only a hundred yards away. He took out his phone and checked the reception again: one bar. He scrolled down to Schmidt's number and dialled it. It rang, then another ring. He had to pick up!

'Stam!'

'Where are you?'

'I'm en route to Herdweg.'

'Good, how far away?'

'I'm turning off the main road and will be on site in thirty seconds. What's going on?'

'I think we found the killer, or they found us. I'm in pursuit. Head for Thomas Lahm's lodge.'

'I'm driving up to it now. Wait, what?'

'Just stay alert!' Stam shouted, through deep breaths.

Stam came out of the forest ten yards up from the lodge that belonged to Thomas Lahm and who he now knew was Thomas's brother, Max. He put his phone in his pocket and replaced it with his gun. Cold sweat was starting to run from his forehead onto his face. He stayed focused and approached the rear of the lodge. The door that had been slightly ajar as they ran after hearing the scream was now closed. He climbed onto the porch and tried the door: locked. He backed away with his gun trained on the door. He slowly walked around the side of the building: no movement or noise from inside. He carried on and came to the front of the lodge. Schmidt's car was parked further up the road. He was standing in front with his gun drawn, and Stam beckoned to him to approach.

'Did you see him?' Stam asked without looking at him, still focused on the lodge.

'No, no one came out. No movement inside either.'

'He must be inside. The door was open when we left earlier and now it's closed and locked.'

'What do you want to do?'

'Call backup and an ambulance. I'll stay out the front and you take the rear. They have to be in there.'

Stam stepped back as Schmidt walked forward, but they both stopped at the same time. A bullet had smashed through the living room window from the inside and missed their heads by inches.

Both men dived for cover and scurried behind the parked car.

'We need back up now!' Stam said.

Schmidt took out his phone and called for backup.

'What's the plan?'

'We can't approach; he'll pick us off like sitting ducks.'

Schmidt was about to reply when Stam stopped him by raising his hand.

'What?' he asked.

'Can you smell that?'

'No, what is it?'

'It smells like petrol,' Stam replied.

They both crouched and looked over the front of the car.

'I can't see anything,' Schmidt said.

'Neither can I, but I can smell it.'

They watched for a few seconds. No smoke, but Schmidt could now smell the petrol too.

Then, against the black backdrop of the forest, there was the slightest trickle of smoke, white and floating upwards.

'Shit! He's setting the lodge on fire!'

Stam got up and ran for the rear of the lodge. 'Check the front door! We have to get him out!' he shouted.

Schmidt ran to the front of the lodge and tried the door, but it was locked. He pulled at the handle, but the door didn't budge. He threw his shoulder at it with all his weight behind it, but still nothing. Just as he had raised his foot to kick the door, Stam appeared from the side of the lodge.

'Both doors are locked, and the flames are blocking me from getting in.'

Schmidt stared at him.

'What're you waiting for? Kick it in!' Stam shouted.

Schmidt raised his leg and drove all his weight down through his leg and into the door, but as before, the door didn't budge. Stam checked through the large window next to the door. The smoke was billowing out from what he assumed would be the utility room at the end of the hall. He noticed the layout was the same as Muller's, but it was difficult to see inside as the smoke was so thick. He knew that they had to get inside soon or anyone who was inside wouldn't make it out alive, and Stam did not want that to be the outcome.

He took his gun and fired into the bottom corner of the large window. The glass exploded and the shards littered the floor. The air that was now being sucked into the lodge was quickly forced back out by waves of smoke. Both men retreated and covered their faces as the smoke escaped into the sky above them.

Stam entered the lodge through the now-open window and pulled his collar over his mouth. The heat inside was already intense, even though the flames were at the opposite end of the house. He headed onwards, one arm keeping his coat collar over his mouth and the other out in front of him, like some kind of shield against the heat.

Stam could see most of the living area from where he had entered the lodge, and he could see that no one was there. He carried on towards the hall, which was almost pitch black with smoke. The flames at the far end of the hall were all that gave off light. His eyes were stinging now and he could feel smoke in his chest, but he had to carry on. No way could he let the person responsible escape, but he knew he was running out of time. He fought the heat and reached the first door in the hall. He pushed the door open, but it was empty, with nobody inside, and no flames either. He stepped out and felt the heat rise the closer he got to the end of the hallway. Far off in the distance, he could hear the wail of sirens, police backup or an ambulance. He carried on, the heat encompassing his body, pressing in on him. He had taken another step towards the second door on the right when he saw movement in the darkness. The smoke swirled as it was pushed to the side. A hooded figure stumbled from the room and fell against the wall. The hood came down and Stam could see their face, but he didn't recognise them. It was a man in his late twenties with light hair and clear blue eyes that were clouded with smoke, fear and panic. The man slid from the wall down to the floor. Stam watched as he hung his head with the realisation of his predicament. Stam took a step and stopped dead. The man lying slumped against the floor looked up at him, half a smirk on his face. The reason for the smirk was in his left hand, resting on his lap: a Walther P-38 handgun. Stam knew the gun right away and knew that it must have been the weapon that had killed Mr and Mrs Langer.

Stam's weapon was holstered, and he knew that reaching for it was suicide. Instead, he stepped back. The man on the floor coughed from the amount of smoke he had inhaled. Stam flinched and almost reached for the gun but resisted. He would bide his time.

'You should have stayed away. We didn't want any of you here. Why did you come?' The man coughed again, louder this time.

Stam took another step back, slowly retreating.

'It's our job. We had to come.'

'No, you didn't. I had it under control until you came.'

'Had what under control?'

'Everything.'

Stam could see that the man had begun tapping the side of his leg with his free hand.

'I don't understand,' Stam said.

'No one does. I have to protect them.'

'Protect who?'

Stam took another step back, when suddenly a loud explosion from inside the utility room sent flames roaring out into the hall. Stam fell to the floor but quickly got up again. The man still lay on the floor with the gun in his hand.

'You have to come with me! Put the gun down!' Stam shouted over the roar of the flames that were now spreading up the hallway.

'I told you. You shouldn't have come.'

The man looked up at him again.

'Neither of you should have come.'

Stam took another step back, confused, when he felt his foot hit something behind him. He glanced round to see someone at his back, but it wasn't Detective Schmidt.

Chapter 54

Detective Muller was bleeding badly, and she knew she couldn't lie in the forest much longer or she would bleed out. She was positive the bullet had passed straight through, from the burning sensation she had on the back of her leg. She pushed herself up and snarled at the pain.

'Where are you going?' Monica said. She was still behind her and looked terrible.

'We can't stay here. We have to move.'

'My dad will come back for us.'

'I'm not waiting on that possibility.'

'You have a hole in your leg!'

'Which is another reason why we can't stay here.'

Monica understood why Muller wanted to get moving and came round to face her, hauling her up. The bandage that was tied tight around the wound to stop the bleeding was saturated with blood.

Monica took Muller's arm, placed it over her shoulder, and took her weight on the side where she had been shot. They took a step, and Muller howled in pain.

'You want to stop?'

'We can't. I'll be fine.'

They continued. Each step was followed by another howl of pain. After five long, slow minutes, they reached the dip in the forest floor. Monica hesitated, but Muller moved forward. Just as they were about to navigate the slope, Muller heard movement to her left-hand side, not too far away either. She immediately slumped to the floor and pulled out her gun. Monica instinctively copied her movement.

Muller focused on the trees in front where she had

heard the noise. Her leg was throbbing, along with her head, but the gun in her hand was steady. They sat for thirty seconds, hearing only small sounds from the forest: animals, wind blowing and trees cracking. Then a voice.

'Officer here. Is anyone there?'

They immediately recognised the voice of Detective Lahm.

'Here!' Monica shouted instantly in a shaky voice that was filled with trepidation.

Detective Lahm eventually appeared from behind a group of trees and saw them both lying on the floor.

'What's going on?' he asked.

Monica tried to explain, but it was taking too long and she was in shock. Muller couldn't waste any more time listening to her.

'We have to get out of here!' Muller interrupted.

'Is everything okay?'

'Apart from the fact I have a hole in my leg, yes. I think we interrupted the killer. Detective Stam has chased them into the forest. We have to follow in case he needs help!'

Detective Lahm took out his gun and looked into the darkness towards Herdweg. He then turned and looked at Muller and Monica for a long moment, thinking.

'We have to get out of here, Thomas!' Monica shouted frustratedly.

Monica pulled Muller up from the ground and lifted her arm again to support her weight.

'Wait,' Lahm said.

'For what? We have to move.'

'Are you sure it was the killer you came across?'

'Of course it was! They tried to bury me alive!' yelled Monica.

'Did you see the person, though?'

'No. Who else is going to be out stalking in the forest at this time of night? Why are you saying this?'

Thomas said nothing.

'Why are you asking this?' said Muller.

'I just don't want to think that the killer could still be out here.'

'That's why we have to move!' said Muller.

They went to walk forward when Lahm turned again.

'What made you head for Herdweg in the first place?' Lahm asked.

Muller knew that the best policy at this point was honesty, and they needed to be moving.

'We believe that the killer is Max, your brother,' she admitted.

Monica and Lahm both turned towards her with shocked looks on their faces.

'We heard a scream coming from the forest when we got to your lodge and noticed there had been a disturbance. We set off for the forest and came across Monica buried alive. Then when we were leaving, we saw a figure and Stam gave chase.'

Lahm went from looking merely annoyed to looking angry. He gripped the gun that was in his right hand, tight.

'We have to move!' Muller said with authority.

They turned and began walking, but all three of them stopped in unison. High above the tree line, not quite smothered by the darkness, were clouds of smoke. Thick smoke that must be coming from a nearby fire.

'Stam!' Muller shouted.

'Dad!' Monica cried out.

'Max!' Lahm called before taking off running into the trees and out of sight.

***

Stam froze in shock when he felt someone's foot under his own. As he turned, he was surprised to see Detective Lahm, who was panting.

The flames were getting bigger and the smoke thicker. He knew he had to get out, but he was aware that if he tried to run, he would almost certainly be shot in the back.

'What are you doing here? Get out! It's not safe!' Stam roared over the noise.

'He's my brother!' Lahm shouted.

The force from the heat was forcing them backwards down the hall.

'I know he is. That's why I'm trying to get him out, but he won't leave!'

The fire was now spitting small flames out of the room that Max was facing. Stam knew the heat must be unbearable. The gun in Max's hand was still pointing directly at Stam.

'Max!' Lahm shouted. 'It's Thomas! What are you doing? You have to get out now!'

Max looked up for the first time since Thomas had arrived. He stared at him.

'Max, you have to get out!'

The fire was beginning to surround Max from all sides. Pieces of wood could be heard cracking and falling from roof joists above. The wail of the distant siren was growing louder.

'Max!' Lahm roared.

Max lifted his gun from where it sat in his lap and held it outwards, still pointed at Stam.

'All I have done is protect you. All I have ever done is

313

protect you. And this was no different,' Max said.

He pulled the gun back towards himself.

'Max!' Lahm screamed.

Stam knew this wasn't good. Instead of fearing for his own life, he now wanted to get Max out of danger and brought to justice for his actions, in the right way.

Max turned his head again, this time looking past Stam and at his brother.

He placed the gun under his chin, with his finger on the trigger. Lahm tried to push by Stam as the fire roared and the smoke billowed out. Frantic steps. Grabbing at Stam to get by him.

'I didn't protect her, and I'm sorry for that,' Max said.

'No! Wait! Please!' Lahm screamed. But he was too late.

Max pulled the trigger.

Chapter 55

It had taken the fire crew over an hour to extinguish the flames completely and for the embers to fade out. Not all of the lodge had been engulfed, however; the damage had largely been to the rear, to the utility room, the toilet and the two rear bedrooms. The kitchen and living area were all but untouched by the fire, but both were covered in thick black ash.

Detective Stam had got out with Detective Lahm, with only mild smoke inhalation, and they had been checked by the paramedic on site as the fire crews were dousing the flames. Almost the entire town had come out to watch the events unfold before a cordon was set up.

Inspector Schmidt had taken control of the scene and organised officers to be stationed throughout the night. He had also called in the forensics department to gather evidence from the lodge. There were mountains of paper in one of the rooms, which would be removed after the charred remains of Max Lahm were taken to the coroner's office, where Dr Park would run a postmortem on them. Any other evidence they were able to salvage from inside the lodge was boxed to be sent to the church in Schwaberwegen to be checked.

As soon as Stam had left the lodge, his immediate thought was for his daughter and Muller. He had run back into the forest but only got twenty yards when he saw them both making their way out. A weary-looking Monica was carrying Muller. The bandage he had applied to her wound was soaked in blood and they both looked chilled to the bone. They had gone straight to the hospital; Monica had been treated for shock and a laceration to her head that needed stitches. She was also checked for pneumonia and had a lung X-ray taken, and she was told she would spend the night in the hospital.

Detective Muller was operated on that night to repair internal bleeding from the gunshot in her thigh. She received several stitches to the wounds and also had to spend the night in hospital.

Detective Lahm had to be physically removed from the lodge after what he had seen happen to his brother. He was immediately transferred into a waiting ambulance and given sedatives to calm him down. After an hour, the anger he was showing began to fade, replaced by grief. Stam had arranged for him to be taken to his cousin's house on the outskirts of Forstinning.

Before everyone departed, Detective Stam arranged with Inspector Schmidt for a meeting at 9 a.m. the following morning in the church in Schwaberwegen. Everyone who was able to attend regarding the case was told to be there. Detective Lahm was excused, but he insisted he wanted to be there.

As the fire crews finished and the coroners packed up the evidence and headed back to Schwaberwegen, Stam and Schmidt called it a night and left the officers in charge of the scene. Schmidt headed home and Stam headed to the hospital to be by his daughter's side.

He pulled out of the driveway, turned the car, and headed for the empty darkness in front of him. In the rearview mirror, the sky was lit up with the flashing blue lights of several patrol cars, the smoke from the dying embers floating between them and circling up into the night sky.

***

Early the next morning, Detective Stam and Inspector Schmidt were standing at the foot of the Victorian bridge at the bottom of Schwaberwegen. Schmidt was sipping from a coffee cup, Stam was smoking, and they were both in a contemplative mood.

By all accounts, the case had been closed and the killer had been found, even though he couldn't be held accountable for his actions. But the people of Schwaberwegen were relieved by the knowledge that the killer was off the streets, and so too was the media.

Detective Stam, however, was less than satisfied with the outcome. Something still wasn't sitting right with him. The fact that the one responsible couldn't be questioned and that two other people had been killed during the investigation meant that for him, it was anything but positive.

'Look, Stam, we caught the man responsible. He won't be able to kill anymore, and that's our job. We keep the public safe,' Schmidt said, sensing the frustration that hung in the air around them.

Stam looked beyond the bridge and out into the forest. The trees creaked and groaned as the morning sun rose and began to seep through them. Up ahead, in the centre of town, swarms of reporters had begun to descend, once again, on the sleepy town as news broke that the killer had been found in nearby Herdweg and that the police were still using the church in Schwaberwegen as the headquarters for the investigation.

'I'm still not seeing the connection between the original case in Munich ten years ago and the killings now,' said Stam after regaining his focus.

'It has to be a copycat,' replied Schmidt.

'But how? Details were not revealed to the media.

Unless it was someone on the inside, someone with knowledge of the …' Stam stopped talking.

'What?' Schmidt asked.

'Have forensics arrived with all the evidence from Detective Lahm's lodge in Herdweg?'

'They were just bringing it into the church as I arrived. Why?'

'We need to go.'

'What is it?'

'I'm not sure yet.'

Inside the church, the officers had set out four long tables in the centre of the floor. Inside were Helen from the forensic team, her assistant, and Dr Park, who had been asked to assist with the examination of Max Lahm's body. She had accompanied the forensic team to the church to help in any way she could.

She greeted Stam and Schmidt as they entered. 'Hey, how are you both?'

'Fine now,' Schmidt replied.

Stam was distracted and didn't engage in the greetings. He went to the first of the tables and began to look through the bundles of files that sat on top of them.

'How's Karl?' he said eventually without looking up.

'He's good. He got checked out last night by a doctor and was cleared. This morning he returned to his offices in the Reichstag building to speak with the chief. He called earlier to say that charges were being brought against Mikael Schultz and a statement will be released in the coming days.'

Stam looked up from the table. 'Good to hear,' he said, before returning to the files.

'So, what is it we're looking for?' asked Schmidt,

looking at the sheer volume of the documents that were sitting on the four tables. 'We may need more bodies.'

'I can help,' a voice said from the front of the church. It was Detective Muller. She was being pushed in on a wheelchair with her strapped leg sticking out in front.

'Muller!' Schmidt said. 'You shouldn't be here! You got shot, remember?'

'I do remember, actually,' she said with a smirk. 'I either sit on my sofa doing nothing, or I sit in here and help in whatever way I can.'

Stam looked up from the file he was holding and nodded at her. She nodded back. He knew he had been right about her from the start.

'So, what's the plan then?' she asked.

Stam stood back from the table as everyone looked to him for an answer.

'It came to me outside on the bridge just now.'

'What did?' asked Muller.

'When we knew that Hans Fischer couldn't have been responsible for the recent deaths in the Ebersberger Forest, I knew there had to be a connection, but I couldn't figure out what it was.'

Everyone stared at him, intrigued.

'The one thing that connected them all was Heidi Winter.'

'How?' Schmidt asked.

'We know she was aware of the original case from working with Angela in the coroner's office in Munich, so she had knowledge of the case and the killings.'

'Was she involved?' Muller asked.

'Not directly. I noticed when we left the lodge in Herdweg earlier that the files that were being removed were copies of murder cases from years back. Heidi

Winter must have been taking them home to study, and eventually became obsessed by them.'

'We didn't know or allow this in the office. She must have been sneaking them out,' Angela said defiantly.

'I would assume so,' Stam replied. 'And then when I discovered the yellow Bug was in her name, my focus was on finding Monica. Now that I've had time to think it through, I've made the connection.'

Everyone stared at the files on the table. Thousands of sheets of paper, all bundled together.

'So, Max studied them as well?' Muller asked, unsure.

'Maybe, maybe not. Maybe Heidi spoke of the serial killer who drilled through the skulls of their victims more than any of the other cases she brought home, and it stuck with him. Maybe she was excited to be involved in such a big case and couldn't help but discuss the details with her fiancé over a glass of wine at night.'

'And this led to murder?'

'Revenge, I would say. Max somehow discovered the identities of the officers responsible for the death of his girlfriend. We now know that that is the link between the four names in the file that Karl came across, and he must have decided to execute his revenge by killing them in the same manner he had heard about night after night from Heidi.'

'I can't believe this,' said Angela. 'I remember her being a great student, engaged and always asking questions.'

Stam walked to the next table and lifted another case file. Inside it, each page was covered in writing and scribbles, with notes at the sides of the pages.

'Can it be proved?'

'If he was as clinical as he was with the first two

bodies, then I'd say it would be very difficult to find any evidence. Remember, this is ten years in the making. He could have been planning it in his head soon after that fateful night in Karlsfeld.'

'Is that why he set the lodge on fire, to hide evidence?'

'I'm guessing he knew that we would find the files. Fortunately for us, they weren't all destroyed,' Stam replied.

Just then, Helen approached them with another box. 'This is the last of the boxes. No more files, though; it's personal letters and correspondence. Most got burned in the fire, and this is what's left.'

Helen set the box down and left. Stam was still scrolling through files, along with everyone else.

'I think I've found something,' Dr Park said. 'This looks like copies of the original files, right enough. There's handwriting on it that's not Karl's or my own. I imagine it's Heidi's.'

Stam and Schmidt came over to have a look at them. The paper was faded but clear, and the handwriting was neat.

Stam was about to speak when the stillness inside the church was broken by the ringing of Inspector Schmidt's mobile phone. He answered it and walked over to the makeshift interview room.

After a few minutes, he returned.

'That was Franz calling,' he said sombrely.

'What is it?' Stam asked, recognising his tone.

'He's been granted access to the government files, and in doing so, he has discovered that it was Max who was with Heidi Winter on the night she was killed. He's also confirmed that it was Theo Schultz who strangled her. The other three men were involved in the sexual assault, but it was Theo who killed her.'

Stam watched as Angela lowered her head. Stam could feel the rage building inside him again.

'He also said that he had found that the inspector on shift on the night of Heidi Winter's death attended the scene. They were the ones who initiated and then orchestrated the cover-up.'

'Do we have a name?' Muller asked.

'Franz is confirming it. He'll send confirmation through in a few minutes,' Schmidt replied.

Stam headed over to the box that Helen had brought in and opened the lid. Inside were more pieces of paper, but this time it was mostly letters and cards. Some of the edges of them were burned and covered in ash. He reached in and lifted a handful out.

The first letters he looked through were mostly bills for phone lines or credit cards. All were addressed to the lodge in Herdweg. He also found some wage slips and several letters addressed to Max Lahm, which were mostly to do with doctor's appointments or prescriptions.

'How's Thomas doing?' Angela asked.

'He's doing okay considering,' answered Muller. 'I called him on the way over here. He's at his lodge in Herdweg, gathering any personal belongings that weren't damaged, but I don't think there was a lot, to be honest.'

'Was he alone?'

'I think so. I'll call him now.'

Muller took out her mobile and dialled Lahm's number. It rang three times before being answered.

Stam lifted out more greetings cards from the box. The first one was a birthday card from years ago. It was from Max to his brother, with a large green dragon on it, holding a balloon. The second card was from their parents to Thomas on his birthday.

He lifted out another bunch of cards and flicked through them as Muller began talking on the phone.

'Lahm.'

'Hey, Muller,' he replied.

'Are you okay?' she asked.

'As can be. I've just cleared out the lodge and I'm heading to a friend's house to stay.'

'Is your friend with you?'

'No, Inspector Klose is with me. He was clearing up at the scene and offered me a ride back to Schwaberwegen. My car got damaged in the fire yesterday.'

Stam was half listening to the conversation in the background as he continued to look through the cards.

The next bunch he looked through were more recent, maybe ten years old or so. They had pictures on them, some with teddy bears and some with love hearts and cute animals holding flowers. Stam opened the first one up.

'Are you coming to the church first?' Muller asked.

'Yes, I believe we are,' Lahm replied.

'Okay, see you soon,' Muller said and hung the phone up.

'They're on their way,' she said.

'He okay?' asked Schmidt.

'I think so. He sounded adamant. If you can sound that way, that is.'

Stam looked at her.

'Grief can do funny things to people,' she said.

The latest bundle of cards were mostly anniversary cards and Valentine's cards. Some of them had long messages inside, declaring undying love for the recipient, and some had just a few words.

'Who's coming to the church?' Schmidt asked Muller, but his phone pinged with a notification before she could answer.

Schmidt opened the message and read it before looking up.

There were even more of the cards, all signed with a declaration of the sender's love, or how much the other meant to them, or that they couldn't live without them, then signed at the bottom. The one Stam was reading now was an engagement card. The message read,

I can't believe how lucky I am to have found you and how happy I am for you to be mine. I count the days until I can call you my wife. I love you.

Stam froze for a second, then took out his notepad. He took the copy of the note he had taken days ago, after the discovery of the first body, and laid it on the card next to the message. He compared the handwriting on it. He studied it.

It looked the same, thicker writing on the card, but the same. The slight slant to the right, the circle above the 'i' as opposed to a dot, and the exaggerated flick on the 'y'.

'Franz has just confirmed that the inspector in charge of the scene back in Karlsfeld regarding Heidi Winter was Head Inspector David Klose,' Schmidt said with as much shock in his voice as there was anger.

Angela and Muller stared at him, then at Stam, who wasn't looking at any of them. He was staring down at what looked to them like a greetings card laid out on the table in front of him.

Stam looked from the note in his pad, then to the card, and then back again. There was no denying it: the handwriting was the same. He wasn't an expert, not by a long way, but he knew they were the same.

'Stam, did you hear me?' Schmidt said.
Stam heard him but he didn't reply.
Every card he took out was signed in the same way. With the same handwriting.
He took another of the greetings cards out and looked at the bottom. Then another, and another. They were all written out to the same person, *Heidi*, the name written in the top left-hand corner of each card.
The cards had not only been written out to the same person, but they had also been sent by the same person too, every one of them signed in the bottom right-hand corner with a message attached. A specific message that was written to let the recipient know how much they loved them. Maybe one of them had written it in a card at the start of their relationship and it stuck. Maybe they had even had it tattooed on them as a declaration of their love.
However, the one thing from the cards that had Stam staring in shock was the name of who had sent the card. It wasn't who he had assumed it was sent by. His head began to spin. He looked up at the others, who were all staring at him, waiting, wondering. Stam closed his eyes and held his breath as he read it again to be sure.
He finally let out a deep breath.
'Who did you say was bringing Detective Lahm to Schwaberwegen?' he said, his face pale with panic.

'Inspector Klose,' Muller answered, fearing the worst from his expression.

'Get him on the phone now!' Stam shouted back.

'What is it, Stam?' Schmidt asked.

Stam ignored him and returned to the card on the table to read it for the third time.

The card read,

To Heidi.

I can't believe we have been together for three years already, and I can't wait to be your husband.

Happy anniversary. All my love, Thomas.

You have no idea xx

About the Author

Scott Carlin is from Scotland and lives with his family in a small village between Glasgow and Edinburgh. He started expressing his creative side in his teenage years, writing songs and performing live with his band.

He has always enjoyed reading thrillers and eventually began to write his debut novel, 'A Falling of Snow,' published by Blossom Spring Publishing.

Scott's interests outside of work include travelling, which has allowed him to experience different cultures and foods and has enriched his creativity, enabling him to incorporate his encounters into his stories. Scott also enjoys engaging in a wide range of sports including golf and football. He loves music and taking long walks in the countryside with his much loved springer spaniel, Poppy.

www.blossomspringpublishing.com